A PREVIOUS TIME

GG SHALTON

OTHER BOOKS BY GG SHALTON

Amelia's Deception
Running From Past Roses – coming spring 2018

CHAPTER 1

LEAH JOHNSON GLANCED THROUGH THE dirty bookstore window onto the London streets. Rays of sunshine peeked through the clouds giving hope that the brisk air outside would not sting. She wiped the dust from the window, clearing the view. This was her last chore until she could finally take a quick break. She glanced at the clock hoping the time would go by faster.

Cleaning the store was her least favorite part of the day. She daily swept the floors, put away books, and organized the desk. She'd finished stacking the newest novels that came in that morning over an hour ago. Working in her family's bookstore was against her grandmother's wishes. Properly bred women did not work, she warned. Leah relished in the written word, and helping her mother in the bookstore enabled her to read the newest novels. Her marriageable options were limited without a dowry, and the lack of a social life made it nearly impossible to find a match. Though reaching nine and one without an offer did not exactly put her on the shelf… yet.

Her family was not noble, although at one time they were financially secure. Her working-class status could be her future. Convincing her family that the concept of marriage was optional was her next battle as her father felt marriage was a woman's only choice.

Finishing her dusting, Leah said goodbye to her mother assuring her she would not be gone long. She was going to visit her mother's friend Ellen who worked at the corner dress shop. Ellen was a seamstress, an honest profession for a widow with no inheritance. She had been a family friend since Leah could remember, and her love for romance novels was a passion they shared. Leah tucked the books for Ellen into her arms and held on to her cloak.

Traffic was bustling by swiftly as she darted through the streets toward the small dress shop. It was a windy day in London causing her to hold the books tightly against her chest to keep the pages from blowing. Squeezing through the crowds, she rushed up the street as fast as she could. Relieved to make it to the entrance without blowing away, she pulled open the door just as the wind caught it, jerking her arm back.

"Good afternoon, Leah." A joyful, middle-aged woman motioned for Leah to join her.

Leah used her body to shut the door. "Good day, Ellen." She suppressed a smile noticing the woman's hair falling out of the pins.

Ellen's face lit up at the books in Leah's hand. "I see you brought me gifts from the bookstore. I have more books to send back."

Leah grinned at the older woman while watching her straighten the dresses on the large oval table. She handed her the new books, admiring the beautiful designs of the latest fashions. There were a few ladies in the store piling their arms full of clothes. A twinge of jealousy tugged at her chest as she wished she could afford a new gown. The bookstore barely made enough money to support her family as her father was ill. At one time, he was a sought-after solicitor, but bad health and some risky investments had cost her father his livelihood.

"How is the shop today?" Leah asked as she heard more ladies enter— their conversations regarding the newest balls and soirees echoed throughout the store.

Ellen looked at Leah. "It's a good day, my girl." Leah had known Ellen since she was a child. She was an old neighbor of Leah's mother and they grew up together. She had no children of her own and often coddled Leah.

"I have a surprise for you that I hope you'll like."

Leah crinkled her brows as she waited curiously for her surprise.

Ellen went to the back of the store and returned with a brown bag. "I made a dress for a girl about your size, but the spoiled child didn't like the way it fit, so the mother decided not to buy it. I was told by Mr. Barnes, the owner, that I could try to sell it or buy it at a discount. I bought it for you."

Leah's mouth fell open as she admired the beautiful silver and blue colors. It was very fashionable and could be used as a dinner dress. Knowing the dress cost Ellen a small fortune, she kindly declined her gift. "I can't take this, Ellen. It's too expensive. Besides, I have no reason to have such a beautiful gown."

Ellen snorted at her modesty. "Nonsense. You deserve to have it. You are young and should be joining your friends at those country dances or dinner parties."

Leah hesitated as she ran her fingers over the gown. The fabric was silky smooth, and the embroidery displayed a beautiful attention to detail. The lace collar included a scoop neck and silk gathered at the waist to accentuate the curves of the woman who wore it.

"You could at least try it on. I think it would be perfect for you."

Leah knew she should refuse such an offer. "I shouldn't." Her voice wavered showing her interest.

Ellen smiled as she took her arm and led her to the dressing room. "It won't hurt just to try it on."

Reluctantly, she took the dress and entered the small room.

A few minutes later, Leah shyly approached Ellen.

"Oh my, Leah! You look so beautiful. You must go show your mother!"

Leah panicked, looking around the store hoping not to attract any attention. "I can't go out in this."

Ellen raised her eyebrow. "Why ever not? Have you seen yourself?" Ellen brought her to the looking glass.

As they approached the glass, Leah barely recognized the woman staring back at her. Her dark blond hair was swooped up in a practical bun. Some of her hair came down in tendrils along her face. Her blue-green eyes stood out even more noticeably because of the blues in the gown.

"You must go and show your mother. This dress was made for you. Besides, you don't have time to change. You're due back at the bookstore in a few minutes." Ellen practically shoved her out the door.

Leah reached for the return books and the bag with her old dress in it as she hurried outside. She didn't have time to put on her bonnet leaving her hair falling around her shoulders. Rushing through the crowds, she tried to hold on to her package and the books—a daunting task on the busy streets of London. Picking up her pace, she tried not to think of her mother's wrath regarding her tardiness. She quickly dismissed images of customers waiting in line while her mother frantically tried to assist them all.

Many carts and horses blocked her path. She had to step around them swiftly, causing the books to fall out of her hands. The wind blew her bag open and she tried to grasp it tighter to avoid dropping it. Inevitably, for all her effort to carry everything, she dropped the books. Rushing to pick them up, she bumped into a stranger.

"Oh, pardon me!" Leah didn't make eye contact with the stranger.

Her balance wavered, and she fell onto the cobblestone, tearing her gloves when she landed. A few trickles of blood soaked through the material. She rubbed her hand wincing in pain. Cautiously, she pulled down on the glove to assess the damage and recover from her debacle. She quickly stood up while trying to gather the books with some dignity.

From the corner of her eye, she saw the stranger hold out a book to her.

She reached for it and looked up into the most beautiful pair of brown eyes she had ever seen. The stranger drew his brow with concern looking down at her as her breath caught in her throat. Trying not to stare, she could not help but notice his very white teeth and broad shoulders. He wore his brown hair slightly longer than the fashionable London society. It blew in the wind allowing her to see his whole face.

"Are you well? How is your hand?" Finally breaking the silence, Leah noticed that the stranger had a low, raspy voice and his eyes held a mix of concern.

"I am well, thank you." Leah was at a loss for words as the stranger was very handsome and meticulously dressed. *Maybe he is an aristocrat trying to be honorable.* The thought made her want to disappear.

"What are you reading?" The stranger inquired as she held the books tightly to her chest almost in a protective manner.

"It's not for me, they are for a friend." Leah's face burned as the stranger read the title of the romance novel that she was holding.

"I think my sister reads the same type of books." He winked and chuckled as another gentleman came up behind him.

Leah was getting ready to turn on her heel when the gentleman said, "Miss Johnson? Is that you?"

Leah looked at the gentleman not recognizing him. "Yes, my name is Miss Johnson. Am I acquainted with you, sir?"

The gentleman smiled down at her. "I previously worked with your father on some business a few years ago. You were always in the bookstore next door, and I remember purchasing some books one day. My name is Lord Preston."

Leah took a better look at Lord Preston's face, faintly remembering the gentleman who brought her sugar sticks as a child. "Oh yes, Lord Preston. I remember the sugar sticks that you brought me when you visited my father. I apologize for not recognizing you right away."

"It's quite all right, Miss Johnson. May I say that you have grown up these last few years? I gather from the books in your hand that you still work at the bookstore with your family?"

Leah looked at him and the stranger beside him who was following their conversation. His gaze hadn't left her eyes as if he was trying to read her mind. It was unsettling.

"Yes, my lord. I work with my mother in the bookstore. My father had to sell his business as he has been too ill to work." Leah clutched the books tighter in her hands, itching to get away from the conversation. Sneaking a look at the stranger, his eyes were still locked with hers. She quickly looked away concentrating on Lord Preston.

Lord Preston gave her a look of sympathy. "I am sorry to hear that, Miss Johnson. I hope he recovers." He glanced over at his friend, suppressing a smile. "Miss Johnson, may I present my friend—His Grace the Duke of Wollaston."

The duke nodded to her. "It's a pleasure to make your acquaintance, Miss Johnson. I hope you can forgive me if I frightened you. I was only trying to help you with your books."

Leah felt her hands go weak and took a deep breath. He was a duke? Awkwardly, she shook her head. "The fault is mine, Your Grace. I was in a hurry to get back to the bookstore. I should have paid more attention." Leah forced a smile at them both, trying to hide her embarrassment. "It was a pleasure to see you again, Lord Preston. I will give my father your regards. If you will excuse me, I must get back to help my mother." She curtsied to both men and turned on her heel, rushing to the store.

The Duke of Wollaston looked on the ground and noticed another book that Leah forgot. He picked it up and smiled. Lord Preston raised his brow at the duke's look of interest. "She can barely be out of the school room, and hardly runs in the same circles as you."

The duke smiled. "She was breathtaking."

Lord Preston sagged his shoulders in defeat. "That she was, but innocent, Your Grace."

The duke adjusted his gloves as he carried the book with him to his horse. "I think I will return her book tomorrow. There can be no harm in that."

Lord Preston sighed deeply but kept his opinions to himself. He mounted his horse and they rode to visit the duke's house.

Leah entered the bookstore peeking back through the glass window. She watched the duke and Lord Preston walk up the street to their horses. Taking a deep breath, she watched them ride away. He was a duke. Of all the people she could have fallen in front of—she humiliated herself in front of a duke! Leah dropped the books on the table and went to the washbasin to take off her gloves and tend to the scrapes on her hand. She shuddered at the sting and patted it dry with the towel. The state of her ruined gloves worried her. A dwindling savings account could not afford a new pair.

Her mother came in the room shortly after hearing the bells on the door ring. "What are you wearing, Leah?" A look of concern crossed her face as she eyed her daughter's dress.

She looked down at her dress. "Ellen gave it to me as a gift. Apparently, someone ordered it and did not buy it."

Her mother raised her brow concerned over the expensive gown. "Couldn't they sell it off the table?"

Leah shrugged her shoulders. "Perhaps, but Ellen insisted that I take it."

Mrs. Johnson sighed then shook her head. "Leah, I know it's been a rough year with our debts piling up. But we don't need charity."

Leah's face fell as her mother kissed her on the forehead. "However, it's not nice to return a gift. We must thank her properly and invite her to dinner this week."

Leah smiled. "Yes, Mama. I will invite her to dinner."

Mrs. Johnson kissed her on the cheek and left the room.

Leah hid her hand and torn glove from her mother behind her back. She had enough worries without the expense of buying a new pair of gloves. Leah couldn't help but notice her mother's golden blond hair was turning gray and worry lines creased her forehead. It wasn't fair that her family had suffered this year and could not afford the luxuries they once had.

The next day the bookstore was full of children as Leah finished her weekly reading group. She enjoyed making the stories come alive for the children. Her mother organized this class each week to entertain the youngsters while their parents or governesses shopped for books. Leah was happy to oblige as she enjoyed watching their faces when she read. Many of the children would hug her after they were finished, anxiously awaiting next week's story.

"Leah, you should consider the theatre. You read with such animation." Mrs. Lawrence, one of the children's mothers, addressed her with a big smile.

"You're too kind, Mrs. Lawrence." Leah smiled at the children as she bid them a good day. The bell chimed in the bookstore again. A man with a package and flowers in his hand entered as many of the group's members were departing.

"Good day to you. I have a delivery for a Miss Johnson." The man had a short stature and a long beard. Leah did not think he looked like a delivery worker but smiled at him all the same.

"I am Miss Johnson, sir." Leah took the flowers and the packages from his outstretched hand as she thanked him. She glanced around to find her mother and noticed that she was engrossed in a conversation with a governess from the reading group. Leah carried the package and flowers to the desk in the back of the store to look at the card. It read, *please accept these flowers as a token of my apologies for running into you yesterday. Regards, The Duke of Wollaston.*

Leah gasped before tucking the card into her sleeve for safekeeping. How would she explain the flowers? People may get the wrong idea. She would have to hide his card and then display the flowers with no sender.

Hesitating, she looked over her shoulder. Her mother was still speaking with patrons, so she carefully unwrapped the package. The paper crinkled as she pulled it off the box. She slowly opened it before peering inside and letting out a gasp in surprise. Inside the box was a fancy pair of lady's gloves. Leah's eyes widened at the personal gift. She knew such a gift was inappropriate and her mother would be shocked if she accepted a present from a man she did not know. But they were beautiful. Leah recognized the gloves as a pair in the Martin's store window. She knew they were very expensive as they were the highest quality.

She quickly disposed of the paper before taking the box up the stairs to the family's personal parlor above the bookstore. She went to fetch her reticule to hide the gloves in there. As she removed them from the box, Leah noticed another note.

Miss Johnson, I would be in your debt and consider it a personal favor if you would accept these gloves. I felt most fretful that I may have caused you to ruin yours. Your acceptance of this small gift relieves me of that debt. Best Wishes, the Duke of Wollaston.

Leah bit her bottom lip while searching around the familiar parlor. She sat on the settee and took out one of the gloves, trying it on. The material was smooth and felt so soft against her skin. Her conscious was playing havoc in her mind. How could she explain the new gloves to her mother? Her other gloves were practically ruined, and still barely passable after she was up half the night trying to mend them.

Her mother's voice startled her as it echoed across the store below. She quickly put the gloves back into her reticule. Walking down the back stairs to the bookstore, she found her mother by the desk admiring the flowers.

"There you are, my dear. What beautiful flowers! Who are they from? There was no card."

Leah's heart beat faster watching her mother put her nose to the flowers and take in the smell. They were yellow roses and their fragrance filled half the bookstore.

Leah shrugged her shoulders innocently at her mother. "They are beautiful." The omission wasn't exactly a lie.

Her mother wrinkled her nose. "I guess we will just enjoy them for now. It may have been delivered by accident or from a customer that we helped recently." Her mother began stacking the books before turning back to look at Leah. "I must go early today to meet with the doctor. He is going to the cottage to check on your father. I must speak to him about the new medication he wants him to take."

Leah tried to keep up a strong stance as her mother's devotion to her father was touching. "Of course, Mother. I can handle the bookstore and will catch a ride with Ellen on the way home."

Mrs. Johnson looked with pride toward her daughter. "I am not sure what I would do without you." She touched her face. "I am so happy that you help me, but I also want you to enjoy your friends. You work too much, my dear. You need to find some time for amusement."

Leah laughed. "Nonsense, I am fine, Mama. Don't worry about me."

Leah's mother retrieved her shawl and bonnet, bidding her a good day.

CHAPTER 2

THE AFTERNOON WAS TEDIOUS FOR Leah. She had not seen a customer in over an hour and was anxious to get home to finish her game of chess with her brother Travis. He was one year her junior and her closest sibling. He wanted to go to Oxford, but with her father's deteriorating condition, the family was unable to afford such expenses. The circumstances caused him to study at home and work at a shop nearby.

Leah was stacking books on the back table when the door opened, and a customer came into the store. Looking up, she sucked in a breath. Standing in the middle of the bookstore was the Duke of Wollaston. Straightening her shoulders, she walked slowly toward him. He wore a dark blue jacket with gray trousers and a perfectly tied cravat. She curtsied trying to swallow her nervousness. "Good day, Your Grace."

He bowed. "Good day, Miss Johnson." His deep voice resonated throughout the store causing chills on her arms.

She felt faint.

Trying to break his stare, she looked down. "Um… May I help you with anything?" His presence filled the room, and Leah's voice betrayed her with a stutter as she tried to control her nervousness.

He smiled, handing her a book that she didn't realize he was holding. It was another romance novel. "I believe this belongs to you. You missed it yesterday when you were collecting the others." His voice was low, almost a whisper.

Leah accepted the book without looking at him. She quickly dismissed the thoughts of hiding under the desk. "Yes, well… uh… thank you." Walking to the table, she put it under another book.

Trying to compose herself, she finally made eye contact. "I wanted to thank you for the flowers and the gloves. It was unnecessary, and I really should not accept the gift."

He held up his hand. "Please, do not return my gift. I felt most at fault over your unfortunate fall yesterday, and as I said, I feel in your debt." He lifted the corner of his mouth dangling a smile.

She chewed on her bottom lip. "Of course, as you wish, Your Grace." Finding it hard to stay still, she busied herself with stacking the books.

He looked around the store. "I would also like some help finding a book for my sister. She probably likes the same kind that you enjoy."

Leah stared at him for a few seconds, suddenly feeling less nervous. Realizing he was teasing her, she took on a sarcastic tone, "Does she? I guess I could show you the *secret* girl section of the store." She regretted the word *secret*. Would he think she was flirting? Did she know how to flirt?

He laughed, seeming surprised at her banter. Leaning down toward her ear, he whispered, "I would never tell anyone." He held up his hand in a promise. They walked to the middle of the store as she guided him to the shelf of books that were romance. Leah heard the store door open.

She looked up. "Please excuse me for a moment."

The duke pulled out a few books to look at. "Of course, I will see you soon."

Leah walked to the front of the store and saw that her childhood friend Melissa had just come in. Melissa was dressed in a pretty, light blue gown and matching hat. A few of her dark curls fell out from her bonnet.

Melissa smiled while hugging her excitedly. "I have the best news!"

Leah looked at Melissa. "What news?"

"I was invited to my sister-in-law's family's house party."

Leah smiled. "That is great news and sounds like fun. I am sure you will enjoy yourself. You must tell me all about it."

Melissa touched Leah's arm. "You do know that her father is *Baron* Morgan. I happen to know that he has invited Captain Shockley. He is bringing some of his fellow officers. One friend, who specifically asked if you would be in attendance." She smirked evaluating Leah's reaction. "Oh, please say you will come. I secured you an invitation and they said you were most welcomed. You know my family adores you."

Leah looked down. "I can't Mel. My mother needs me in the bookstore."

Melissa crossed her arms. "Nonsense, I already spoke to your mother earlier. She practically insisted that you go."

Leah hesitated, shaking her head.

Melissa grabbed her hands. "Please Leah. Captain Jackson asked to see you again. He remembered you from my mother's garden party a few months ago, and that is the only social gathering you have attended in months. I had to practically threaten you to attend that one. You are too young not to enjoy life. Your mother worries that you spend too much time at the bookstore and will never meet anyone to marry."

Leah felt defeated and wanted to make her friend happy. "Oh, stop graveling... I will go." She did remember Captain Jackson, although did not realize he would ask about her. Their introduction had been brief and included a vague conversation focused around the refreshments.

Melissa shrieked very loudly. "Oh, yes! It will be so much fun!"

Leah warned her friend. "I am only staying for few days and not the entire time."

Melissa creased her eyebrows. "Oh, very well... At least we will have a few days."

Melissa was chatting nonstop about the events scheduled for the party. Her family was not titled, but rich. Melissa's father owned several factories and was involved in trade. He was the third son of a viscount and had relatives within the *ton*—a term used for England's high society. Melissa had met Leah when her father was an active solicitor. Their families became friends and dined with each other on occasion. Melissa and Leah became instant best friends and she stuck with Leah when her father lost his practice.

Leah was listening to her friend when she heard someone clear their throat. Startled, she looked behind her. "Forgive me, Your Grace. Have you made your selection?"

"I think I will take both books, you never know with my sister."

Leah took a deep breath, meeting his eyes slightly before looking away. "Very well, I can wrap up your purchases at the table."

Melissa looked between the two, peering inquisitively at Leah.

Leah noticed the look of her friend. "This is His Grace, the Duke of Wollaston." She glanced at the duke, "Your Grace, this is Miss Baldwin."

Melissa curtsied, lowering down in her most polished curtsey. "Nice to make your acquaintance, Your Grace."

The duke bowed. "The pleasure is mine."

Leah felt nervous with Melissa's questioning gaze. "We met yesterday when I accidentally bumped into him on the street."

Melissa stared at them. "Indeed?"

The duke looked at the exchange. "Yes, I was most fortunate that Miss Johnson was not hurt and has accepted my apologies."

Leah blushed looking away. "He is most generous with the incident as it was my fault."

He put up his hand. "Nonsense."

They stared at each other for a few seconds in silence. Melissa cleared her throat and gave them a smile. "Well, I am just happy that you both are well. I must be on my way." Leah bid her friend a good day as she walked out the door.

The duke handed Leah some money and she put his purchase in a brown wrapping. "Thank you, Miss Johnson. My sister will be most pleased." He turned and left the store.

Leah took a deep breath and locked the store door to go home for the night. The day had proved exhausting.

CHAPTER 3

T HE DUKE OF WOLLASTON'S TOWNHOUSE was bustling with servants preparing for the night's festivities. He'd forgotten the invitations that had been sent out a fortnight ago, inviting Lady Jane and her acquaintances along with some of his closest friends. His sister Caroline had agreed to host the dining party and spared no expense as far as he could see. She lost her husband a little over a year ago, so the duke tried to keep her busy with any task he could find.

His best friend John Smith, the newest Earl of Shepley, had just arrived to claim his spot on the duke's favorite chair.

"Joseph? Don't look so grumpy, I am sure your mood will change once Lady Jane arrives." His friend raised his eyebrows and grinned. Lady Jane was sought after by most the men of the town. Her pursuit of Joseph was no secret, making him envied by many noblemen.

Joseph was not looking forward to the dining party. Lady Jane could offer some temporary comfort—perhaps even a distraction—yet he found her unappealing. She was a typical debutante with a pushy mother trying to make a match. Secretly they didn't know that he wasn't exactly on the marriage market.

Thoughts of the bookstore girl Leah were consuming his mind, and the last thing he needed was to spend the evening with a bunch of giggling women playing whist. He had to find a way to get an invitation to Baron Morgan's house party gracefully. He wanted to see her again.

"Forgive me, my friend. I have a lot of business to work on. You will soon learn what it is like to have all these responsibilities now that you are an earl." Joseph accepted some mail from the footman who entered the room then bowed to leave.

John shrugged his shoulders. "I may now be an earl, but I still know how to have fun. You have become quite boring, Wollaston. Soon you will be married and won't be able to play at all. Loosen up the cravat tonight and enjoy the company. Your mother is out of town, and Caroline thinks you need as much entertainment as I do." John sat up and took some tea biscuits lying on a tray in the corner. He stuffed two in his mouth. "You need to enjoy your last few months of bachelorhood until you get leg shackled."

Joseph looked down, taking a deep breath. "Give me a few hours to finish up some correspondence, and I will join you for some drinks before the guests arrive."

John stood up. "Very well, *Your Grace*." His sarcastic tone and over-exaggerated bow went unnoticed as he left the room. Joseph was preoccupied with a letter he needed to write to his man of business. He wanted him to check out Baron Morgan and find out about his background. If he could learn his business interests, he may be able to find a mutual acquaintance. He felt almost like a schoolboy again, competing for the attention of a female.

Joseph's jaw tightened as he thought back to John's comments regarding his upcoming engagement. He tried to push the thoughts out of his mind. The promise he made to his father on his deathbed plagued him. An arranged marriage was common in the *ton*. The late duke always told him that he was not like other men. His marriage would secure their livelihood and those that depend on him. It was his wish he would marry Lady Roslyn when her family arrived back from Italy. They'd lived abroad for the last year, and he had only met Roslyn once during a brief visit with her parents. Their families were old friends and arranged the meeting with the expectation they would suit. They only courted for a fortnight and the deal was made. She was a very proper girl and would make a great duchess. But he felt no love interest with their brief courtship—yet he agreed to his father's dying wish. They signed the marriage contract, and both agreed to announce it when she returned to London.

Joseph ran his fingers through his hair and groaned inwardly. He thought about his growing infatuation with a girl he barely knew. She was beautiful, even in her work attire. Her gray frock did not show off the delicious curves that he had seen the day before, but she could not hide her beauty. Thoughts of her wrapped in silk and diamonds played in his mind. It was not just her beauty, but her unspoiled innocence. It was unreasonable given their brief acquaintance, but he was determined to spend some more time with her before he had to face the circumstances of his future marriage.

Lady Caroline, the duke's sister, proved to be a delightful hostess. The servants set the tables with vases of roses and feathers with gold candlesticks. They also prepared eight courses which included three fancy desserts that were accompanied by fine wines. The guests listened to violin players as they enjoyed each other's conversations. Many compliments were given over the grandeur of the dining room. Caroline sat on the right side of her brother who was at the head of the table. John sat on his left side. Many toasts were made and received until the end of the dinner was announced. At that time, Lady Caroline led the ladies to the drawing room while the men enjoyed their port.

"Most of the prominent members of the ION club are here tonight. Should we talk about the shipment to India next week?" Lord Rinehart asked before taking a drink.

"You know the rules, Rinehart. Meeting notes have to be taken, and this is a social gathering." The Marquis of Wyatt was serious. The investment club, shortened to ION, was exclusive and many wanted to join. Joseph and a few of his close friends ran the club. They would pull their resources and money on many business ventures. One interested in joining needed the committee's nomination and approval to be a member.

"Wollaston, have you lent any support to the Earl of Halters and his newest cause?" Sir Jackson chuckled as he poked Lord Riverton in the ribs.

"We may have some deals that can be made Jackson, but we must wait and see." Joseph took a drink of his port. He eyed his friends as he tried to casually change the subject from the usual politics, as he wanted to find out what they knew. "Have any of you heard of a Baron Morgan?" Joseph tried to look nonchalant in his quest to find a link to the man's business interests.

Riverton drew in his eyebrows in thought. "Did you say, Baron Morgan? I believe he is friends with my father, and they might have gone to school together. He is a nice old man, and I have met him on occasion. Terrible shame what happened."

Joseph could not mask his interest. He quickly asked him. "What shame?"

Riverton cleared his throat. "He lost a lot of money on some risky investments, and I don't believe he participates much in polite society anymore." Riverton took a drink. "Why do you ask?"

Joseph was not sure how much he should reveal. "What kind of risky investment?"

Riverton shrugged his shoulders. "I don't know exactly, something to do with horse racing. Apparently, he raises horses on his estate. This business venture was for some new saddle or something that makes the saddle stronger. Unfortunately, the device that goes on the saddle did not work properly, and he lost all his investment. It was very sad. My father lent him money to keep him afloat."

The duke's interest peaked. "You say he raises horses? A business associate of mine may have an interest in purchasing some good stock and his name may have been mentioned. Do you think you could arrange an audience with me to look at some horses? Perhaps in a few days?"

Riverton drew up the corner of his mouth. "I can ask my father, but there are probably better horse breeders to choose from. The old baron may not be the best investment."

The duke cracked a smile trying to hide his true intentions. "I do remember my associate mentioning his name, and I would at least like to look at his stock. Perhaps on Saturday." His voice remained steady. The last thing he wanted was any attention at his eagerness to attend a country house party with the lower gentry.

Riverton nodded his head. "Of course, I will arrange it and accompany you."

The men finished their port and made their way into the drawing room. The ladies stopped their chattering and welcomed them. Lady Jane marked her territory by looping her arm around Joseph.

"You must play whist, Your Grace." She rubbed his arm touching him ever so slightly.

"Of course. I have already claimed the winning partner." He reached out and took his sister's hand. Lady Jane curtsied in defeat eyeing the siblings. Caroline was the safest partner—he did not need any romantic hassles with the other women who were pining for his attention.

CHAPTER 4

LEAH TOOK THE CARROTS OUT of the pot and added them to the beef stew. The smell of the beef made her mouth water. The extra carrots would make the stew go further as everyone was hungry. Miss Freemont, the family's only servant, put the bowls out for Leah to scoop the stew into. A few of the bowls were chipped but had stood strong for many meals throughout the years. The family used to have a cook, three maids, and a groom before Leah's father took ill. The small manor house that she shared with three siblings and her parents had steadily declined without the proper upkeep. The roof needed repairs and two windows were cracked. They didn't have money in their budget to buy the supplies to fix the manor. Leah was the oldest in her family and helped Miss Freemont with the household chores when she wasn't working in the bookstore.

"Where did you get all those carrots, child?" Miss Freemont laughed deeply as Leah put more into the pot. Her red hair with specks of gray fell around her face. Perspiration beaded on her forehead from the heat of the kitchen.

"Mr. Wilcox made me take a bag. He told me he had a lot of extra vegetables and didn't want them to go to waste." Leah shrugged her shoulders as she tasted the stew.

"Hmm… Mr. Wilcox may be a bit smitten with you. Last week he offered you a bag of potatoes and the week before he had two extra chickens." She raised one of her eyebrows. That look was embedded in Leah's childhood memory. It was Miss Freemont's way of asking a question that she already knew the answer to.

"You think that means he is smitten? I think he is just nice." Leah stirred the pot of stew. "Besides, he's an old man. He is at least forty." Her wedding day dreams were not of men twice her age.

"Forty and single and it's not just food. He sent flowers yesterday as well." Miss Freemont carried the silver tray to the counter.

"Flowers? Those were for the family, not just me." Leah picked out the spoons and put one in each bowl.

"Please child, what man delivers flowers to a family? It's part of his pursuit. Betty is far too young, and your mother is married. It's you he is interested in. You are a beautiful girl even though you try to hide it. He has his own house and inherited a small living from his grandfather. He could make a good match." Miss Freemont smiled at her as she took the water pitcher to pour water into glasses.

Bewildered, Leah stopped working in the kitchen to look at her. A realization that Miss Freemont may be right hit her like a ton of bricks. A match with Mr. Wilcox was not impossible. After all, many young girls married older men. She reminded herself to be more attentive to the man's charitable deeds as he may expect a payback from her. Albeit, he never made any forward advances, he could be planning a pursuit. She had mistakenly taken his attention for her family as being a good neighbor. It was true she was of marriageable age, but a courtship was out of the question. She must be more careful not to encourage him.

"I am not interested in a match with Mr. Wilcox or any other man. I want to take care of my family and work in the bookstore." Leah fumbled with her apron as she looked at Miss Freemont.

Miss Freemont carefully looked at Leah. "Leah, your parents want to see you settled and know you will be taken care of. You must not dismiss a good offer if one should come." Miss Freemont's eyebrows furrowed with concern.

Taking the bowls to the table, she thought about what Miss Freemont had said. She hadn't thought about her marriage as a relief to her parents. It would take a burden off them if she would marry, but they still needed her. Didn't they?

Leah looked across the room at her younger brother Travis as he entered the front door. He had hoped to follow in his father's footsteps and attend Oxford, but the family could not afford it. He hid his feelings well and contributed most of his income to the family budget. Leah felt pride in her brother and hoped that someday he could attend the university.

Her youngest brother Jasper was lying down on the settee. He had dreamed of being an officer in the military, but Leah feared they would never be able to afford a commission. He helped with the chores outside and kept the animals fed. He was one and six and could handle horses better than anyone Leah knew.

Betty, her youngest sister, planned on being a writer. Leah had enjoyed writing when she was younger but had to give it up to help the family. She couldn't find enough time to write when she had her chores and the bookstore to take care of. Betty was only one and four and dreamed of poetry and a white knight who would rescue her someday.

Leah called her family to the table, so they could eat together. They tore into the beef stew and threw compliments at Miss Freemont and Leah regarding the meal. She prepared a special bowl for her father, so he could eat in his room. He often got a chill when he left the bedroom and chose to take his meals on a tray near his bed. Leah would sometimes read to him while he sat in a chair, but he did not venture outdoors and rarely outside of his room.

Leah savored the beef as she tasted the rich juice surrounding the stew. Her siblings were laughing as they were talking about Jasper chasing some chickens that morning. Leah took in their faces, enjoying her time with her family.

The duke woke up late the next day and tried to ignore his valet's rude opening of the curtains. The man persisted that he get out of bed, but Joseph felt he needed much more rest. He stayed up late the night before with his friends from the dinner party.

The valet told him that he had a visitor from his solicitor's office in the drawing room that insisted on speaking with him. Joseph moaned inwardly as he raised his head off the pillow and forced himself out of bed to wash up. He dressed quickly with the help of his valet and made his way down the grand staircase that overlooked the massive marble-wrapped foyer. The duke entered the drawing room and greeted his visitor.

"Mr. Smith, so glad you could come. I apologize for my delay as I am most anxious for your news. Please join me in my study." The duke was curious to see what Mr. Smith had uncovered. He worked as a detective for his solicitor and had Lord Morgan checked out. He gestured to the study doors and both men entered the room.

"Good to see you again, Your Grace. Mr. Dickerson asked me to deliver the news in person. I am sorry to disturb you in the morning hours, but I am leaving for Kent soon and wanted to deliver our report first." He raised his eyebrow as he took the paperwork out of his case.

The duke dismissively flicked his hand. "It's quite all right. What did you find out?"

Mr. Smith took a seat in the wing back chair on the other side of the duke's desk. He took a deep breath. "Well, it seems that Baron Morgan did indeed lose his fortune in a busted business venture. His oldest son and heir, George, is now engaged to a rich merchant's daughter from America. I verified that they have deep pockets and are paying for the house party next week. It seems there was a hefty bride price for their daughter to marry a titled gentleman. Although I was not able to find out the exact amount."

He shook his head as he took another paper from the pile. "What the merchant does not know is that Baron Morgan has been out of polite society for a while now. Not quite what the merchant paid for in my opinion."

He shifted and adjusted his spectacles looking again at the paperwork. "He raises horses and hopes to sell some of them soon to subsidize his income." Mr. Smith leaned back in his chair. "It seems Mr. Hogget, the merchant, has invited some of his business associates as well to the party. Lord Morgan extended an invitation to his son's military chums. His daughter's husband sent invitations to a few titled gentlemen. None of which have accepted the invitation as of yesterday."

The duke flexed his jaw as his plan came into action. He grinned at the detective. "I applaud your work and must thank you. I know you want to get an early start for Kent."

"Of course, Your Grace." Mr. Smith stood and bowed as he left the room.

The duke rubbed his chin. He had visions of Leah on his mind wondering what she must be doing at that moment. No chit had ever filled his mind as much as she had the last few days. He hoped his plan would come together and Riverton held the key. He had to visit Riverton soon about the arrangements and would feign interest in purchasing some horses in a deal that must take place at the same time as the house party. If things went well, he might even purchase a few of them in good faith.

Lord Riverton's townhouse was not far from Joseph's. He was anxious to meet with him regarding the house party and his new interest in acquiring horses from Baron Morgan.

"Wollaston, is anything amiss?" Riverton showed up in the drawing room in his robe. His hair was disheveled, and his eyes were droopy. "What brings you here at this early hour? Is someone dead?"

Joseph smirked at his friend and patted him on the back. "Business, my friend."

Riverton shook his head. "Give me a few minutes, and I will dress and be back to join you to break my fast. The servants will be in shock that I am up this early."

Joseph smiled, taking a seat on the settee to wait for Riverton's return. He looked through the paperwork one more time as his thoughts turned to Leah. If any of his friends knew the length that he went through to secure an invitation to this party, they would never let him live it down. He had a reputation among the town as a cad. What would they think of him now? In the back of his mind, he knew that his upcoming engagement would be pressing, but he didn't want to think about it.

Riverton returned dressed and with his hair combed. Joseph followed his friend into the dining room for a quick bite to eat.

"So, what business could not wait?" Riverton asked while stuffing a breakfast cake into his mouth. Joseph smiled at him, taking a sip of coffee.

"Well, my man of business has confirmed with me that Baron Morgan does have some quality stock horses for sale that I could probably get at a great price due to his financial situation. However, there is a rumor that his eldest son is marrying soon and receiving a substantial amount of money. When this happens, Lord Morgan may not be impoverished for long. I heard there was a small house party this weekend, and I need you to secure an invitation for a few days. Your family is the only one that seems to know him among the *ton*."

Riverton creased his brow puzzled at his friend's request. "Wollaston, you are a duke with a huge fortune. Why do you care about the baron's stock of horses? You can buy them anywhere. Besides, the money from the bride's family will only be enough to keep him out of a debtor's prison."

The duke took a bite of his eggs and shrugged his shoulders. "I heard his stock is one of the best and he may not be aware of it. I must admit that curiosity has taken hold of me and I want to see what he has to offer."

Riverton swallowed some tea. "As you wish. I will send a missive today, and I may even join you to see what stock he has available. I wouldn't mind a few days in the country and a nice house party, although most of the guests will not be our usual acquaintances."

The duke cracked a half smile. "Don't be so proud. A few days won't kill us. It will probably have more amusements that the ton parties."

CHAPTER 5

LEAH WENT THROUGH HER WARDROBE one more time. She was going to be at the house party for only a few days and did not have enough clothes. Melissa told her there would be dancing and a ball on one of the nights. She only owned two decent day dresses that fit her—the others she outgrew a few years ago, and her family did not have the funds to buy new dresses for the house party. She regretted accepting the invitation.

Leah packed the dress that Ellen had given her and the new gloves. That would cover the one night at the ball. She owned one Sunday dress that could possibly be worn as another dinner gown. She packed the two day dresses she wore for special occasions and settled on two work dresses that would have to make due. One was brown, and one was gray, and she wore them for her chores around the house, but she had nothing else in her closet except the old riding habit that Melissa gave her last year.

"Leah?" Her mother interrupted her packing and walked into her room.

"Hello, Mama. I was just packing my trunk." She continued to fold her clothes and didn't notice the dress in her mother's hand.

Mrs. Johnson smiled at her. "I have something for you. It's an old day dress of mine that still looks new. I grew out of it after my last pregnancy, but I thought the green color would bring out the color of your eyes."

Leah smiled at her mother's thoughtfulness. The dress was out of fashion, but still beautiful. Her eyes burned with tears as she basked in her mother's kindness throughout their tough times. Mrs. Johnson had sold most of her jewelry and nice dresses to help pay the family bills, but she must have kept this dress and Leah was thankful.

"Oh, Mother! It's beautiful. I will wear it my first day." Leah held it up and spun around. Her mother smiled, hugging her daughter.

Leah was thankful to know she had one more dress to wear for her journey. She had enough money to purchase some new stockings and perhaps a bonnet. Ellen had given her some lavender perfume for her last birthday that she could use. She took the old silver chain her grandmother had given her out of her jewelry box and put it in her reticule. It was the only jewelry she owned.

Leah sat on her bed and had second thoughts on whether she should cancel her trip. It was silly to go through all this work for a house party full of people that she did not know. Baron Morgan had a title and Captain Jackson probably would not even speak to her. She was no one to them.

After tossing and turning for most the night, she decided to go. She'd made a promise to her good friend and would reluctantly attend. But she refused to get her hopes up that she would have a good time.

<hr />

The duke and Lord Riverton took three carriages to the house party to carry all their luggage and valets. They rode their horses outside of the carriage for the journey. Their grooms would join them later. The estate was not too far, and they should arrive there by late afternoon.

"I hope the food is good. I am famished." Riverton rubbed his stomach looking at the duke.

Joseph laughed at his exaggeration. "Me, too."

Riverton grunted. "I heard Morgan was ecstatic that a duke was going to be at his house party. The messenger told me that Lady Morgan was most pleased to be the hostess. She is hoping to be mentioned in the society pages."

Joseph rolled his eyes. "Happy I could oblige."

Riverton stretched his back while he was riding. "I hope this trip is worth it—I gave up cards tonight at the club."

Joseph thought about Leah. "I am sure it will be full of surprises."

The trip lasted a few more hours before they arrived at the estate. The main house was of modest size but starting to show its age. It was surrounded by two more houses with the same worn exterior walls. In the back of the estate, there were two large stables surrounded by fenced pastures. The duke was impressed at the size of the stables and looked forward to seeing the horses.

Several footmen met the party and helped them with their trunks. Their hostess Lady Morgan, an older woman with brown hair and a heavy frame, greeted them at the door and escorted them inside. The crest on the carriage gave away their identity and many servants came out to service them.

"Lady Morgan, you have a beautiful home and I am most grateful that you extended an invitation to stay with you for a few days."

She chuckled and leaned down for a lopsided curtsey. "Your Grace, the pleasure is ours. The house party began yesterday, and my husband is attending to some guests. I will have George show you to your rooms, so you can freshen up and my husband can meet you shortly for luncheon."

The duke thanked her, and they were shown to their rooms in the main house. His room was huge and displayed royal blue carpets with gold tapestries. The four-poster bed had velvet coverings with the same blue and gold color theme. The window at the back of the room gave a glimpse into the garden where he could see some guests playing yard games. He searched the area to see if Leah had arrived yet. The ladies held parasols making it difficult to locate if any of them were her. He was anxious to make his presence known and went to join the guests for lunch.

Baron Morgan was of small stature with red hair and freckles. He greeted the duke with a bow and welcomed him to his home. The luncheon was served buffet style on the terrace. Many guests were filling their plates as the baron took a seat with Joseph and Riverton.

"Your Grace, I am anxious to show you some of the stock. We have organized a horse race for tomorrow afternoon that should display some of the skills of my thoroughbreds."

The duke grinned at him. "I am looking forward to it, Lord Morgan."

Joseph took a bite of cheese with bread, before washing it down with a drink of water. Glancing around the terrace, he noticed a light green gown and dark blond hair that shimmered in the sunlight. His breath caught for a few seconds when she turned to a man with a blue coat on. It was Leah.

"Excuse me for a moment, gentleman. I think I see someone I know."

Joseph walked across the terrace to speak to Leah as she was smiling at a man in whispered conversation. Interrupting the young couple, he stepped beside them, "Pardon me, Miss Johnson? Is that you?"

Puzzled, Leah looked up to a familiar face. "Your Grace? What a surprise to see you here."

"Yes, I have some business with Lord Morgan. He has invited me to stay a few days."

Leah locked eyes with the duke, surprised by his presence. Trying to recover from her shock at being the center of attention, she remembered her manners. "That is great news. I hope you enjoy yourself." She looked over at her companions, "May I introduce you to the Duke of Wollaston? Your Grace, this is Captain Jackson and Captain Shockley. They are a part of the Royal Navy."

The duke nodded at them. "I am happy to make your acquaintance."

They bowed, "Your Grace."

Leah looked at Melissa. "You remember, His Grace?"

She smiled at the duke. "Of course, from the bookstore. Nice to see you again." She bent down in a curtsey.

Captain Shockley looked at Melissa and Captain Jackson. "Should we depart?"

Melissa agreed, "Yes, let me tell my sister-in-law where I will be."

The men excused themselves and walked away. Melissa followed them but stopped to look back at Leah. "Are you coming? We are going to the river."

"Yes, I will meet you in a moment." They walked away and stopped to wait for her at the bottom of the hill as she turned back to the duke.

"I must go now. It was nice to see you again." She curtsied to take her leave.

"Miss Johnson?" The duke stepped closer to her.

Leah was taken off guard as he leaned down to whisper near her ear. She felt the warmth from his breath tickle her cheek. "The pleasure was mine." He reached for her hand and kissed it. Leah was dazed and stood still.

The duke seemed to enjoy keeping her off-balance. "I will see you at dinner." He turned on his heel and left.

———————

Leah stared after him for a moment before strolling down the hill. She thought about the exchange in her head. Surely, the duke was just being polite, but the kiss on her hand made her face feel a bit warm. Why would he be at the same house party as her? After all, he was a peer and a prestigious duke.

When she approached the group, she noticed that Melissa gave her a prying stare. Leah shrugged it off and smoothed her dress as she took the arm of Captain Jackson and they walked to the river.

"You have friends in high places, Miss Johnson." Captain Shockley lifted the corner of his mouth and grinned.

"He is a not a friend. Just a customer at my mother's bookstore. I am barely acquainted with him."

Leah did not like his suggestion. They strolled for over an hour talking of pleasantries when Leah heard the water rushing. It was a small river and reminded Leah more of a creek.

Melissa clutched Leah's arm and they ran to the water laughing. Leah stopped near a big rock and stepped onto it. Captain Jackson stepped on the rock beside her. The breeze from the water was a welcomed reprieve as it cooled them down after running. Leah could see fish jumping near the other side. Melissa and Captain Shockley walked farther down the creek leaving Leah and Captain Jackson alone. Captain Jackson stepped off the rocks and helped Leah descend to the shore.

"Have you ever seen a rock skip?" He looked down at her and smiled. Leah thought he was handsome in a rugged way. Years at sea had given him a bit of a worn look making him look older than he was. His dark hair matched his eyes and the tan on his face was apparent from his time at sea. He was clean-shaven for the house party but donned a beard at the garden party she had attended. She liked the way he looked.

"I don't believe that I have, Captain. Will you show me?"

The captain looked around and chose some flat rocks. He took the rock and threw with a side motion across the creek causing the rock to bounce several times.

Leah giggled. "Show me how you did that."

The captain took a step toward Leah then took her hand. His hands were rough and strong as he placed a rock in her hand. He stood behind her and guided her hands with the rock as they threw it together. The rock bounced three times and Leah squealed with excitement. Captain Jackson did not let go of her hand for a few seconds.

Leah turned around and looked up at him. "That was so much fun."

His grin turned serious as he studied her face. "Your enthusiasm is refreshing. I must take you to the river more often." He bent down and tucked a piece of hair behind her ear and kissed her cheek. Leah's heart leaped at the affectionate gesture. She turned around to see if Melissa had noticed, but she did not see them. She looked back up at Captain Jackson and bit her bottom lip.

"Do you fish?" She was nervous and did not know how to respond to his kiss.

He had amusement in his eyes and probably knew she was nervous. "I have on occasion when I was younger. The military doesn't allow much time for such outings."

"Are you going to sail anymore? Melissa told me you were resigning your commission and going to America."

He walked to the trees near the shoreline, took off his jacket and laid it beside him. He motioned for her to sit on it under a big tree. Leah followed his gesture and sat beside him.

"I have a job offer in America to run my own ship. My uncle owns a fleet of them and offered me a lucrative opportunity with his company. I have a few weeks to think about it." He lay back on his elbows and closed his eyes.

"It must be exciting that you could live abroad. Think of all the adventures you will have." Leah imagined the sights and people he could meet.

He gazed up at her from the ground. "Some sights here are better than all others."

Leah was not sure what he meant. "What kind of sights?"

Captain Jackson sat up and took her hand. "You, Leah."

Leah's eyes enlarged, and she looked away from him. She was embarrassed by his compliment and use of her Christian name. He touched her chin and turned it to him.

"You're blushing." He licked his lips and bent down, softly brushing his lips across hers.

Leah closed her eyes as her heart skipped a beat. The kiss was soft and quick. She slowly opened her eyes and he released her chin.

"I... haven't decided about America yet. I have some unfinished business here."

Leah looked at him with a serious face. Hearing voices, the couple turned around and saw Melissa coming up the hill. She was running from Captain Shockley laughing. "I told you I could beat you."

Captain Shockley was out of breath. "You cheated."

She looked at Leah. "Tell him I didn't cheat."

Leah and Captain Jackson stood up and walked to meet the couple. Captain Jackson reached for Leah's hand and put it through his arm. "We should head back for dinner."

CHAPTER 6

LEAH PUT ON HER SUNDAY dress for dinner. The dress had a fitted bodice and a lace collar and was in a shimmery rose color. Melissa and her lady's maid Lucy came across the hall to help Leah fix her hair. She wasn't used to such luxuries and thanked them for the assistance. Lucy put some tiny flowers through her hair and Melissa let her borrow a pearl necklace. The girls giggled as they made finishing touches to their look.

Leah could hear the voices in the drawing room as the guests were served drinks getting ready for the dinner announcement. She strolled across the foyer and was caught by a voice behind her. "Miss Johnson?" Leah turned around with Melissa and noticed the duke dressed in some deep brown coat and brown trousers. He had a handsome friend beside him with brown hair and a tan jacket.

"Your Grace, how are you this evening?" She felt pressure on her chest trying to mask her nervousness as her eyes met his.

The duke studied her face with admiration in his eyes. With the smoothness of a duke, his throaty response dripped with flirtation. "I am better now, Miss Johnson. You have brightened the room. I would like you to meet my companion, Lord Riverton."

Both girls curtsied. Leah's face burned with embarrassment. The duke openly complimented her, causing Melissa to stare at her, suppressing a giggle. Leah swallowed hard and addressed Lord Riverton. "Nice to make your acquaintance."

She looked at Melissa who was grinning at him. "Lord Riverton."

The duke's expression turned serious. "Miss Johnson, I was hoping to see you before dinner. You see, Riverton and I are in a predicament. We don't have any female acquaintances at this party and I need to escort someone to dinner."

Leah slanted her head trying to understand his concern. "I am sure many lovely ladies would be more than willing to assist you, Your Grace."

The duke gave an exaggerated sigh. "If only it were that easy. I am hoping that you may be able to help me since we are already acquainted. You see, I would feel more comfortable if you would do me the honor of escorting you to dinner." Riverton looked at Melissa with a smirk and then looked away.

Leah rubbed her lips together, contemplating his request. After a few seconds, she straightened her shoulders. "As you wish, I would be honored."

The duke took Leah's hand and put it in the crook of his arm. "Shall we get a drink before dinner?" He led Leah to the drawing room and took two glasses of sherry.

Leah took the glass of sherry while the duke was called away by Lady Morgan. She let go of the duke's arm and took the opportunity to speak to Joslynn, Melissa's sister-in-law.

Lady Morgan touched his arm. "Your Grace, we would like to introduce you to our son, Mr. Morgan and his lovely fiancée, Miss Shepherd. They should be married within a few months."

"You're a real duke?" Miss Shepherd looked inquisitively at him while displaying her American accent.

He squinted his eyes at her. "I hope so. That's what my father told me." The small crowd laughed.

The next female waiting for an introduction was Madelyn Printer. She was an attractive girl with dark hair and blue eyes. Everyone knew she was the daughter of a knight as she told everyone that would listen. Her father had a modest fortune and she was always dressed in the latest fashion. She did not like Leah or Melissa and tried to make sure that Leah knew her place.

Madelyn batted her eyelashes. "Your Grace, it's nice to see you at our humbled country gathering. I am sure it does not compare to the parties that you are accustomed to."

The duke grinned, assessing the young lady who was showing her interest. He was tired of the many debutantes who threw themselves at him for a chance to be a duchess. He would not encourage her with any flirtation. His response was polite but short. "Lady Morgan is a great hostess. I have enjoyed myself."

Lord Riverton entered the room and went to stand by the duke. Madelyn held her companion's arm. "This is Lady Krystal, and her father is the Earl of Searcy. Perhaps you know him?"

The duke smiled at her shy friend. "I don't believe I've had the pleasure."

Lord Riverton cracked a smile interrupting. "I believe I have been introduced to him. His family is from Bath?"

Lady Krystal looked down. "Yes, my Lord."

The group spoke about the city of Bath and the duke interrupted the conversation. "I must speak to Lady Morgan for a moment if you will excuse me." The group nodded their heads and then resumed their discussion.

The duke walked to Lady Morgan by the fireplace. "Hello, my lady. Would you perhaps do me a favor?"

She acknowledged him with curtsey. "Of course, Your Grace."

He smiled, "I need to speak to Miss Johnson about a mutual acquaintance and would like very much to have my dining card placed next to hers at dinner. Can you arrange that for me? I would also prefer not to formalize the dinner by rank. Is that acceptable?"

She curtsied. "As you wish."

The duke looked around the crowds to find Leah and noticed her speaking to the same man on the terrace. He had forgotten his name and did not like the way he was looking at her. As he walked to her, he saw Madelyn standing with Riverton and Lady Krystal.

Madelyn blocked his path to Leah and leaned toward him showing off her low neckline. "Should we go to dinner together?"

The duke was annoyed by the presumptuous young woman. The footman made the dinner announcement and couples came together to enter the dining room. The duke leaned down to Madelyn. "Thank you, but I already have a prior arrangement." He turned and walked to Leah. He smiled at the group she was speaking with as he approached her. "Shall we go?"

Leah smiled and looked back at her companion. "I will see you after dinner. I had accepted his escort to dinner earlier." The man nodded his head and the duke guided Leah to the door.

"Did I tell you how lovely you look tonight?" He patted her hand that was on his arm.

She whispered near his ear. "Thank you. I was not sure what to wear. This is my first house party."

Her sweet nature was refreshing. He grinned, and leaned down to whisper in her ear. "You outshine every female here. Don't let anyone tell you different."

Leah choked on a laugh. "You do tease me, Your Grace."

They arrived at the table as the couples were reading the place cards and men were escorting the women to sit down. Leah found hers and Joseph pulled out the chair for her to sit.

He picked up his dining card. "Look, Miss Johnson. My card is next to yours."

The dining room was decorated with roses and the smells from the kitchen were making Leah's mouth water. Madelyn Printer sat across from Leah with Mr. Palmer, a local solicitor, on one side and Mr. Jones, a friend of the baron's, on the other side. Captain Jackson sat at a different table. Melissa sat on the other side of Mr. Palmer with a look of concern as she noticed the duke whispering in Leah's ear.

"Tell me Miss Johnson, what is your favorite food?" The duke gazed down when he whispered to her.

"Actually, I have many favorites. If I had to choose only one, it would be roast beef, although we only have it on special occasions. What about you?" She smiled as the footman delivered turtle soup.

"I think roast beef is my favorite too." He smiled and winked at her taking a spoonful of the soup. Leah looked down at the soup and moved her spoon around the bowl. "You do like to tease me."

He chuckled. "I only like to see your beautiful smile." Leah turned to her soup and lifted the spoon to her mouth. She tasted the spices and enjoyed the warmth of the broth.

Leah noticed Madelyn watching her exchange with the duke. She raised the corner of her mouth in a half-grin and Leah had a sudden bad feeling in the pit of her stomach. "Miss Johnson, what a pleasant surprise to see you here. I didn't realize you were on the guest list." Her voice carried across the table with a condescending tone. Some of the other guests stared at Leah.

Leah shifted in her seat covering her lap with her napkin. Her thoughts took her back to the time when her friends, including Madelyn, turned their back on her when her father lost his business. She did not know how to answer but took a deep breath and whispered, "Melissa invited me." Leah tried to turn to Melissa and ignore Madelyn.

Madelyn tilted her head. "Indeed?" Madelyn looked over at Melissa and then back to Leah. "Are you still *working* at the bookstore?" Madelyn took a drink before putting her cup down and staring at Leah.

Leah's mouth went dry and she noticed the other guests were waiting for her reply. Women who worked were looked down upon in some circles. Certainly, in the duke's world, who sat right beside her. Leah's heart pounded in her chest. She looked at the duke and saw his eyes glowering at Madelyn.

She turned back to Madelyn. "Yes, I do help my mother at her bookstore." Leah turned her head to the duke and smiled. "I meet the most interesting customers."

The duke's soft brown eyes held interest in her. "I found the store enchanting, but it could have been the help." He took a bite of bread and gazed at Leah.

Madelyn's body tensed at the duke's comments. "Hmm, that's an interesting necklace you have on Leah. Where did you get it?"

Leah bit her bottom lip. "Err... actually, Melissa let me borrow it."

Madelyn cracked a smile. Her eyes rested on the tinted pearls with a spark of recognition in her eyes. "Oh, so kind of her to help out a friend with lesser means. You know, you're welcome to borrow a piece from me if you need to. Having no jewelry would be awful."

Leah's mouth dropped open as her face burned in embarrassment. Melissa looked at Madelyn. "Stop it, Maddie."

Madelyn placed her hand on her chest and looked at Melissa. "I was only trying to be nice and this is how I am treated?"

Leah was mortified at her suggestion. Everyone knew that her family was penniless, but to suggest in front of the other guests that she had to borrow jewelry was embarrassing. Leah could not even look at the duke.

The duke looked at Madelyn and smiled. "Actually, it's hardly fair to the jewels if Miss Johnson wears them."

The guests looked confused. Melissa looked at the duke. "Why is that, Your Grace?"

The duke had given Madelyn a scowling look and moved his eyes to Melissa to address the question. "Her beauty outshines them."

Madelyn looked down at her plate and was silent. Mr. Palmer held out his glass of wine. "I will drink to that, Your Grace."

Leah's heart could not take any more of their pity. She was humiliated and put her napkin on the table. Avoiding eye contact with the others, she stood up addressing Melissa. "If you will excuse me, I am not feeling well."

The duke and the other men around her stood as she left the dining room. The duke went to escort her, but she put her hand out. "Please, finish your meal. I will be fine." He hesitated but nodded taking his seat again. Leah didn't notice as she left the dining room, but the duke's eyes shot daggers at Madelyn.

Leah rushed to her chamber sobbing loudly as the tears poured down her face. She rested her head on her bed contemplating not joining the others for the stargazing they had planned for later in the evening. She did not want to face the duke or Captain Jackson. The last thing she needed was anyone's pity for the circumstances of her family. She just wanted to go home but knew she had to get herself together to be able to join in the festivities and hold her head up high in front of the others.

Captain Jackson approached Melissa after dinner. "Is Miss Johnson unwell? I saw her leave the table after the first course."

Melissa touched Captain Shockley's arm and looked back at Captain Jackson. "I will go try to find her."

They looked up the stairs as Leah was coming down to them.

Her face was flushed, and she gave a guarded smile. She glanced at Melissa. "I am well." She refused to let Madelyn ruin her time. Captain Jackson held out his arm to escort her.

The duke walked by the couple. "Miss Johnson, are you feeling better?"

Leah looked up at the duke and his friends not wishing to talk about her humiliation. "Yes, Your Grace. Thank you."

She quickly turned away touching Captain Jackson's arm. He looked between the duke and Leah. Leah squeezed his arm and smiled back at the group trying to mask her discomfort. "We are going to look at the stars on this beautiful night. Captain Jackson is going to teach us the constellations."

"Indeed?" The duke grinned, taking Leah's hand and lifting it up to his lips. "I will see you later, Miss Johnson. Enjoy."

The duke watched after them as they walked away, his grave expression gave away his dislike for Captain Jackson.

Lord Riverton let out a laugh and the duke glared at him. "Your Grace, were you just given the cut?"

The duke narrowed his eyes. "Watch it."

Lord Riverton smirked and accepted two glasses of brandy from a footman. "Drink up, Your Grace. Let's play some cards."

The duke agreed and followed Lord Riverton to the cardroom. He hesitated by the window peeking out to watch the couples walk away from the estate.

The air felt cool on Leah's face. She snuggled a little closer to the captain feeling warmer. The foursome walked up to the hills in the back of the estate to get a better view. Melissa had brought a few blankets for them to rest on while they stargazed. Her maid and two footmen walked behind the group. Captain Shockley found a spot of grass for the group and spread the blankets out. He helped Melissa lay back to look at the stars. Captain Jackson sat down beside Leah. He pointed out different constellations and told her stories from the days he served in the Royal Navy. Leah liked the sound of his voice and his knowledge of the sky. After an hour, the group sat in silence as they gazed into the blackened universe. It was getting colder and Leah shivered. The captain took his jacket off and put it over her shoulders. Leah put her head on his shoulder smelling the woodsy scent on him.

A drop of rain fell on Leah's cheek and then two more drops. Melissa yelped. "It is starting to rain. We should head back."

Captain Jackson groaned. "Leah, keep my jacket over your head and let's hurry." Leah smiled at the use of her Christian name. She shook her head. "I can't take your jacket, you will freeze."

He pulled her closer to him. "Nonsense, I will hold on to you to keep warm." Leah laughed as they ran together to the main house. When they arrived on the terrace they stood beneath the stone shelter. Melissa and Captain Shockley caught up with them.

"It is pouring now. We should get inside to change." Melissa reached for Leah. "We need to get out of these wet clothes." The girls hurried to their chambers after asking her maid for some hot tea.

Once inside her room, Leah removed her drenched clothes and folded her body up in a quilt. She sat on the window seat and watched outside. The glass was fogged up from the passing rain and she swiped the pane with her hand to enhance her view. The darkness provided cover to the estate as her eyes adjusted to the stable in the background. A tiny beacon of light broke through the blackness showing the outline of a window. The stillness of the night caused her eyes to droop when she saw a flicker in the bushes.

She widened her eyes trying to get a better look. The light reflected from the window resting on a small creature rolling in the grass. It had stopped raining making her vision clearer. Leah squinted trying to focus on the creature realizing it was a kitten—a baby kitten that was all alone. Leah's chest filled with anxiety thinking about the harm that could come to the baby animal. Her heart beat faster watching it fall into a nearby bush. Leah stepped away from the window and dressed quickly. She placed a shawl over her shoulders and headed to the rear servant stairs.

The night air was freezing with dampness causing a chill. She pulled her shawl closer walking around the back of the house to the stables. Her motherly instincts in protecting the kitten took hold of her. The stone path in the dark was barely visible, but the lights from the terrace helped her locate it. She made her way down through the bushes and called for the kitten. After several attempts, she looked through the bushes and finally heard a faint cry. Leah smiled with relief and picked up the kitten. She held the kitten close to her chest to keep it warm and gave it small kisses. When she backed away from the bush, she ran into a solid body and quickly turned around letting out a gasp.

"Miss Johnson? What are you doing out here?" The Duke of Wollaston was standing in front of Leah.

"Oh, you frightened me, Your Grace." Leah held the kitten protectively in her arms.

The duke looked at her with bewilderment. "What are you hiding?"

Leah looked down. "It's a kitten that I saw from my window. There must be a mother somewhere nearby. He may be lost, and I wanted to keep him safe."

The duke smiled. "You came out in the cold to rescue a kitten?"

Leah creased her forehead, surprised at such a question. "Of course, I couldn't let it fend for itself."

The duke petted the kitten in Leah's arms. A bit of surprise mixed with amusement showed through his stare. "Very well, Miss Johnson. Let's go into the stable and see if we can find the mother or somewhere the kitten can stay tonight."

He walked to the stable and Leah followed. The light from a lantern hanging in the window enabled them to look around the stable calling out for the mother. The duke climbed up to the loft to see if there were any other kittens.

"Leah, I think we may be in luck tonight. There are a few others here in the corner, so the mother can't be far away." The duke reached down from the ladder and Leah handed him the kitten. He carefully took the kitten and Leah followed him up the ladder trying not to rip her dress. Thankfully, it was loose enough to allow her to lift her legs to climb. She tried to gracefully crawl with the duke across the hay into a corner where a few other kittens were sleeping. Leah watched him lay the kitten next to the others, and they quietly backed away.

He crawled over to the ladder climbing down and then assisted Leah down. He laughed at their situation. "Not the most proper position to be in. We better get you inside before propriety is broken."

She reached for the hay stuck to her dress and wiped it away. "Yes, I think that may have been a problem the minute we entered the stable."

Leah walked behind the duke to the stable door. "Your Grace?" He turned around and looked at her.

"Yes?" He gazed down at her causing her to slightly lose her balance.

Leah bit her bottom lip. "How did you find me?"

He examined her face closely, hesitating before speaking as if he changed his mind before he spoke, "I happened to come out on the terrace for some air, and I saw you going to the stable alone at this hour. You couldn't blame me for being curious. You should be more careful, Miss Johnson. Not everyone has good intentions."

She looked down at his warning. "I know I didn't use my best judgment. I could only think about the welfare of the kitten."

He stepped closer to her and brought her chin up to look at him. Without saying a word, he cupped her face bending down to press a soft kiss on her lips.

Leah froze.

She could not bring herself to look at him. Did he just kiss her? The duke touched her face.

"Look at me, Leah." He used her Christian name—a common occurrence this evening between the duke and Captain Jackson.

Leah hesitated as she was embarrassed. Slowly, she lifted her eyes to meet his gaze. He locked her eyes for a second and wetted his lips. For a moment, she thought he might kiss her again. "Will you go riding with me tomorrow morning?"

Not making a sound, she managed to nod her head as she stared into his eyes. He smiled at her and offered his arm to walk to the main house. As they approached the terrace, the duke stopped short and pulled her back.

"I will wait here, and you can go up the back stairs. After a few minutes, I will go inside the terrace doors, so no one will know we were together. Meet me at the stables tomorrow morning. The races will be after lunch, and I will need your help in deciding which ones to buy."

He held both her hands and kissed them. Leaning toward her ear he whispered, "Sweet dreams."

Leah curtsied and turned to leave. She never said a word and practically ran to the servant's entrance being careful not to look back. Once she turned the corner and was out of view from the duke, she leaned against the house to catch her breath. Closing her eyes, she touched her lips. She must be mad to let him kiss her.

The back entrance was empty, and Leah tried to sneak up the sides of the steps to prevent the creaking noise. She made it to her room without incident and jumped into her bed. She caught her breath and began to think about the duke when she heard a knock on the door.

She squirmed out of her dress and threw the covers over her shift. The knocking did not cease, and she covered herself with a blanket to peek out the door. It was Melissa.

"Where were you?" She questioned rushing past her into the room. She placed her hands on her hips demanding an answer.

Leah let out a yawn. "I was lying down."

"I came for you earlier and you were not in bed. I searched the house too. Captain Jackson has to depart."

Leah gave a surprised look at her friend. "Forgive me if I worried you. I stepped outside for a few minutes for some air and came back."

Melissa suspiciously eyed Leah. "Indeed? Captain Jackson wanted to bid you farewell. He is leaving at dawn for a family emergency."

Leah hesitated and went behind the dressing screen to change into her gown. She slipped on a brown day dress and covered it with her shawl. She accompanied Melissa out the door and into the foyer to wait for Captain Jackson.

The captain came shortly afterward with a sober look on his face. He nodded to Leah and stood in front of her. "Miss Johnson, thank you for meeting with me. May I request a private audience with you in the parlor?"

Melisa smiled at them both. "I will keep the door cracked for propriety while I sit outside."

Leah took the captain's arm and he escorted her into the parlor. Melissa, true to her word, kept the door slightly open and took a seat outside of the room.

The captain sat on the settee with a disheveled appearance. Leah took a seat beside him turning her body to see his face.

"Miss Johnson, forgive me, but as you know, I must depart earlier than I want to. I received a missive that my grandmother has taken ill, and my father asked me to make haste as soon as possible."

Leah touched his hand. "Of course, you must go at once."

The captain took her hand and kissed it. "You must know that my intentions are for us to get to know each other better and I would like to speak to your father about courting you."

Leah took in a deep breath. "Let's talk about that when we return to London. I would like for you to call upon me."

The captain stared at Leah. He tilted his head and gently kissed her lips. He groaned not seeming to want to pull away. "Leah, my dear. You are lovelier with every moment."

She felt like a trollop. How could she kiss two men the same night after never being kissed before?

Leah caught her breath. "You flatter me."

He winked at her, kissing her forehead. "I must let you go for now, but I will see you soon in London." His kindness warmed her heart. She tried to push thoughts of the duke aside. He escorted her out of the parlor to speak to Melissa who was accompanied by Captain Shockley, and they said their goodbyes.

CHAPTER 7

L EAH WOKE EARLY THE NEXT morning to prepare for the outing with the duke. Confused about his intentions, she quickly dismissed any misplaced thoughts she had about him. True, he was a wealthy duke. Whispers of his fortune and prestige were the talk of the house party. Surely, he was only bored and asked her to accompany him due to his lack of companionship. Perhaps he was a bit foxed the night before and that is why he kissed her. She touched her lips thinking about their kiss. Determined to stop her woolgathering, she quickly dressed in her old riding habit. She washed her face with rose-infused water and donned her silver chain. After pinning up her hair, she pinched her cheeks before exiting the room. Her stomach was unsettled, so she ate a piece of dry toast and tea to break her fast. She put a few sugar cubes in her pocket and left to go riding.

Leah spotted the duke at the stables. He smiled and waved. "Good morning, I have picked out a horse I would like you to ride to test out for me."

"I will do what I can, Your Grace. She is a beauty." Leah patted the horse and the groom put on the sidesaddle. She fed the horse the sugar cubes from her pocket.

"Are you ready for our ride? I have asked Thomas to chaperone us." Leah looked at the man in brown trousers and a white shirt. He was a groom from the duke's estate and tipped his hat at Leah. Not exactly a chaperone, but she would not complain. Her mother and most of society would accept no less than a maid or companion.

"A chaperone? Of course." Leah smiled, taking the duke's hand. He took her waist and lifted her up on the saddle. He turned to his horse and put his foot in the stirrup to lift his leg over the saddle. He nodded to the groom and they rode off toward the open fields.

Leah giggled when the horse went faster and held tightly to the reins. The groom stayed back so she and the duke were alone. After several minutes, she turned around and could not see the groom any longer. The duke kept pace with Leah until they came across a lake. He helped her dismount, so the horses could get a drink and they could rest.

After the horses had their fill, he tied them to a tree to graze while he sat on a nearby rock. He motioned for Leah to sit beside him as he leaned back looking at her. Taking a deep breath, he confessed. "I love the fresh air and miss my country estates."

Leah could smell his cologne, a scent that made her think of masculinity. Being alone with him was not proper, especially the way he was looking at her. She looked around the area feeling uncomfortable. "I think we may have lost our chaperone." She glanced down at him through her eyelashes.

He lifted his eyes. "Are you scared to be alone with me?" His voice was deep and tantalizing.

She swallowed hard, not sure how to answer. "Should I be?"

He sat up reaching for her gloved hand. "I hope not. I just wanted a chance to apologize if I was untoward last night."

Leah's stomach dropped. "Untoward?"

He rubbed the back of her hand. "When I kissed you."

Leah looked away with embarrassment. Perhaps he wasn't foxed last night. After a few seconds, she released her breath feeling his hand touch her arm.

Her bare arm. The touch scared and enticed her at the same time.

He whispered tenderly. "Leah? Are you okay?"

Her voice cracked. "Of… Of course." She faced the lake not wanting to look at him. He was so handsome, refined, and mature. Her palms were starting to moisten being so near him.

The duke leaned closer to her and she could feel the heat of his breath near her face. "Look at me, Leah."

She slowly turned to him. Their faces were close, practically touching. He caressed her cheek, spreading warmth through her. His eyes were closing as he bent down to brush his lips against hers.

Leah's body shivered as the duke tilted his head, kissing her again. She was afraid to breathe and found it hard to open her eyes.

His face was serious as he took her hands to kiss them. "You are so beautiful." He rubbed her hands, looking deep into her eyes.

"I… I am unsure of what to say?" She looked down and bit her bottom lip.

He placed his forehead on top of hers. "I could spend all day out here with you, but I think we need to get back on the horses. The races will start soon."

Leah agreed and took his hand to stand up. He took a step backward as his foot twisted in a hole. He lost his balance as he was assisting Leah and tumbled into the mud. Leah gasped trying to catch him but lost her balance from the force of the fall. The duke tried to catch her by rolling his body to protect her from the ground. But her head hit his chest.

"Forgive me, I did not mean to injure you." She looked up at him holding her head.

He held onto her. "Nothing to forgive. I was hoping that you would land on me and not in the mud." He gently touched her head.

Leah sighed. "Are you hurt?"

His face winced as he grabbed near his ankle, lifting his pants to check for swelling, he shook his head. "Nah, there is no swelling. Only my pride hurts."

The couple sat in the mud for a few seconds assessing their state of dress. Leah's hair had partially fallen out of the pins, and his trousers were ruined. He looked at the ground as he sank deeper into the mud.

Smirking at first, he began to laugh. Leah bit her bottom lip biting back a giggle. Spurts of mirth escaped her mouth. He reached over pulling her closer to him as he stroked her hair with his fingers. Gently, he cupped her face kissing her again. The kiss deepened as he opened her mouth with his tongue. The sensation surprised Leah as she had never kissed in this way. His skillful mouth taught her to open wider as the intense kiss took her breath away. Her kisses with Captain Jackson were nothing like this, and she could feel her body responding to his touch. As their kisses slowed, he nibbled on her bottom lip letting out a breath. "Leah, you're making me forget myself. We must put you back together."

Leah tried to scoot off him. But he pulled her back. Smiling, he leaned near her, "Maybe just one more kiss."

He gave her a soft kiss and stood up to help her off the ground. The pressure of his injury caused him to limp as he stretched out his legs.

Leah searched the grounds to find her pins and bonnet. She straightened out her skirt, and he tried to get as much mud off him as he could. He grabbed his coat and adjusted his clothes.

Smugly, Leah tried to suppress a grin. "What story will we ever come up with, Your Grace?"

The duke looked at her with tongue in cheek. "We will tell them the truth. I fell off the horse and you rescued me."

He walked over to her, putting his arms around her waist to assist her back onto the horse. Kissing her forehead, he whispered, "Will you call me Joseph when we're alone?"

Leah stared at him in silence for a few seconds. She had to be mad to call a duke by his first name and could not allow this charade to go further. Lifting her eyes up, she stared at him. "Your Grace, I can't call you Joseph. And I also should not allow such liberties between us. Forgive me if I have given you the wrong impression."

Joseph slanted his head. "I don't have improper intentions toward you, Leah. The truth is that you have intrigued me since the first time I met you. You're not like the typical debutantes trying to gain a rich husband. You're different, and I enjoy your company. I only want to get to know you better, and I will not allow your reputation to suffer. I asked you to call me Joseph because I am more than my title and you are more than your station. Please allow us to at least be friends."

Leah took a step back from him. "Friends?" After giving it some thought, she nodded. "I would like that."

He stared at her for a moment then held out his hand. "May I assist you on to your horse, my friend?"

Leah agreed and took his hand. He lifted her up to the saddle keeping a hold of her hand tightly.

He kissed her hand before letting go. "Thank you for today."

Leah smiled. "Thank you." She cleared her throat and took the reins. Joseph turned on his heel and mounted his horse. They rode at a brisk pace and did not speak again. When they arrived close to the stables, the groom met up with them and escorted them to the stalls. Leah thanked them both and went to the house to get ready for the races.

Melissa was by the doorway of her room when she saw Leah. She covered her mouth. "What happened? Why are you so dirty?"

Leah walked past her and opened the door to her room. Melissa followed behind her. "I went riding and fell in the mud. I asked the footman for some water for a bath."

Melissa sat on her bed. "Who did you ride with?" There was a knock at the door and the footmen entered with a tub and some hot water. Leah thanked them and turned to Melissa.

"If you will excuse me, I must wash up." She took off her bonnet and let her hair down.

Melissa stood up from the bed. "Was it His Grace?"

Leah took off her gloves and turned away as she gathered some new clothes to wear to the races. She sighed. "Yes, Mel. I accompanied His Grace on a ride. He wanted my opinion on which horses to buy."

Melissa snorted sarcastically, "Indeed? What is his head groom here for?"

Leah put her hands on her hips. "Please Mel, I must bathe."

Melissa walked to the door. "I will meet you on the terrace before the races start." She sighed and rubbed her lips together. "Honestly, I hope you can forgive my frankness, but I don't want to see your reputation ruined. The duke is showing you attention, but his intentions are not honorable despite what he may tell you. No duke will marry below his station. You don't want to ruin a chance with Captain Jackson. He could be your love match. He is very handsome and will make a good living."

Leah looked down at the floor for a few seconds before answering her friend. "We have made no promises to each other. We are barely acquainted." She took a drying cloth and went to close the door. "Thank you, Mel, I know you are my friend. His Grace is only my customer at the bookstore and nothing else. I asked Captain Jackson to call on me when he returns to London."

Melissa smiled and reached over to hug her friend. She backed away when she noticed the dirt on her dress. They both laughed, and she closed the door.

CHAPTER 8

THE GREEN FIELDS WERE FULL of the houseguests as tables were set up for a late luncheon. The races were to start soon, and Leah wanted to get a good spot. Several blankets were put under trees for the guests to relax while watching. The banners were set up at the bottom of the hill and Leah could not help but to look for the duke among the gentlemen.

The spectators filled the lawns waiting for the horses to race. Leah spotted Melissa and joined her and Captain Shockley on their blanket. The clouds swarmed down threatening to end the fun, but the rain stayed at bay. Leah searched the crowds for Joseph, not able to find him. She chatted with her friends and eagerly waited for the races to begin. Some of the other military officers joined their group making comments about the baron's stock. The enthusiasm was contagious, and Leah found herself cheering for each race. One horse was all white and could not keep up with the others. Her heart went out to the horse as she knew it would be looked over during the sale.

Many of the men came together talking about which horses they thought would win. They placed wagers. It was easy for Leah to establish the guests that won their race and those who lost by the expressions on their faces. She snickered to herself but stayed quiet.

"Miss Johnson?" Leah jumped, startled at someone calling her name. She looked behind her and saw Joseph's smiling face. "Did you enjoy the races?" Bending down beside her, his closeness combined with his deep voice gave her chills. He was out of breath, and she realized he was one of the riders. His flushed face made him even more handsome.

"I did, Your Grace. Did you make your selection?" She wetted her lips unconsciously staring back into his eyes.

He focused on her puffy lips lifting his mouth into a half-grin. "I am waiting for you to help me."

She smiled, trying to focus on the conversation. His nearness made her off-balance. "I am sure your groom is more qualified than I."

He shook his head. "Tsk, tsk. I think I need a lady's opinion."

Leah blushed, a female opinion she would give him. "If you must know, then I think I would pick the white horse that lost the race."

"Indeed? Why may I ask?" He took his finger placing it on his chin.

"The winning horses will add to your vast possessions, but the white horse would be the most loyal. She may have lost the race, but she has a great spirit, and that is the one I would choose. That horse would prove to be the most trustworthy companion." He took a moment staring at her.

"What? It is true, Your Grace." Leah's face felt warm as she looked away.

His gaze on her was unmistakably seductive with a bit of admiration. "I have no doubt. I never met a woman with so much compassion. You have convinced me, and I will purchase her with the others."

She smiled basking in her triumph. He stood up and offered her his hand to help her stand. "Care for something to drink?"

Melissa looked over and raised her eyebrow. "Leah? Do you want to join us for a walk?" Leah looked back at Joseph.

"Thank you, but we were going for some lemonade. I will meet with you later." Melissa shook her head and went with Captain Shockley.

Joseph handed Leah the glass. "Your friend looks out for you?"

Leah sipped a drink. "Yes, she invited me to the party and feels responsible. Although I don't need her protection."

Joseph walked her near some trees, so they could talk privately. "Where is the captain that took you stargazing?"

Leah looked away, she didn't want to speak about Captain Jackson "He um… He had to leave unexpectedly. His grandmother is ill."

Joseph touched her arm. "I am sorry to hear that. I hope she recovers well." He stepped away from her and held out his arm. "Would you like to take a walk? We could visit the white horse."

Leah accepted his arm as they walked to the stables. The white horse was in its stall eating some oats from a bucket. The grooms were busy preparing the horses and washing them down. Joseph watched her petting the horse. "If you will excuse me for a moment, I must speak to Baron Morgan and finish our transaction. I will return in a moment."

Leah nodded her head. "Of course, I will wait here." She watched him walk out of the stable to meet with Baron Morgan and a few of his associates. Taking notice of his persona and confidence as he presented himself to the group of men, anyone could tell he was a man of importance and demanded respect. She watched the men as they patted each other on the back and grinned as they exchanged paperwork. Turning away, she petted the white horse wishing she had some sugar cubes. Whispering in his ear, she enjoyed his good nature. "How are you today?" She smiled running her gloved hand over the horse's coat. "You are so beautiful."

Joseph came up behind her, touched her waist and whispered in her ear. "Not as beautiful as you."

Leah jumped, feeling his arms going around her waist. She twisted around as their faces touched. He bent down brushing his lips with hers. "So, my friend. I have a favor to ask you."

She lifted her eyes taking in his brown eyes with anticipation. "You see, my stables are very full now. I was hoping that you could take care of the white horse for me? She is yours."

Leah covered her mouth with her hand. "I could not possibly. It would be improper for me to accept a horse from you."

Joseph stepped away from her. "You insult me, and I am wounded." His mouth curled into a grin. "I asked you to do it as a favor for me. I agree with you that she would be very loyal. I just don't have room for her."

Leah parted her lips to protest and the duke covered her mouth with his finger. "Shh. She is a gift. I bought her for you. Either way, she is going to your home." Joseph pulled her into the stall next to them and hugged her tightly.

"My mother may swoon, but I thank you." She smiled kissing his cheek. He took her hands and brought them to his mouth kissing her knuckles.

He let out a breath. "We should go back to the house and get ready for the ball."

Leah smiled, a bit worried over how to explain the horse to her family. "Yes, it's my last night. I have never been to a ball. I went to an assembly dance once, but never a ball."

Joseph raised his brow. "Wait. Did you say you're leaving?"

Leah nodded. "Yes, I could only stay a few days. I have to work in the bookstore."

Joseph's face dropped in disappointment. "You don't say? I am leaving tomorrow too. Have you arranged transportation?"

She stepped away from him and smoothed her skirt. "Yes, well I mean, Melissa's father graciously offered to hire me a coach. One of Melissa's servants agreed to escort me."

Joseph crossed his arms. "Nonsense, you can ride with me. I am taking my carriages and the grooms from my estate are escorting the horses. I will have my valet hire a chaperone to escort us."

Leah looked away. "I appreciate your generous offer, but that will not be necessary. I can find my own way. I don't want you to hire a chaperone just for me."

Joseph pulled her closer to him. "Let me help you, Leah. I insist." She was lost in his eyes. He smiled, pulling her against him—kissing her. He opened his mouth wider to deepen the kiss. Her body arched naturally into his like she was meant to be there. She felt the pressure of his embrace growing tighter when they heard a few voices.

Joseph let go of her, spying a few grooms coming down the path to the stable. He looked back at her. "It's only grooms from my estate. I don't think they saw us." Leah straightened her bonnet and walked outside with Joseph.

The grooms tipped their hat. "Your Grace." Joseph walked back up the hill to the house with Leah. She said her goodbyes and walked to her chamber. Leah didn't know that after she left him, Joseph sent his valet on a shopping trip in town. He had a surprise for her.

She tried to take a nap before the ball, but her slumber was interrupted by pounding on the door. Leah sat up startled, trying to get her eyes to adjust to the light in the room. She approached the door and unlocked it as Melissa swung past her. With groggy eyes, she faced Melissa. "What's amiss?"

Melissa sat on her bed looking grimly. "We need to talk, Leah."

Leah sat beside her trying to focus on her friend as she let out a yawn. Melissa faced her with anger in her eyes. "Leah, I know about the horse. My father overheard the baron arranging transportation."

Leah paused trying to think of an excuse. "I… um… tried to tell him that I couldn't accept it, but he insisted." She panicked at the implications of accepting personal gifts from the duke. Personal gifts from noblemen were usually reserved for a wife or worse—a mistress.

Melissa touched her hand speaking in a motherly tone. "I have no doubt, Leah."

Leah's eyes grew moist and she placed her hand on her forehead. "What will happen?" She thought of her parents and if this could ruin her family.

Melissa shook her head taking a breath. "Don't fret. My father will tell no one, but he was just concerned."

Leah looked away from her. "I know what you're thinking."

Melissa kept a hold of her hand. "Do you?"

Leah pulled her hand out of Melissa's by standing up. "Yes, that I am a fool for spending time with him. That I don't know that our different stations could never make it possible for us to be friends."

Melissa raised her brow. "Friends? Indeed, Leah. That is not what I am thinking." She grunted. "Look at me."

Leah looked at her.

Melissa took a deep breath trying to choose the right words. "He is *seducing* you. You are just too naïve to see it. You shelter yourself in that bookstore living in those romance novels that you read. Stories of happy endings are fiction, Leah. He will never be honorable toward you."

Leah held her stomach. She knew her friend was right. Melissa stood up and reached over to hug her. "Forgive me for being so curt. You are my closest friend. I see how he looks at you. You are a conquest to him, and that is all. Your beauty intrigues him, but he won't marry you. His reputation proceeds itself. He is a rake. *He* will not suffer when his interest moves on, but you could ruin your reputation and never marry."

It felt like a bunch of bricks fell on her chest. "Of course, you are right. I truly believe it's only that we are forced to be together at this house party. After tomorrow, I doubt I should see him again."

Melissa opened her mouth to say more but quickly closed it. "It's good you're leaving tomorrow. The ball should be the end of this farce. I will send my maid to help you dress in a few hours."

Leah agreed, escorting her to the door. Once the door shut, tears pooled in her eyes. A feeling of sadness overwhelmed her. She knew that Melissa spoke the truth. Allowing herself to fall for a peer who was unable to take his pursuit seriously was madness. Society would call her *loose* to spend time with a man who had no marriage interest.

There was another knock at the door and Leah went to open it as she thought Melissa had more to say. She pulled it open to see a well-dressed man with a small box in his hand.

He inquired, "Miss Johnson?"

Leah crinkled her brows in question. "Yes?"

He grinned. "I have a delivery for you." He handed her the box, bowed, and then left.

Leah shut the door and took the box to her bed. She opened it to find another box and a letter. She untied the letter:

> *Dearest Miss Johnson,*
>
> *Please accept this gift as a token of my appreciation for sharing your time with me these last few days. A woman such as you should not have to borrow pearls. It would give me great honor if you wore these tonight. Please don't consider returning such a gift. My only wish is that you save the waltz for me.*
>
> *Yours,*
>
> *J*

Leah's stomach fluttered as she removed the inner box and popped it open to find a velvet cloth. She unwrapped the cloth that held beautiful pearls strung together forming a beautiful necklace. Covering her mouth, she sucked in her breath in surprise. The pearls were so smooth—almost like silk. It would not be possible to accept such a gift. Especially after Melissa's visit. How could she explain them to her? Taking a deep breath, she closed her eyes as she rubbed her thumb over the pearls again. Contemplating, she convinced herself that she could wear them just for tonight and tomorrow she would be brave and return them.

Leah dressed with help from the maid. She wore the gown she met Joseph in and hoped he didn't remember it. It was the only fancy gown she owned. The colors in the gown complimented her coloring, giving her a glow. Her hair cascaded in tendrils down her back with parts of it pinned up. Her new gloves highlighted the outfit, giving it a polished look. She donned the pearls along with a couple dabs of rose water. She was ready.

The ballroom was a flurry of activity. Streams of decorations filled the room as twinkling lights illuminated off the windows. It was full of guests laughing, dancing, and eating refreshments. Leah's palms perspired with fear as she tried to find Melissa. She was self-conscious of the way she looked, hoping that she would not be alone for long.

A few minutes later Melissa appeared with Captain Shockley touching Leah's arm. She twirled Leah around giggling. "You look beautiful, Leah." Leah's face felt warm in happiness over the compliment. Melissa's smile faded as her eyes fell upon her neck.

Captain Shockley bowed.

"I wish Captain Jackson could see you." Leah grinned accepting some champagne from a footman.

Mr. Hogget, a friend of Baron Morgan, asked Leah to dance. She received his arm, following him to the dance floor. He was a tall man with a long mustache smelling of brandy when he leaned down to speak to her. Leah was grateful for the distraction and invitation. The couples lined up on either side to perform a popular country dance. She was happy her mother insisted on dance lessons when she was younger. Her elated feeling was contagious as many men asked for her dance card. Leah did not leave the dance floor for four more dances when she finally told her current partner she needed to take a break. He bowed and escorted her back to Melissa.

Leah tried to find Joseph but did not see him. Captain Shockley excused himself to get some lemonade for Melissa. She turned to Leah with nostrils flaring. "Are you mad? Did he give you those pearls?" Leah reached for her neck—feeling the pearls.

"Mel, listen… he um…"

Melissa crossed her arms as Leah stuttered. A touch on Leah's shoulder took her attention away from Melissa. It was Joseph.

"You are popular, Miss Johnson." He took her hand and kissed it. Leah tried to hold back a smile, but it escaped. She glanced over at Melissa from the corner of her eye. She stumbled over her words. "Hello, Your Grace. It's nice to see you."

Joseph turned to Melissa. "Miss Baldwin."

Melissa curtsied. "Your Grace."

He smiled at her playfully. "Do you mind if I steal Leah?"

Melissa looked straight at him with a sober expression. Propriety would not let her be rude. "As you wish." She glared at Leah before turning on her heel to leave.

Leah turned to him as he touched the necklace. "I see you are wearing them. They look great on you. I wonder what diamonds would do?"

Leah groaned. "You are too generous. You know that I can't keep them."

He protested. "I know no such thing. I refuse to take them back. Seriously, you are the most beautiful girl in this ballroom—probably in all of England. They look great on you, and it would be a shame if you gave them back." He winked at her. "I heard the next dance is a waltz. May I have the honor?"

Leah curtsied. "As you wish."

He put her hand in the crook of his arm as they entered the dance floor. Pulling her close to him, he led her around the dance floor. Her stomach fluttered as she was afraid to waltz. Her friends had taught her, and she practiced with her cousins on occasion, but not with an audience of this size. He kept his eyes on her, tempting her with his gaze. She looked away, observing the other couples, concentrating on her steps. His scent was mesmerizing, making her lose herself in the dance.

Drawing her close to him, he bent down to whisper. "Where are your thoughts? You are very quiet."

Her rapid breathing subsided. "Just enjoying the dance."

He twirled her around until the couples stopped dancing. "Will you walk with me in the garden?"

Leah hoped to make her escape without Melissa's watchful eye. She took his arm as they walked out the terrace doors. The garden contained lit up paths and other couples were strolling about. Leah held his upper arm, feeling his muscles under his waistcoat. She never experienced this type of closeness before, and she longed to kiss him. To touch him. She was unable to steady her thoughts when she was near him.

"Leah?" he softly spoke in her ear. She stopped walking, and he took both of her hands and held them to his mouth. "I wanted to get you alone all evening."

Leah swallowed trying to calm her nerves.

He creased his brow. "What is amiss?"

Leah looked at her hands. "I don't understand." She raised her chin. "What is it you want from me? You said you wanted to be friends, but you kiss me. You gave me pearls, not to mention a horse."

He grunted defensively. "A horse is very romantic." He chuckled. "I am quite taken with you, Miss Johnson. I only wish to spend more time with you."

She closed her eyes as he moved his lips on top of hers. He gently caressed them bringing her against his chest. Opening his mouth, he claimed her lips, tasting her, and kissing her more passionately. Leah became liquid in his arms unable to stand straight. Finally breaking his kiss, he moved his kisses to her jawline and caressed her neck with his mouth. She was losing herself—afraid of what she would let him do to her—knowing that she was sealing her fate. He finally brought his head up breathing hard, and touched her face. "I wish to see you again."

Leah stared at him unsure how to answer. That kiss made her knees weak, and she needed a second to compose herself. "My mother—she wouldn't understand your intentions."

He licked his lips. "Understood. But my intentions are honorable. Please say you will spend time with me, Leah."

She should say no. The smart answer was no. She looked down at her gloves—the gloves he bought her. "I would like that, Your Grace." She could not believe she agreed to see him again.

His eyes sparkled. "You have made me very happy."

CHAPTER 9

T HE DUKE'S CARRIAGE PULLED OUT front displaying his ducal seal. Leah stood with Melissa, watching her trunk carried by a footman. Melissa's Aunt Thea needed to go back to London and agreed to chaperone Leah. Leah was relieved the duke would not have the expense of hiring someone. His generosity to her was a subject of whispered gossip.

"Miss Johnson, you look lovely this morning." Leah curtsied and took his hand for assistance to board the carriage.

Joseph turned to Thea. "Mrs. Trundle, may I assist you?"

Thea blushed while taking his hand, and upon boarding selected the seat opposite of Leah. The duke and Lord Riverton rode their horses beside the carriage. Leah relaxed in the plush seats covered in red velvet. The luxurious carriage was spacious, allowing her plenty of room. Melissa said only a few words to her that morning, but she did accompany her outside and said goodbye as the carriage pulled out onto the cobblestone drive. Her expression was guarded as she watched the carriage drive down the road. Leah knew her friend disapproved of her accepting Joseph's invitation. She should of taken the hired carriage generously offered by Melissa's father. She knew the risks, but her heart would not let her decline.

The time went by fast. Thea slept most of the way leaving Leah with her thoughts and some sewing she brought. Leah gave the driver instructions to her family's cottage when they stopped for a break. She tried to decline the duke's escort, but he insisted on personally seeing her home. Lord Riverton parted company when they reached the city limits.

Leah's family was not at home when the carriage dropped her off. She could only imagine Joseph's thoughts of her family's small cottage and farm. His vast estates may have spoiled his view of the common accommodations most working-class people owned.

He opened the door to the carriage. His manners were impeccable, and he displayed no visible judgment of her lodgings. In fact, he insisted on escorting her to the front door. She opened it for the footman to place her luggage inside the drawing room. He took her hand. "It's been a pleasure. I hope to see you again soon."

Leah curtsied. "I do as well."

He mounted his horse to leave, and before vanishing from view, turned back to wink at her.

Leah watched the carriage depart. An empty feeling filled her chest as she turned to walk inside. Her first thoughts were of her father, and she went to check on him finding him sleeping peacefully. Closing the door quietly, she headed to the kitchen to don an apron to prepare dinner. She found fresh vegetables and began chopping them, trying to get a head start. A few minutes later, her mother and brother came into the kitchen.

Her mother grinned. "Leah, you're home. You must tell us all about your trip."

Leah smiled as Miss Freemont joined them. "So, sorry, my walk took longer than I thought. Let me help you, dear."

"It was wonderful. We had many fun things to do and delicious food. I am very happy that I went." Mrs. Johnson beamed at her child.

Travis walked up next to her and hugged her. "It's good that you're home. We must play chess tonight."

Leah poked him. "If you're ready to lose. Where are Betty and Jasper?" Travis looked at his mother, and she gave a little nod. Miss Freemont left the family alone for some privacy to fetch some eggs from the barn.

Mrs. Johnson sat on the chair, patting the seat beside her. Leah was confused by the serious demeanor of her mother and brother. She sat down slowly. "What's amiss?"

Her mother cleared her throat. "Leah, Betty went to stay with my sister for some time. My sister will take diligent care of her. It's only temporary until we can pay some of our debts. Jasper is helping Mr. Wilcox on his farm assisting with stable chores."

Leah crinkled her brows. "I don't understand. He is only one and six and educated. Why would he be a farmhand?"

Travis sat in the chair beside his sister. His eyes faced the floor. "Leah, we can't afford to pay the mortgage next month. Our father's debts are too much. All of us must sacrifice. Papa is doing worse, and the doctor gave him only a few more weeks. I may be taking a room in town. We may all have to prepare to move."

Leah's voice cracked. "Why did you let me go enjoy myself if our family situation is so dire?"

Mrs. Johnson took in a breath. "Stop it. It was my wish that you could have a few days of happiness. We have a few months at least before they make us close the store. I just hope that the debt collectors will give us some more time."

She reached for her daughter's hand. "Leah, we do have good news for you. Mr. Wilcox came to see your papa and he has made an offer for your hand. Your papa wants you to accept."

Leah felt the stomach contents coming up into her throat. The room was spinning. She looked at her mother. "Marriage? To Mr. Wilcox?"

Her mother squeezed her hand. "Yes, is it not wonderful? He owns a lovely home and inherited a good living, not to mention that he is quite taken with you. He would be good to you. We are so grateful to him for all his help with Jasper, and for the food he brings each week."

Leah's mother must have seen the expression on her face by the grimace she gave her. She knew that their family needed Mr. Wilcox's financial help, and her mother tried to plead with her. "Leah, it's a decent offer. My sister can't take us all in. She has agreed to look after Betty and has a temporary room for me if we lose the farm. Jasper will stay in the stables at Mr. Wilcox's. Your choices are limited."

Leah sucked in a breath. "I don't see him as a husband. He is an old man!" The sobs came out as she tried to hold them in. Looking between Travis and her mother she begged, "I can work longer at the store and make more money."

Mrs. Johnson let go of her hand and stood up. "Leah, we are women. We can't afford to refuse such offers. You have no dowry. Mr. Wilcox doesn't care about that. He will be a good provider. He will be by later after dinner to take you for a walk. The store is not making money, Leah. I am not sure how much longer we can keep it open."

Leah closed her eyes as she panicked. "What if I received another offer?"

Her mother tilted her head. "Have you?"

Leah put her head in her hands. "Not exactly, but I think one may be coming from Captain Jackson." She removed her hands, wiping tears from her eyes. "He had to depart the party early due to his grandmother's illness but will call upon me soon in London. I think he may make an offer."

Her mother rubbed her lips together. "Very well, we will give him a few weeks, but if he doesn't, then you will marry Mr. Wilcox. Tell Mr. Wilcox you require some more time."

Travis sighed and changed the subject. "Do you know anything about a horse? A groom came by a few hours ago and said it was a gift for you."

Leah's heart beat faster. "Oh, yes. I forgot about that. It was an unexpected prize for picking a horse. It's really a long story, and I want to rest before dinner."

"Of course, rest, my dear. We will see you for dinner in a couple of hours."

Leah excused herself to her bedroom. She lay on her bed crying into her pillow. If she were a man, she could run away. A woman had no choices. Mr. Wilcox was a nice man, but he did not make her heart skip a beat. Captain Jackson was her best hope to escape the marriage. The only man she pined for was Joseph, but that was impossible. She did not have time to waste on that dream.

A few hours later, Mr. Wilcox came to the door to call upon Leah. Her mother went to her room and bid her to come down for her walk. Leah washed her face in the basin pulling a shawl over her shoulders. She met Mr. Wilcox's eyes as she walked down the stairs, quickly looking away from his gaze.

He wore a gray overcoat with black boots. His black hair was combed back with a few gray hairs at his temples. His brown eyes widened when he saw Leah approach. "Miss Johnson, it's a pleasure to see you. It's a beautiful evening for a walk. I was hoping that you would join me?"

Mr. Wilcox stepped near her. Travis shook his hand turning to Leah for her reply.

"As you wish, Mr. Wilcox." Leah stood in front of him, looking down at the floor.

"Very well then, shall we go?" Mr. Wilcox offered his elbow and Leah slowly placed her hand in the crook of it. She bid her family goodbye.

The fresh breeze stung Leah's cheeks. She shivered, and Mr. Wilcox removed his coat offering it to her. "You are cold. Please take my jacket."

"Oh no, I have my shawl." She tightened the shawl around her.

He placed his coat around her. "Nonsense, you are shivering. I insist."

She smiled. "Thank you."

They walked in silence for a few minutes. Leah was unsure how to speak to him. He finally broke the quiet. "I heard you were at a party this week?"

Leah's throat went dry. She did not want to discuss the party. "Yes, my friend Melissa invited me to spend a few days in the country with her family. I enjoyed the fresh air."

He nodded his head, slowing their pace. Leah looked around when he stopped walking. He faced her as she dropped her hand from his elbow. "Miss Johnson, I hope you don't think me too forward."

Leah held her breath. She was not prepared for this conversation.

He wrung his hands, looking at the ground nervously. "I wish to ask your permission to call upon you tomorrow? The truth is that I want more than that." He looked into her eyes. "Since I bought the manor house down the street a few years ago, I watched you turn from a darling girl to a beautiful woman. My real wish is to make you my wife."

Leah bit her bottom lip. She looked away from him, hoping for a distraction.

None came.

The silence was deafening, and she knew he deserved an answer. "I... don't know what to say."

He grinned. "I understand. I know you are probably unsure of my intentions. I promise you that I will take care of you. I will be a good husband and try to make you happy. I have enough money from my inheritance to live comfortably. You would not have to work. You could stay home, taking care of the house and children. Jasper will be taken care of as well... He can live in the house with us once we are married."

Leah's heart sank. Did he say, *children*? What would happen to Jasper if she declined? She needed to think, and couldn't with him standing in front of her.

She inhaled a breath. "Mr. Wilcox, I have much respect for you. You have been very kind to my family. I have not thought about marriage until now. Can you give me more time?"

He paused before answering. "Of course. At least you didn't say no."

She smiled. "My answer is not *no*, and I just need to think about marriage."

He pushed out his elbow and escorted her back to the house. At the doorway, he turned to face her, holding her hands and laying a warm kiss on both. He rubbed her hands. "I would like to invite you to dinner this week. Are you free Thursday? I don't think you work late that night."

She creased her brows and he laughed. "I asked your mother for your schedule."

"Of course, Mr. Wilcox. Thursday is good."

He stared at her, fidgeting with his hat. "Can you call me Ray? After all, I asked, you to marry me and we needn't be so formal with each other now."

She grinned. "Yes, Ray. Please call me Leah." Leah felt she could not be rude. His poor head beaded in sweat. She knew he was nervous. She saw that he was a good man. After all, he provided food for her family on many occasions and gave Jasper a job. Her heart hurt with the thought of hurting his feelings. She smiled up at him. "Good night, Ray."

CHAPTER 10

JOSEPH RETURNED HOME, COLLAPSING ON the settee in his study. John came in to join him shortly afterward. "Joseph, what gives? You went to a house party without me? I heard Preston talking about it."

Joseph snorted at his friend. "Hardly a house party. I went to buy some horses, and there was a gathering at the residence. No one you would know. Riverton and I stayed a few days for amusements and races. You would have been bored after a few hours."

He shrugged his shoulders taking a drink of brandy. "Very well, let's go to Barton's tonight. I was lucky at the tables last night."

Joseph yawned. "Not tonight my friend. I am in need of a bath and bed. Do you know where Caroline is?"

John snorted. "Last I saw her she was yelling at me for knocking over a vase. I am staying clear of her wrath. I will see you later."

Joseph searched the house for his sister and found her on the terrace reading a book.

She smiled when she saw him. "You're back. How was it?"

He took a seat on the chair next to her and smiled. "Intriguing."

Caroline raised her brow. "Interesting choice of words. How so?"

Joseph pondered her question. "I may need your help."

Caroline tilted her head. "Joseph, what's amiss?"

"Caroline, you know me better than anyone." Pausing, he bit the inside of his cheek. "I have been thinking about the responsibilities that I must face soon. My upcoming nuptials weigh heavily on my chest."

Caroline interrupted him. "Joseph, marriage is not a prison. You were given a choice."

He grunted. "A choice? Hardly. Father bringing Roslyn's family here for that fortnight was only a formality. I was pressured into the marriage proposal. It made a dying man happy. I have not seen her since. Father didn't care if we suited, only that she had noble blood and was his Oxford friend's daughter. Our engagement will not be announced until she returns from her trip abroad. I still have a few weeks left. I never gave it a lot of thought until now."

Caroline took a drink of her wine. "Why now?"

He glanced at her, pausing before he answered. "I met someone."

Caroline's eyes widened. "Joseph, no. You can't do this."

He sighed loudly. "Don't I deserve to be happy? Does being a duke mean that your life is destined to be horrible?"

She squared her shoulders. "Being a duke is a privilege. Joseph, you inherited a fortune and have many lands, titles, and money. You will hardly earn anyone's pity. Happiness depends on the person. You can choose to be happy."

Joseph's anger boiled over. He reached for his glass of brandy and threw it, shattering it into pieces. Caroline gasped. "What is wrong with you?"

Joseph's voice cracked. "You don't understand. I know my obligations and I complied with the marriage proposal. For the first time in my life, I met someone who makes me feel like a person and not just my title. She is different than other girls of our acquaintance. She works in a bookstore."

Caroline touched her brother's arm. "A bookstore? Your right, I don't understand. Are you looking for a mistress?"

He removed her hand from his arm. "No! She is innocent. I don't wish to use her in such a way. I am not sure what to call it, but I want to spend time with her. Please, Caroline. I need your help."

She took a deep breath. "It sounds dangerous and I don't want you to get hurt."

He grabbed her hand. "Please Caroline. I understand your concern, but it's my choice."

She made a deep sigh. "What type of help?"

Joseph leaned over and kissed her on the cheek. He smiled. "I will give you all the details once I work it out." He jumped out of the chair and ran into the house leaving Caroline out on the terrace shaking her head at his behavior.

The children's reading group ended early. Leah cleaned up the chairs and returned the books to the shelves. Touching the shelves brought tears to her eyes. The store may be sold within a few months and her love of working in the store would be a memory. Leah patted her eyes, taking in a breath as she returned to completing the inventory. She would need to speak to her mother about limiting the stock, so they could save money. The front bell rang, alerting her that a customer had entered. She smoothed her dress walking around the corner. Her eyes widened with surprise. Joseph stood in her doorway accompanied by a beautiful woman. Leah's heart went into her throat at the instant jealousy she felt seeing the woman at the duke's side.

"Miss Johnson, so nice to see you again." The duke took a few steps closer to her. He motioned to the woman. "May I introduce my sister, Lady Caroline."

Relief drained through Leah. She curtsied to Caroline. "It's so nice to meet you, Lady Caroline." Caroline's regal presence was intimidating. Leah was sure that she had the envy of women around her with her golden curls and porcelain skin.

She laughed. "Please call me Caroline. My brother tells me that we share a love of the same books. I wanted to personally thank you for helping him pick out the books he brought me."

Leah's voice strained. "Of course, please call me Leah."

"I wanted to invite you to tea tomorrow afternoon if you are free?"

Leah looked up at Joseph and he smiled at her. "Please say you will come."

Caroline watched their exchange as Joseph stepped closer to Leah. "We can send a carriage for you."

Leah was shocked by the invitation. Lady Caroline's name was associated with the elite of the *ton*. Not wanting to sound ungrateful, she nodded her head. "Thank you, Your Grace. I accept. The carriage may pick me up here as I am working tomorrow."

Caroline clapped her hands together. "Very well, I look forward to seeing you."

Leah walked them to the door. Caroline left, leaving Joseph and her alone. He turned to her leaning down to whisper. "I have missed you."

His warm breath against her cheek made her stomach flutter. She looked directly into his eyes and responded, "Me too." He kissed her hand and left the store.

Leah gulped looking around to make sure that no one saw them. She was grateful the store was empty. She peeked out the window as they departed. Travis would be there soon to pick her up. She needed time to think about Lady Caroline's invitation to tea. It was unwise of her to accept knowing that rumors could begin about her reputation. The smart decision would be to send a letter and decline feigning a forgotten engagement. Her time would be better spent considering Mr. Wilcox's offer. After all, her family was counting on her to make a match. Her father's failing health pushed her into this situation. Leah shoved her feelings aside to finish cleaning the store. As she completed her task, she donned her bonnet as she heard Travis approach to pick her up to go home.

CHAPTER 11

L EAH DRESSED WITH EXTRA CARE the next morning. She borrowed an older dress from her mother that Ellen had altered for her, adding some embroidered sleeves and lace. Ellen dropped it by and visited with the family.

She was frantic telling her mother and Ellen about the tea invitation from Lady Caroline. Mrs. Johnson was surprised at the request to have tea with her as Joseph's family was well known in the society papers. The invitation to such a gathering was not common within her class. She voiced her concern, but Leah convinced her that Caroline was a customer and wanted to thank her for her help in picking out books. They enjoyed the same books and would discuss them over tea. Ellen told her mother that it was silly to worry.

The day was slow. Feeling restless in the afternoon, Leah checked herself in the upstairs looking glass several times. She thought she would die of old age before the footman finally showed up to fetch her. Leah was thankful that her mother agreed to let her go. Leaving with the footman, he assisted her into the duke's carriage along with Caroline's lady's maid who chaperoned the trip.

The duke's townhouse resembled more of a mansion. Leah's heart beat faster as they pulled into the drive. Another footman greeted her, assisting her out of the carriage. Lady Caroline came to the foyer to greet her after being announced.

Caroline hooked her arm with Leah's and led her to the drawing room. "Leah, it's so great to see you."

Leah smiled. "Thank you for inviting me. You have a lovely home."

Caroline grinned. "Thank you. It's my brother's. I only stay here when I am in London."

Leah gazed at Caroline. She had heard of her tragedy, but dare not mention it in polite company. Caroline motioned to the drawing room. "Please come in, the tea was just served."

Leah couldn't help but marvel at the spread displayed on beautiful china dishes. Many desserts and crumpets were decorated with the utmost attention to detail. She felt a bit guilty at the amount of food for only the two of them. Leah took a seat on the settee, trying to focus her attention on her host, yet her mind wondered if Joseph would join them.

"Do you take sugar in your tea?" Caroline turned to Leah.

"Yes, please."

"None for me." A deep familiar voice sounded behind her. Leah knew that voice. She tried not to turn around to avoid looking too eager.

Joseph came around the settee taking the seat beside her. "I will take some tarts, too." He smiled at her. "You look fetching today."

Leah blushed while Caroline laughed. "My brother—the flirt."

Just then, another handsome man appeared at the door. "I taught him everything he knows."

Caroline turned around surprised. "Oh no, look who is here. He must have smelled the free food."

The man snorted. "I take offense to that." He reached over grabbing some pastries, pushing them into his mouth. Caroline handed him a cup of tea as he winked at her. The man swallowed a mouth full of food and turned his attention to Leah. "Now, who do we have here? I don't believe we have been introduced because I never forget a pretty face."

Joseph grunted at his friend's flirtation. "She is a friend of Caroline's. Her name is Miss Johnson." He turned to Leah. "Miss Johnson, may I introduce the Earl of Shepley."

Leah nodded. "My lord."

Leah noticed that Joseph's smile turned to a scowl when the earl took a seat in the chair next to her. "So, tell me, Miss Johnson, where have you been hiding? Is this your first season?"

The duke stood up abruptly offering his elbow to Leah. "Let's go for a walk in the garden." Leah stood up taking his arm.

John smirked when Leah got up to leave. "I hope we can meet again, Miss Johnson."

Leah nodded as Joseph pulled her away.

John turned to Caroline who was sipping her tea. He raised his brow. "What's amiss with Joseph? He acts like he knows the chit."

Caroline smiled. "He introduced us yesterday and I invited her for tea. I guess he met her at a bookstore then spent time with her at Baron Morgan's house party."

John finished his tea in a big gulp. "That sly dog, he told me that house party was boring. He never mentioned her. If the ladies looked like her, no wonder he was glad that I didn't come. He may be a duke, but I am an earl with more charm."

Caroline choked on her tea. "As you wish, John."

The garden was marvelous—the grounds immaculate. Joseph led her through a path, rubbing her hand on his arm. When they arrived at a fountain, he motioned to a bench and they took a seat.

"I couldn't wait to get you alone." He took her hands kissing them. "How have you been?"

Leah melted at his affection. "I am well, thank you."

He touched a piece of her hair, placing it behind her ear. "Can you stay for dinner?"

Leah's chest hurt to withhold information from him, but she couldn't stay for dinner tonight because of her promised dinner to Mr. Wilcox. She didn't want to tell Joseph about him just yet. Her voice cracked. "I um… would like to, but I have to decline. I have a previous engagement later tonight."

Joseph studied her face for a few seconds. "Of course. Perhaps another time."

Leah nodded at his suggestion and looked away hoping not to give away her discomfort.

After a few moments, Leah looked up at him as he stared at the garden hoping she didn't upset him. She tried to think of something to say. "Your sister is kind, and your friend is nice."

Joseph glanced at her. "Caroline is kind—she is a little lost since her husband died. It has been over a year, and she needs to join society again, but is not quite ready yet. At least, she is out of mourning clothes and attends smaller social events. As far as John, I have been friends with him since Eaton. He is a bit of a rogue, but a loyal friend. You must not take him seriously."

Leah laughed. "I bet he got you into a lot of mischief."

Joseph cracked a crooked smile. "You have no idea. It all started with one of our teachers at Eaton."

Joseph stood up from the bench hunching over pretending to be the teacher. "He walked like this and wore a fake beard that often fell off into his soup. One day, John and I were eating, and the teacher lost his beard. John took it and tried to give it back to him. He got into trouble and when I tried to defend John, we both got extra chores for a week. We became the best of friends during that time and were inseparable after that." Joseph's demeanor changed, he was no longer a duke, but an actor on the stage. His reenactment was so real that Leah could not stop laughing.

He joined her until Leah took a big gasp of air. "Oh stop, you are making me laugh too hard."

Joseph grinned watching her. "The sound of your laugh is the best sound in the world to me."

Leah caught his stare as the laugh ended in a smile. "Your words are too kind, but my siblings poke fun at my giggling all the time."

He reached over taking her chin. "My words are true." He leaned down brushing his lips with hers. She put her hand on his chest as the kiss deepened. Leah almost forgot where she was as she pulled away out of breath.

Joseph stayed close to her. "I could kiss you all day."

Leah's eyes widened at his endearment. She whispered, "I feel the same."

Joseph let out a sigh. "We must go back inside. Caroline and John may kill each other if I don't stop them." He winked as he escorted her back along the path.

John and Caroline were arguing over a book she was reading, but no physical violence had happened. Joseph led Leah to the settee and sat beside her. Caroline offered to ring for more tea, but Leah declined. "I need to be going as my family expects me at home soon. Could I trouble your footman for a ride back to the bookstore?"

Joseph's brow came down. "So soon?"

Caroline shot her brother a look, then nodded to Leah. "Of course. I enjoyed seeing you again."

Joseph cleared his throat, "Yes, I believe we have plans to go the theatre on Saturday. Caroline was just saying how she needed a friend to accompany us as she lacks female companionship within our party. We are three men and one woman. Lord Preston, with whom I believe you are acquainted, will be attending as well as John. If you have no other *previous engagements*, we would like you to attend."

Leah swallowed hard at the way he stressed the words *previous engagements*. It was obvious that he did not like her excuse for dinner. How could she accept an invitation to the theatre if she had no dress for such an occasion?

Caroline smiled. "Yes, I would be much obliged if you could come. Please say you will."

Leah's fears came across her face. "I um… will need to check with my mother. I can send a message tomorrow and let you know."

Caroline looked at her and replied, "Of course, we will anxiously wait for your reply."

John watched the exchange curiously but did not contribute to the conversation. Leah stood, and the men joined her as she walked to the door. The mood in the room became somber. Leah turned to her hostess as she reached the doors to embark onto the carriage. "Thank you for the tea. The cakes were delicious."

She turned to Joseph. "Thank you for the walk, Your Grace."

Joseph gazed at her and bowed to bid her a good day. Caroline walked her the rest of the way to the carriage without Joseph.

Caroline whispered to her as they reached the door to carriage. "Leah, forgive me if I appear too forward. Do you not want to attend the theatre?"

Leah's face reddened with embarrassment. "Oh, please do not think I am not grateful. Honestly, I would not even know what to wear. And my mother needs help in the bookstore. I will speak to my mother and send a message tomorrow."

She smiled at Leah reassuringly patting her arm. "Of course, we will await your reply."

The carriage took Leah away as Joseph watched from inside. Caroline walked back toward the house. She stepped into the doorway and Joseph immediately approached her. He touched her arm. "What did she say?"

Caroline tilted her head questioningly. "I have never seen you this way. You're acting like a schoolboy instead of a man of seven and twenty."

A rumble of laughter interrupted them. "Stop with the mystery. Who is she? I thought you would call me out with pistols at dawn when I spoke to her."

Joseph scowled at his friend while turning to Caroline. "Well?"

Caroline looked at John and then back to Joseph. "Let's talk privately in your study."

John held up his hand. "No need. I was just leaving." He walked out of the room.

Caroline turned around to face her brother. "Joseph, I don't pretend to understand your infatuation with this girl. Yes, she is very pretty—her kindness is evident. But she is very young and seems a bit lost. If people found out about the two of you, it could be bad for her as well as you. Please don't encourage this girl. Society will know you are not serious about her due to her station—they will think it's a scandalous reason why you are with her."

Joseph shook his head determined to uphold his decision. "It's none of your business. Let me deal with the consequences."

Caroline was shocked at his announcement. "Joseph?"

He closed his eyes. "Please Caroline, that is why I need you. You are the reason society will think she is with us. Caroline, please help me."

Caroline sighed loudly. "I don't like this." She wrung her hands anxiously. "But I won't deny you. I will do this only if you promise this charade will not last much longer. Your engagement will be announced next month, and your soon-to-be fiancée will be arriving within a fortnight."

Joseph held up his hand. "I promise."

Caroline rubbed her lips together, deep in thought. "I think she wants to go to the theatre, but there is a reason she won't accept. A dilemma neither of us has experienced."

Joseph was losing patience with his sister. "Stop speaking in riddles— is she going or not?"

Caroline lifted the corner of her mouth. "Perhaps, if she had a dress to wear."

Joseph lowered his brow. "A dress? I would buy her dozens of dresses if she would let me."

Caroline smiled at her brother. "Exactly, she won't let you. Her face was flushed when she told me she wouldn't know what to wear and had never been to the theatre. I will go to the bookstore tomorrow. Perhaps she will take a dress from me?"

Joseph raised his brow. "Buy anything she needs and send me the bill."

Caroline put her hand on his shoulder. "Joseph, I will do it. I just hope she doesn't get hurt."

CHAPTER 12

LEAH MADE IT HOME JUST in time to sit with her family as they ate dinner, though she did not participate in the meal. Mr. Wilcox expected her to dine with him.

After the main course of roasted chicken, Mr. Wilcox arrived and graciously greeted her family. He brought them a basket full of pastries and escorted Leah to his carriage. One of his maids was in the carriage as a chaperone. Mr. Wilcox's cologne was strong and overbearing. She couldn't quite place the scent, but it reminded her of the outdoors. She was grateful that the distance was short, and they arrived at his manor quickly without much conversation.

She walked ahead of him into his house as he gestured for her to go inside. The fire illuminated the room, showing the dining table set for two. The house was full of books and old papers that were piled on shelves. There was a musty odor in the room causing Leah to cough into her gloved hands. The furnishings were older but in decent shape. She watched the maid go into the kitchen as an older, male servant offered her some wine and helped her take a seat. The footman came shortly afterward and served the first course of vegetable soup. She ate her soup quietly, as Mr. Wilcox tried to find something to converse about.

"How was the bookstore today?" He sipped his soup awaiting her reply.

Leah's heart skipped as she thought about her day with Joseph. She concentrated on a quiet reply. "Not too busy. I changed around some of the shelves and met with a children's reading group."

Mr. Wilcox stopped eating, putting down his spoon. "Leah that is something I wish to speak to you about. I don't want you working in the bookstore once we are engaged. It's unsavory for a woman to work, especially if she is under my protection."

Leah's eyes widened. "I don't understand? I like working in the store."

Mr. Wilcox wiped his mouth reaching out for her hand. He held it for a second while looking at her. "There is no need. I will provide for you once you accept my offer. I will give you an allowance with pin money. I hope our engagement won't be long—my wish is to marry as soon as possible."

Leah's stomach dropped, she pulled her hand away. "Forgive me, Mr. Wilcox... I mean, Ray. Your request has taken me by surprise. I still need more time to think about your offer, but I don't want to give up the bookstore."

Mr. Wilcox's mouth formed a straight line in disapproval. He stared at her for a few seconds before responding. "I understand your predicament may cause you discomfort, but I assure you that my offer will not last forever. I have already secured permission from your father to marry you, not to mention the debts I have paid on your father's behalf. I would hate to have to ask for payment—a debtor's prison is no place for a sick man. Don't forget that your brother Jasper is provided for too because of my affection for you."

Leah's felt nauseous. "Your kindness to my family is much appreciated, sir. We are all in your debt. I assure you that I don't take proposals of marriage lightly and would like to make sure we are suited."

Mr. Wilcox took a few moments to answer her. "I know that you are very young, Leah. Please understand my desire is to take care of you. As your husband, you must trust me to make decisions for you."

She couldn't eat anymore, feeling her stomach contents threatening to come up in her throat. "I am not feeling well. Could you take me home?"

Mr. Wilcox stood up perturbed. "I will ask Carlton to bring around the carriage. I will escort you home."

Leah stood and touched her face with the back of her hand. "I thank you for dinner. Please forgive my early departure—I suddenly feel ill."

Mr. Wilcox put on his coat then assisted Leah with hers. "Perhaps you should rest." He took her hand and put it in the crook of his arm. "I gave you a lot to think about. I have made my position clear and will expect a reply shortly."

Leah looked down at the floor. "As you wish."

Leah swept the entrance of the bookstore for the hundredth time that day.

At least, it seemed like that much. Her mind was not on her work, causing her books to be misplaced. She had not heard from Captain Jackson, so her options were limited to Mr. Wilcox and she was running out of time. He proved not to be good husband material, the deception of his shyness and mild demeanor was deceiving. If only Joseph could be someone else. He understood her, and his gentleness made her want to spend all her time with him. She stopped herself from thinking about him, knowing that his intentions could not be honorable. He knew they could never be together as man and wife, yet he introduced her to the closest people in his life. Leah sighed as she dusted the bookshelves. She heard the bell ring and a familiar voice asking her mother for her whereabouts.

Leah peeked around the shelf. "Lady Caroline?" Leah threw the dust rag on the floor and straightened her dress. She was embarrassed by the state of her appearance. Lady Caroline gave no indication that anything was amiss. She smiled brightly at Leah. "There you are. I was hoping we could talk for a few minutes?"

Mrs. Johnson smiled with anticipation of an introduction. Leah glanced at her mother. "Mother, this is Lady Caroline. She is the one I told you about that invited me to tea. We like the same authors."

Mrs. Johnson smiled, looking at Caroline. "Lady Caroline, this is my mother, Mrs. Johnson."

Caroline nodded. "It's wonderful to meet you. Your daughter is ever so charming."

Mrs. Johnson smiled. "Thank you, my lady. If you will excuse me, I have another customer."

Leah faced Caroline. "Are you looking for another book?"

Caroline shook her head. "Not yet, but probably soon. I wanted to ask you a favor."

Leah creased her forehead. "Of course, what do you need?"

Caroline looked down and whispered. "You must not repeat my dilemma. I am trusting in your discretion. You see, I purchased a dress that is too small for me. When I heard you wouldn't know what to wear to the theatre, it occurred to me that this dress would be perfect for you. Please say you will wear it and go to the theatre with me. It's a perfect dress, and it would make me so happy that someone was able to wear it. It doesn't seem right that it just stays in my closet never worn. I am too embarrassed to tell anyone that it doesn't fit."

Leah doubted Caroline's story. She had a lovely shape and didn't seem bigger than her. Leah felt like a poor relation but did not know how to gracefully get out of the tale. She thought for a few moments without saying a word, the expression on her face must have given her away.

"Oh, please don't fret, Leah. The dress looks like it was made for you. It's a favor to me. Please say you will."

Leah chewed on her bottom lip. "I don't know if I could. It's not that I don't want to go."

Caroline clapped her hands. "Then you will go. I will have my carriage pick you up early. I thought it would be fun if we got dressed together. I could have my lady's maid fix your hair. She is really good and studied French fashion as well."

Leah hesitated but agreed. "Very well, I will see you tomorrow." Caroline smiled and turned away.

Leah arrived at the duke's residence in style. Caroline sent her carriage and lady's maid to pick her up early from the store. Leah's woolgathering kept her occupied all day dreaming of the theatre. When her father's business did well, her parents often visited the theatre, but at that time Leah was too young to accompany them. This was her first opportunity and invitation—she would be in an exclusive box that overlooked the stage for optimal entertainment.

She followed the maid to an empty chamber. Leah stared into the massive room with pale rose curtains and bed coverings with gold trim. It was beautiful, with a huge four-poster bed. Paintings covered the walls, and fresh flowers scented the room. She was afraid to touch anything as she slowly turned around the chamber soaking in the atmosphere.

The lady's maid guided her near a chair and told her she could put her clothes on the bed. She ordered a bath with scented water and brought out the most beautiful dress that Leah had ever seen. The greens in the silk material would match her green eyes.

"Miss Johnson, Lady Caroline will join you in a few hours. She requested that I help you get settled. Do you need help with your bath?"

Leah snorted amusedly. "I don't think so. I have given myself a bath all my life."

The maid smiled. "Very well." A knock at the door presented three footmen with buckets of steaming water, they filled the tub and left the room.

Leah undressed and bathed. She dressed in a robe that was laid out for her and started combing her hair. The maid came a few minutes later to finish combing her hair, helping it dry by the fire.

It felt good to have someone pamper her. She felt at ease with the maid who was only a few years older than her. She brought her small cakes and chocolate to drink to help her relax.

The maid helped her dress and then fixed her hair. She twisted it in ways that Leah did not know existed, leaving several tendrils cascading down her back. Leah did not recognize herself in the looking glass. She reached for her reticule to find her pearl necklace when there was a knock on the door.

The maid opened it and Caroline entered. She gasped covering her mouth. "Oh, Leah! You look exquisite. My brother will not know what hit him. He may not let you go out looking so good."

Leah's heart beat faster. She did not realize that Caroline knew about their affections. Her and Joseph were just friends. Did she know about them?

Leah sighed deeply. "Thank you. I have never received such grand treatment." She looked down. "I am not sure if His Grace would care about my appearance."

Caroline gave her a motherly look. "Oh, we will see his reaction." She looked at her maid. "I just need some last-minute touches on my hair. Can you meet me in my chamber in a few minutes? I want to speak to Miss Johnson." The maid curtsied and left.

Caroline was holding a box that she gave to Leah. She took it looking confused.

"Before you open it, I am under strict orders that you can't refuse the gift. If you would like to wear it only for tonight, that is your choice. If you decide to give it away or sell it after tonight, it's of no consequence. However, if you don't take the gift with you, then it will be mailed to your home."

Leah laughed at Caroline's impersonation of her brother. She took the paper off the box and opened it. She gasped in surprise. The box held a diamond necklace. It sparkled with brilliance. Her hands shook thinking of the priceless jewels she held. "I can't take this!" She tried to shove the box back into Caroline's hands.

Caroline held her hands up. "Neither can I."

Leah's face frowned in worry as she laid the box on the dresser. She pleaded with Caroline. "You don't understand. I could never explain a diamond necklace to my family. I have a hard enough time hiding the pearl necklace he gave me."

Caroline touched her arm. "Leah, you can't give it back. It would break his heart."

Leah was overwhelmed and frowned at Caroline. "Why? We are just friends."

Caroline tilted her head. "Leah, honestly, I don't understand this connection you have with my brother. You have somehow captured his heart, and he considers you a friend. I don't want either of you to get hurt. I am not sure what tomorrow will hold for you or him. My advice to you is to enjoy the moment if it makes you happy. Take the necklace if it makes him happy. He won't expect you to pay him back in any way. He enjoys giving his friends nice presents. Did you know he gave John a new carriage? He has a fortune and is always giving money away."

Leah stepped away from her to sit on the bed. "I don't understand. Why me? My friend from the house party says he can't have honorable intentions."

Caroline continued to try to reassure her. "Leah, he has no bad intentions. If his affection makes you feel uncomfortable, then I can speak to him. I am not saying that his intentions are marriage, but I know he likes having you as a friend. He has grown fond of you."

Leah was embarrassed at the conversation. She did not want Caroline to think she had hopes of marriage to him. Everyone knew there could be no marriage due to her station. Hearing Caroline say it aloud was like a stab in the heart. Leah's mind was racing, yet she composed herself. This could be her last chance to feign a different life before she was forced into marriage with Mr. Wilcox.

She looked up at Caroline. "Can you put the necklace on me?" Caroline obliged and left Leah alone to finish preparing herself for the evening. Leah straightened out the room to clean any mess she had created, not wanting to make extra work for the servants. An hour later Caroline knocked on the door, ready to escort her down to the drawing room to meet the men. Leah felt nervous as she descended the stairs and walked into the room. She noticed Joseph right away upon entering.

His eyes locked with hers. A slow smile came to his mouth. He stepped toward her taking her hand to kiss it. "You're breathtaking." She could barely move feeling his stare upon her. He placed his hand on the small of her back as his friends approached her.

John approached Leah and took her hand kissing her knuckles. "You look beautiful, Miss Johnson. I may want to take my pistol to fight off all your admirers tonight."

Leah giggled accepting some champagne from the footman. Lord Preston was behind John, and his manners were more refined. He smiled. "I always thought you were lovely even as a young girl. Now you have turned into such a beautiful woman."

He took a sip of brandy, turning to Caroline. "You look beautiful as always. I did not realize you were acquainted with Miss Johnson?"

Joseph shot him a scowl as Caroline smirked at his question. "Recently my lord. We enjoy the same books."

Lord Preston took another drink, carefully studying Leah and Joseph. He turned to Leah. "How is your father?"

Leah sagged her shoulders with sadness. "I wish I had better news. The doctors think he hasn't much time. Perhaps a few months."

He took a breath. "Please give him my regards."

Leah nodded. "Of course, my lord. Thank you."

Lord Preston offered his arm. "May I escort you to the carriage?" Leah looked at Joseph and watched a scowl grow on his face for the briefest of moments. Leah knew it would be rude not to take his arm. "Of course."

Caroline took her brother's arm and John walked behind them. Leah and Caroline rode in one carriage with her maid. The men followed in a different carriage.

Lord Preston stared at Joseph when they entered the carriage. Joseph was jesting with John and looked at him. His smile faded when he saw the expression on Lord Preston's face. "What's amiss?"

Lord Preston looked sternly in his eyes. "What are you doing with her?"

Joseph took a minute to control the conversation. He would not allow Preston to question his intentions. "What do you mean? She is a friend of Caroline's."

He cracked a smile. "Since when?" He leaned back in the carriage studying his face. "Please Wollaston. I told you she was innocent, and her family has lost so much already."

Preston looked at John who said nothing. He lowered his voice, "Don't forget that I know her father. I am the one who introduced you two." He straightened his jacket giving an exhausted sigh. "I stopped doing business with him a few years ago. He made some risky investments and was swindled. He is in heavy debt and dying. Can they really afford to have their daughter ruined? You will cost her any future marriage prospects if you continue this charade. Her station alone should discourage you from pursuing her. What are your intentions? To cost her the only thing she has—her virtue? I feel sorry for the girl."

Joseph was shocked at his friend's admission. His anger rose. "I will not hurt her. We are only friends. I ran into her at a house party and we spent a few days together. I introduced Caroline to her. You're the one being proud, my friend. Do you think we can't associate with her because of her station? Perhaps, we feel sorry for her too."

Preston glared at him. "You have no other intentions?"

Joseph squared his shoulders lifting his chin. "Of course not. I will not make her feel awkward and will offer to escort her this evening."

Preston shook his head mulling over the situation. "It's better if I escort her. We are acquainted, after all."

John chimed in. "I want a turn too. Did you see how she looked tonight? She is probably one of the most beautiful girls in England. I couldn't be married to a girl like that as it would be a constant battle with my jealousy. However, a beautiful woman on my arm can attract other less beautiful women."

They laughed out loud as they pulled up to the theatre.

The men departed their carriage and headed to meet the other carriage in front of them to escort the women. Caroline stepped out and took Joseph's arm. He eyed Lord Preston as he took Leah's arm. His blood rose admiring her beauty once again. Sweat beaded at his neck as he tried to think of an excuse to pull her into his arms.

The crowds of people were staring at Leah. Joseph watched their curious glances as she spoke to Lord Preston and John. The jealousy constricted in his chest as he waited to sit by her in the box. He would not be overshadowed by Lord Preston. He could only take so much honorable behavior for one night.

Many people greeted Joseph including women batting their eyes for his greeting. Joseph's attention was otherwise engaged in Leah's reactions. She had such poise and grace. For a moment, he thought that she would make a great duchess. *What was he thinking? Where did that come from?*

They entered the box and Joseph pushed John out of the way to take the seat next to Leah. He sat behind the three of them to Joseph's delight. John turned to offer Leah his seat in the front row, but she declined. Joseph smiled to himself.

The lights turned down as the performance began. Joseph reached for Leah's hand rubbing her glove. She peeked at him through the corner of her eyes, watching him lift her hand to his mouth as he kissed her glove. She smiled as he leaned down to whisper in her ear. "I love the diamonds on you. Thank you for wearing them."

She whispered back. "It's too much. You should not have given me such a gift."

He held her stare. "Please accept my gift. It is what I wish." His warm breath was so close to her ear, she shivered. He twisted a piece of her hair with his finger. "Your hair smells so good."

She gave him a nervous smile. "Thank you."

Carefully watching their friends seated in front to make sure they did not turn around, he leaned over and brushed a quick kiss on her cheek. Leah panicked trying to be discreet. She was safe for now but didn't know if she could survive the next few hours sitting so close to Joseph.

At intermission, Joseph offered to escort Leah to get some refreshments. Some friends had visited their box, engaging Lord Preston and John in conversations. Caroline declined the invitation to join them, staying instead to speak to a friend. They left the box, and Joseph held her closer. The champagne they received was cold, and Leah finished it in a few gulps. Joseph led her down an empty corridor telling her it was a shortcut back to his box. A few rooms were shut, but one was open. Joseph stepped inside escorting Leah into the room.

Leah's expression was full of apprehension over being caught. It was dark in the room with just a few candles. Joseph lit a candle then closed the door. She looked around trying to decipher her surroundings. Joseph held up the candle. "It's a dressing room for one of the actors. I know him and know for a fact that he is not here tonight."

Leah should have known he was prepared. "You do have quite a list of acquaintances."

Joseph sat on a chair pulling her into his lap. She felt uneasy and looked at the door. He felt her stiffen and chuckled. "I locked it." He stroked her tendrils of hair. "I just wanted a few moments alone with you."

He reached out to touch her face. "Leah, you look so irresistible tonight that I can't watch the play. I find myself watching you."

Leah's heart beat faster. "I am sure you exaggerate."

Joseph leaned down brushing his lips against hers. His touch was so soft and gentle. His mouth opened touching her tongue, and he pulled her closer to him. She tasted of sweetness, and he didn't want to ever let her go as he explored her mouth. Her earlier resistance turned into the response he yearned for as she put her arms around his neck and kissed him back. Leah moaned as he rubbed her arms before finding her hand intertwining his fingers with her. He finally broke away from her. "You have no idea what you do to me."

He put his forehead on top of hers. "We need to go before they send a search party. Lord Preston has proclaimed himself your protector from me."

She smiled, and he led her to the door. He rubbed her hand. "Give me a minute to make sure that we are alone in the hall." She nodded as he checked the hall before escorting her back to the box.

The evening ended too soon for Leah. Caroline gave her a ride back to the duke's, as the men went to their club. Caroline's maid rode with her back to Leah's home. It was a night that Leah would never forget.

CHAPTER 13

THE NEXT DAY MR. WILCOX came to call on Leah after church. He brought a pot of chicken stew that his servants had prepared along with a basket full of bread. The family enjoyed the meal together. Mr. Wilcox asked Mrs. Johnson for her permission to take Leah on a ride. She looked up at her mother pleading with her eyes for her to say *no*, yet she said *yes*.

Leah composed herself, thanking Mr. Wilcox as she took her shawl for a ride in the country. His familiar cologne caused Leah to hold her breath as he assisted her into his carriage. He lingered holding her hand, and she pulled her hand away forcing a smile. He walked around the carriage entering the other side. One of his woman servants crawled into the back to chaperone the couple.

They drove into the country making little conversation along the way. Leah's comfort ended when they pulled along some hills. Mr. Wilcox brought a blanket with a basket full of sweets. He assisted Leah out of the carriage while the servant stayed inside reading a book. She followed him out of sight of the carriage and her palms became sweaty at the thought of being along with him. He spread a blanket under some trees, and then offered her assistance to sit down.

Leah sighed. "It's a lovely view, Mr. Wilcox."

He smiled. "Again, please call me Ray."

Leah fidgeted with her hands, hoping the time would go by quickly. He handed her some biscuits and poured some wine. Leah bit into the biscuit, accepting the glass of wine to wash it down.

"Leah, I know it's only been a few days, but I was hoping you may have a decision for me." He took a drink of wine, leering at her.

She had to buy some more time. "I don't mean to be coy. It's not you. It's the idea of marriage when my papa is so ill. I wish to wait."

Mr. Wilcox tried to hide his resentment. "I thought announcing our engagement would bring him peace."

Tears formed in her eyes. "I can't right now. I don't want to think about good news when my papa has so little time. Please understand Mr. Wilcox... err... Ray." A tear came down her face.

Mr. Wilcox straightened his shoulders, visibly upset. "I don't understand. My patience is running thin. Your father gave his permission."

Leah looked away and her shoulders slumped as she let out a sob. Mr. Wilcox touched her arm. "Fine. You can have a little more time. I hope I don't regret this. I just need a little encouragement."

Leah's body stiffened as Mr. Wilcox touched her face. Leaning down, he kissed her on the mouth, pressing in as she refused to open. She thought she might vomit and tried to mask her revulsion by slowly pulling away.

He smiled, misunderstanding her disgust for innocence. He rubbed her face. "It's okay to kiss me, Leah. I know this may be a first for you. We will take it slow. As your husband, I can teach you many things."

Leah pulled away from him trying to regain control. "Thank you for taking it slow. I am not ready for such affections until after I am married."

Mr. Wilcox licked his lips, studying her. He poured another glass of wine and handed it to her. "This will relax you."

Leah refused, but he insisted. She reluctantly took another drink. After a few minutes of silence, she lifted her eyes to him. "I think we should head back now."

He agreed as he leaned toward her. "After one more kiss."

Leah's stomach dropped thinking of an escape. She quickly kissed him on the cheek, running from the blanket to the carriage. She looked back at his stunned expression. "Catch me if you can!"

Mr. Wilcox shook his head while carrying the basket and blanket up the hill. The servant got out of the carriage to assist them. Mr. Wilcox dare not make a scene in front of the servant. Leah giggled at her quick thinking. "You're faster than I thought."

He glared at her with annoyance. "You like to play games."

Leah ignored him and enjoyed her ride back to her house. When they arrived, Travis was outside tending to her new horse. Mr. Wilcox helped her out of the carriage kissing her hand, speaking to Travis as Leah went inside.

Travis was brushing the horse as Mr. Wilcox approached him. "Mr. Johnson, may I have a word?"

Travis shrugged his shoulders. "Of course, what is it?"

Mr. Wilcox cleared his throat watching Travis with the horse. "How is your father?"

Travis looked down as he stopped brushing the horse. "Not good. He had another episode today. The doctors have only given him a few more weeks to live."

Mr. Wilcox patted him on the back. He looked directly at Travis. "Very well. Leah has asked to wait for an announcement until after your father passes. If we wait until then, she must observe a mourning period. Do you think I should press your mother to make her comply before your father passes?"

Travis shook his head. "No, I think Leah would need to wait. As far as a mourning period, we hardly run in the same circles as nobility. Social norms are not the same. I am sure it will not be a standard mourning period, probably a lot less time."

Mr. Wilcox nodded. "So be it. Good night, Mr. Johnson."

Leah rushed past Miss Freemont and went to her room. She entered, falling on her bed and closing her eyes. She tried to forget about the kiss with Mr. Wilcox. Joseph entered her mind, yet she tried not to think about him either. What was she going to do? She contemplated her choices while thinking of her father lying in his room—how much she needed his advice. Perhaps he would be awake. Leah made herself get up and go to her parents' room. She peeked through the door and caught her father's eye.

He blinked. "Leah?"

She entered, closing the door behind her. "Yes, Papa."

He lifted his hand weakly. "Come closer, poppet."

Leah stepped near him, bending down to kiss his forehead. "Papa, I missed you. You're always sleeping when I come to visit you."

His eyes drooped. "Forgive me, I am just so tired. I wanted to ask you about Mr. Wilcox."

Leah held back the tears. Seeing her father this way broke her heart. A once vibrant man was reduced to a skeleton shape with all the weight he had lost. Leah bent down on her knees beside his bed and held his hand. "Papa, don't fret about Mr. Wilcox. He gave me his offer. But there may be another one soon from a different suitor, so I have asked him for some more time."

Mr. Johnson coughed as Leah patted his back. He moved her hand away. "I am fine, child."

He tilted his head. "Forgive me for not providing for you better."

Leah shook her head trying not to cry. "Nonsense. You gave me the best childhood a girl could hope for. I hope to find a man just like you, so you see, I must wait before I accept Mr. Wilcox's offer because I am not sure that he is the right one for me."

He smiled as his eyes fell shut. He drifted off to sleep. Leah stared at her father for a few moments. She kissed him again before leaving.

CHAPTER 14

LEAH FELL INTO THE CHAIR after working in the bookstore all day. Mondays were always so busy with the reading groups and refreshments. Mrs. Johnson left a few hours ago and gave her instructions to lock up the store early. Her brother Travis would take her home when he finished at the shop. She finished her break then closed the curtains to lock up the store and busied herself rearranging books and cleaning the shelves. The bell rang a few moments later causing her to bump into the bookshelf. She was surprised the door was unlocked and hurried to the door to tell the customer they were closed.

A deep voice stopped her. "Leah?"

Smiling she tried to smooth her skirt. "Joseph? I didn't realize the door was unlocked. We are actually closed."

He smiled warmly at her. "Forgive me. Should I come back another time?"

She laughed. "Of course not, it's just that I am alone." Saying she was alone out loud gave her a mild feeling of panic that she quickly dismissed. "Let me make sure the door is locked." She walked past him to click the lock. When she turned around, he slid his arms around her waist pulling her toward him.

"I missed you." He hugged her and kissed her cheek.

She smiled. "I missed you too."

He bent down and kissed her on the mouth, just a peck as he held her hand walking toward some chairs.

Her mind went back to the locked door and empty bookstore. She hesitated, worried at their lack of a chaperone. "My brother should be here in an hour to pick me up."

He grinned. "Then we have an hour."

She bit her bottom lip. "He can't find you here."

"We will keep the door locked, and I will leave out the back when he arrives. Now don't worry and come here." He sat down and pulled her into his lap, and though he tried to be calm and reassuring, she felt nervous to be completely alone with him.

He rubbed his nose against her cheek holding her tightly. "I am here to invite you to an outing on Saturday. My family owns a hunting lodge a few hours from here. It holds some of my favorite childhood memories and I want to take you there to see it."

Leah shifted in his arms, "Saturday? I will have to ask my mother."

Joseph pleaded, "Please Leah, say you will come. I have it planned so you need not worry. You could meet me at my house for breakfast, and then we can go from there. Caroline will be at breakfast with us, but it will only be the two of us for the outing. I will have her lady's maid and a footman for chaperones."

She nodded. "Very well, I can probably persuade her."

She looked around the room for a change of topic, "Do you play chess?" She got up from his lap, bringing the chessboard to the table near them. She placed the pieces on the board.

"A little." His gaze was more on her than on the game.

She shrugged. "I am not that good, but I like to play. My father taught my brother to play when I was younger, and I paid attention while they thought I was embroidering cushions. A girl can only take so much of that."

He chuckled. "Let us play then."

They sat across from each other playing chess. She moved her chess pieces around the board methodically, causing Joseph to tilt his head. "Not that good? I think you may have tried to swindle me, my dear."

Leah giggled. "You don't like to lose, Your Grace?"

He raised his brow. "You haven't won yet. Perhaps I am letting you get ahead."

They heard someone attempt to open the front door and Leah jumped up. "You have to go! That is Travis."

Joseph took his coat as they heard knocking on the front door.

Leah yelled near the door. "Be there in a moment, Travis."

Joseph touched her arm. "I hope to see you Saturday morning. Please send a message if you can't make it." He kissed her quickly on the mouth leaving out the back door.

Leah moved the curtain and seeing Travis, she unlocked the door. Travis stepped in abruptly. "What took you so long?"

She shrugged her shoulders innocently. "I had my hands full. Let me get my shawl so we can go. I am hungry."

Leah arrived home to find Melissa waiting for her in the drawing room. She was hesitant as their last conversation was about Joseph's intentions. She smiled at her friend. "Mel, it's good to see you."

Melissa smiled, hugging Leah. "We have much to talk about." She held up her hand and wiggled her fingers sporting a diamond ring.

Leah gasped grabbing her hand. "Oh! Does this mean what I think it means?"

She smiled coyly. "Yes, Captain Shockley, or Brian if I may, asked me for my hand. We will have an engagement party very soon."

Leah's heart swelled for her friend. "I am so happy for you! He is a great man."

Melissa sighed. "I know. Sorry, I haven't visited sooner. We were so caught up in courting that I haven't visited many people."

She sat down, pausing to take a breath. "Oh, before I forget… he received a letter from Captain Jackson who included a letter for you. Here it is." Leah accepted the letter without opening it—she wanted to read it later when she was alone. Melissa smoothed her skirt with her hands. "Captain Jackson's grandmother died, so his trip to London has been delayed. Apparently, more family members are going with him to America. They are leaving soon."

Leah's heart fell. She knew that Captain Jackson was her only chance to be saved from Mr. Wilcox. She smiled at Melissa. "I will read his letter later."

Melissa beamed at her friend. "I hope he can attend our wedding. Brian wanted him there, but he may be in America by then."

Leah sighed. "I hope he can attend too."

Melissa stood. "Well, I must get back. Let's have tea soon." She hugged Leah and left out the door.

Leah walked into her room closing the door behind her. She missed sharing a room with Betty. After all those years of wanting a room to herself, she never knew how much she would miss her. She sighed as she opened the seal and read the letter.

Dearest Miss Johnson,

I hope this letter finds you well. Forgive me for my delay getting to London to visit you. Our family has experienced the loss of my beloved grandmother. We are in mourning and will need time to attend to some family business. I should be in London soon and wish to visit with you. Perhaps we can take a ride to a park or enjoy a picnic when I see you.

Yours,
Clyde Jackson

Leah sighed a breath of relief. Captain Jackson was her last hope. She needed to stop this infatuation with Joseph and not see him anymore. He filled her thoughts every day and will eventually cause inevitable heartbreak.

CHAPTER 15

THE WEEK FLEW BY, AND Saturday finally came. Leah's mother agreed she could have the day off from the store. She convinced her mother that she was spending time with Caroline though she didn't tell her that it was only for breakfast. She needed to tell Joseph that their time together had to end. Leah couldn't chance her reputation. She needed to marry.

The breakfast buffet at Joseph's house was unlike anything Leah had ever seen. There were piles of bacon, sausage, and ham, accompanied by rolls, cakes, and fruit. Leah helped herself to a piece of sausage and some bread smothered in butter along with some juice.

John stopped by and piled a plate for himself. At the table, Caroline rolled her eyes at John. "Do you have a home?"

John smirked and took Caroline's hand to give it a kiss. "Yes, but I like the food here better. I need a new cook." She pulled her hand away with a playful look of disgust.

Joseph smiled at Leah. "Is that all you want to eat?"

Leah looked down at her plate. "It's enough for me. Thank you."

John looked at Leah. "Are you going to eat that sausage on your plate?" Leah shook her head and gave him the plate. Joseph scowled at John.

John looked up. "What?"

Joseph shook his head. "Never mind. Leah, if you are finished, we should depart early."

Leah followed Joseph to the carriage. They were alone inside as the maid and footman rode outside of the carriage.

He pulled her into his arms holding her on the ride there. He snuck kisses and took her gloves off to hold her hands. Leah's heart hurt knowing that this could not last too much longer. She was convinced that she was falling in love with him and didn't have the heart to tell him that they couldn't see each other anymore. They talked for the two hours making the time go by quickly. They were so different, yet so much alike.

Leah cracked a smile looking at the hunting lodge that Joseph was so fond of. Her imagination did not prepare her for the size of the house. In her mind, she imagined a small bungalow, but the house was huge with two master chambers and five bedrooms. It was closed, but Joseph took her for a tour anyway. They had a basket of food they took with them on their walk, while the maid and footman spent time in the servant's quarters for the afternoon.

Joseph was like a little kid pointing out all the areas he had adventures in as a child. He showed her a tree house that displayed the words: *"No girls allowed."* Leah busted out laughing at the sign. He took her by the hand to show her inside.

She stopped. "But I am a girl."

He kissed her. "You are an exception."

She climbed the ladder as best she could in a dress. She had to keep pulling her dress down as she crawled into the small house in the tree. He laughed at her as they went inside. Looking out the window, she could see the forest. He came up behind her, holding her around the waist. He kissed her neck as they looked outside together.

He whispered in her ear. "You're the only girl I would ever show my secret hideaway to."

She turned around. "I am honored."

He kissed her again, teasing her tongue, tasting her. He moaned and pulled his face away. "I have a lot more to show you."

He helped her climb down, then took her hand and headed to the lake. They walked out on the dock where he put the basket down. He opened the basket taking out some bread and cheese before giving her a glass of wine. "Do you like being near the water?"

She smiled as she raised her chin up to the sun. "Yes, I just wish I knew how to swim. It's always been a secret dream of mine."

He looked over at the lake. "I could teach you sometime when it gets warmer."

She relished in his attention, and thought of the contrast between her time with Mr. Wilcox and her time with Joseph. She lay down on the dock, soaking up rays of sunshine as the wind blew off the lake. Looking up she found Joseph staring at her.

She smiled, shading her eyes from the sun. "What's amiss?"

He rubbed his lips together. "Can I take the pins out of your hair?"

At that moment, she would let him do anything to her. "As you wish."

He reached over and began slowly taking the pins out while watching her hair cascade down her back. He ran his fingers through the golden strands while bending over and kissing her again. This kiss was passionate, taking the breath from her body. She opened her mouth trying to take all he was giving her. He continued to run his fingers through her hair, moving his kisses to her neck. Leah leaned back as Joseph lay partially on top of her. She placed her hands around his neck, running her fingers through the back of his hair. He moved his kisses down her neck to her chest, moving further down, placing feather-like kisses along the top of the neckline of her dress. Leah stiffened as she felt his hand move along her rib cage, feeling the underside of her breast, and she finally regained her senses. She slightly pulled away causing Joseph to stop the liberties he was taking. He rolled off her and leaned on his elbow. "Forgive me, I lost myself in you. You are just the most beautiful woman I have ever known."

Leah tried to catch her breath and fixed her dress. "I am sure that is not true, Your Grace."

He rubbed his finger along her cheeks. "I am serious, Leah."

She sat up ignoring him and reached for her wine, trying to get a hold of herself and remember her virtue.

Joseph was deep in thought. "I need to go take care of something quickly. Can you wait here for a few minutes? I have an idea."

Leah was curious at his odd behavior but agreed. "Of course." She watched him walk away and took the pins, putting them back in her hair to a more proper style. She chastised herself for falling so quickly for his touch. She took a few deep breaths and leaned back to enjoy the sun's rays.

Several minutes later, Joseph returned and reached for her hand. "Come along. I want to show you my surprise."

She took his hand and followed him up a trail in the woods. He kept sneaking looks at her like he held a secret. After reaching a clearing in the woods, he guided her around the tree until she noticed a carving in the bark. She moved closer, recognizing the words. It read—*Joseph loves Leah* with a heart around their names. He looked at her grinning from ear to ear, but Leah was startled. Did he just tell her that he loved her? She studied his eyes watching him rub his lips together. "It's true, I love you, Leah."

The gravity of his words hit her in the chest. "You *love* me?"

He reached over and hugged her tightly, "Yes. I have never told anyone that before—not even my parents."

Leah kissed him on the cheek. "Oh Joseph! I feel the same way. Thank you for today. I had the best time and I love the tree."

He took her hand and escorted her back to the dock. They gathered their leftovers and headed to the lodge. They had a long ride back and needed to get started. The ride back was full of laughter, games, and kisses. Leah's heart filled with love, and she would not allow herself to think of anything else. Perhaps all their friends were wrong about them. Maybe her station didn't matter. Would marriage be possible?

When they arrived back to his house, another carriage took her home. Joseph told her he would come see her on Monday when she closed the store and challenged her to finish their game of chess.

The duke went to his study after Leah left. Caroline joined him shortly afterward handing him a missive. He looked at her. "What's amiss?"

She was stoic. "Look who it is from."

Joseph looked down recognizing the name. It was the Earl of Rosenberg, his betrothed's father. He broke the seal, reading the message as his face turned pale. He looked up at Caroline. "They're coming next Saturday?"

Caroline touched his arm. "That's not all. Mother is coming back on Friday."

Joseph took a seat while Caroline poured him a brandy.

He sat without saying anything, only staring into the fire. The warm liquid filled his body as he took another drink. Caroline sat on the settee in silence. She finally took a deep breath. "Joseph, you have to tell her."

He looked down into his glass of brandy and gripped the glass tightly. "I know."

Caroline shook her head. "I think the sooner, the better. You don't want her to hear it from someone else."

Joseph glanced over at Caroline. "Impossible. No one knows about the announcement besides John. He won't tell anyone. I will invite her to dinner on Wednesday. I will need you here for propriety, but give us some time alone so I can tell her."

Caroline took a deep breath and looked around the room. "Very well. I just hope it was worth it."

Joseph rubbed his chin looking at his sister. "It was. For the first time in my life, I met someone who made me feel something I never thought possible. I think I love her."

She coughed trying to catch her breath. "Did you say, love?"

Joseph slowly nodded his head.

Caroline stood with a look of concern across her face, and Joseph stood up with her. She walked next to him and kissed his cheek. "I better go to bed."

Joseph nodded as he sat back down staring into the fire thinking about Leah.

CHAPTER 16

LEAH DUSTED THE OFFICE AFTER sweeping the store, anxiously awaiting Joseph's visit. The store was closed, and her brother was due in an hour to pick her up. She took out a package from underneath the counter. She had spent most of her Sunday avoiding Mr. Wilcox by feigning fatigue and instead worked on a present for Joseph.

The bell rang as Leah hurried to the door, looking through the curtains covering the window. She saw him standing there smiling as she opened the door. Leah locked it behind him pulling the curtain closed. He hugged her and lifted her up to swing her around.

"I missed you." He pulled a red rose out of his coat. Leah accepted it, putting it up to her nose. "Thank you."

They walked to the table that had the chessboard set up. Joseph raised his brow. "Are you ready to lose?"

Leah lifted her chin in a challenge. "Are you?"

He took her hand, held it up to his mouth and kissed her knuckles, before taking a seat opposite of her. She reached for the package and handed it to him.

He took it confused. "What is this?"

She grinned, a little afraid to give it to him. "It's a present for you. You are always giving me presents, and I wanted to give you something. It's not much, but I stayed up all night making it for you."

He stared at her seemingly unsure of what to say as he opened the papers. A black scarf laid on the bottom. He grinned as he pulled it out. "I love it." He wrapped it around his neck before standing to walk to the other side of the table. After bending down to kiss her, he broke away and touched her face. "Thank you."

Leah blushed. "I do hope you like it."

He smoothed the scarf with his hand and was about to say something, but was then interrupted by a knock at the door. Leah panicked, staring at Joseph.

"Is that your brother? I was hoping we could talk today?"

Leah shook her head. "He is early. Forgive me, Joseph. We will need to wait for our talk."

He placed his hands on her shoulders looking into her face. "Can you come to my house on Wednesday for dinner? I will send a carriage."

Leah heard Travis yelling her name, and she pushed Joseph near the back door. She lifted her eyes up to him. "I will be there."

He bent down and kissed her before turning on his heel to leave.

Leah rushed to the door to open it for Travis. He came into the store and helped her put everything away, so they could leave.

Leah took extra time dressing on Wednesday night. Her mother let her have the night off hoping she would spend some time with Mr. Wilcox. Leah talked fast and convinced her mother that she could not decline an invitation to dinner with Lady Caroline.

The carriage picked Leah up, taking her to Joseph's. She sunk into the cushions enjoying the ride looking out the windows. The familiar driveway came into sight causing her stomach to flip at seeing Joseph again. She noticed the rain falling again as it had on and off all day. She was hoping that the roads were not too muddy.

Joseph greeted her and escorted her to the drawing room for drinks. John was there along with Caroline. They greeted each other as Leah took a glass of sherry from Joseph.

The butler appeared announcing dinner. Joseph held out his arm, and as she took it, a loud sound of thunder shook the house. Leah jumped with a startled look. Joseph put his arm around her, patting her back. He smiled. "Are you okay?"

She laughed. "That frightened me!"

He rubbed her hand guiding her to the dining room. The oval table was set for four. The place settings were beautiful.

Two footmen brought out dish after dish. Leah savored each course while anticipating the next one. The food was scrumptious, and John proved most entertaining as he told stories of his nights out. Leah's stomach hurt from the laughter. The dessert finally made an appearance when the butler addressed Joseph. "Your Grace. A young man is at the door requesting Miss Johnson. He said it's of the utmost importance."

Leah removed her napkin and stood up. "Please excuse me."

Joseph and John both stood when she rose. Joseph followed her out of the room. When Leah entered the entrance of the home she raised her brow in confusion. "Travis?"

Travis was dripping wet with a serious look on his face. "Forgive me, Leah. You must come home at once. It's Father."

Leah gasped grabbing her stomach. "Is he…"

Travis shook his head. "Not yet. Mother is with him and Miss Freemont went for the doctor. They asked me to fetch you because it could be the end."

Leah tried to catch her breath. "Of course, let me get my cloak."

Joseph stood in shock, but came out of his stupor to introduce himself to Leah's brother. "Mr. Johnson? It's nice to make your acquaintance. If there is anything I can do, please let me know. I will send my carriage for you both."

Travis squared his shoulders. "Thank you, Your Grace, I know who you are. It's not necessary as I have the gig. We just need to hurry."

The front door swung open, two grooms stood dripping wet, along with a footman. Joseph wrinkled his brow. "What's amiss?"

The footman bowed. "Your Grace, the creek has flooded causing the road to flood too. No one should try to go out in this weather until the storm passes."

Leah pulled her cloak next to her body. "We have to go. My father needs me. Travis will find a way out."

The head groom shook his head. "Please, miss. The road is impassable right now. If the water doesn't wash the gig away, the lightning and thunder will scare the horses. Your best bet is to let us put the horses in the stable tonight. We can check on the bridge in the morning. The daylight is the best time to travel in this weather."

Joseph looked at Travis. "Mr. Johnson, please let me offer your sister and you a chamber for the night. I can make sure you are up at first light. Hopefully the water will have receded enough, so you can pass. I think it's the safest solution for your sister."

Travis hesitated but looked outside the window. He turned around to see Leah's face stressed with worry and acknowledged the duke. "Your Grace, may I have a few minutes to speak privately with my sister?"

Joseph nodded. "Of course, the drawing room is the first door on the right. We will wait for you."

Leah followed Travis to the drawing room, closing the door behind her. Travis whispered, "Is there something going on here between you and the duke?"

Leah was startled by her brother's question. She shook her head, frantic that Travis saw something between them. "We are friends. He is Lady Caroline's brother."

Travis looked at his sister in way that made her think that he knew she was hiding something. "Is he why you won't give Mr. Wilcox your answer?"

Leah bit her bottom lip. "Travis, I don't wish to talk about this. I want to see Papa."

Travis hugged his sister as she let out a loud sob. He pulled back looking into her face. "Leah, as much as I want to go home, the duke is right. It's too dangerous to leave right now. I can't do that to you. I think we accept the bed chambers he has offered and leave at first light."

Leah nodded as Travis wiped the tears from her eyes. "Leah, we need to talk about your friendship with the duke. That could be dangerous. Have you no idea of what could happen to your reputation and our family if anyone finds out about this?"

Tears pulled up in her eyes. "Travis, please not tonight."

He took a sigh. "Fine. I won't speak of it tonight, but you need to be careful around him. It looks bad, Leah. I saw the way he was looking at you. It could cost you the chance to make a good match."

Leah didn't want to argue, so she took Travis's arm and walked back into the foyer. Travis did not let go of her arm. "Your Grace, we accept your offer for a room for the night. We will leave at first light. If you would be so kind to have one of your maids show us the way to our accommodations, I will escort my sister."

Travis inserted himself between Joseph and Leah in a protective way, taking his sister's arm.

Joseph excused himself to speak to some servants, leaving them alone in the foyer. Leah tried to speak. "Travis, you sounded a bit rude."

Travis hushed Leah. "We will not speak of this now."

A few moments later two maids entered the foyer and escorted them up the grand staircase. Leah was escorted to one chamber, and Travis wished her a good night. Travis was escorted to a different chamber down the hall.

Leah took in the beautiful, massive chamber. She couldn't believe such a chamber was for guests. The cream wall coverings showed highlights of blue and matched the colors throughout the chamber. The bed was huge with an abundance of pillows. She couldn't wait to jump in the middle of it. A knock disturbed her exploring. She went to open it, eyeing a maid with some folded clothes in her hand.

She curtsied. "Miss Johnson, Lady Caroline thought you might need a nightdress. Please accept this one to sleep in."

Leah accepted the gown. "Oh, thank you. It's perfect."

The basin water was warm, and she changed her clothes for the night. Thoughts of her father plagued her mind. She kneeled beside her bed to say a prayer for him, hoping for some more time. Tears filled her eyes—she was not ready to say goodbye yet.

Joseph watched Leah walk upstairs with her brother. He needed to tell her the truth. His time was running out. She consumed his thoughts night and day. Not wanting to face his sister's questions and insistence, he said goodnight and waited in an adjoining room for Travis to say goodnight to Leah.

Leah had settled herself in bed when she heard a knock. Looking at the door, she realized it was coming from the wall by the wardrobe. She rose from the bed to investigate, turning the nob on the wardrobe, she jumped back to see Joseph standing there.

He laughed. "Surprise!"

Leah let out a breath. "What are you doing? Is this a secret doorway?"

Joseph held the door open. "Yes… from years ago. I wanted to put you in the duchess chamber, but I thought Travis would not like that. I remembered these chambers having the secret doors, so I gave this one to you for tonight."

Leah whispered, "Joseph, you can't be in here. It's not proper." Leah covered her nightgown with her arms, wrapping them around herself.

Joseph's face became serious. "Leah, please don't send me away. I only want to comfort you. I am so sorry about your father, I do know what that feels like." He reached for her hand and held it. "I promise I will not touch you improperly. Please just let me hold you."

His eyes fell upon her nightgown, admiring her curves more clearly than in the dresses she wore. She was magnificent.

Joseph wrapped his arms around her. She snuggled her face into his chest, absorbing the warmth of his body. He kissed her head. "Leah, let me hold you while you sleep. I promise I will be a gentleman."

Leah was reluctant but allowed Joseph to guide her to the bed. He sat on the bed pulling her with him. He scooted to the middle and laid her on his chest. He kept his word—only wrapping his arms around her—and stroked her hair.

He took a breath. "I hope your father will be okay. I could send my doctors if you think it would help?"

Leah sniffed her nose. "Thank you for your concern. But he has had great physicians that all say the same. He will not last more than a few weeks. Maybe even less now based on what my brother has said."

Joseph squeezed her. "I would like to help if I could. Please let me know if your family needs anything."

They sat in silence and he listened closely as Leah's breathing steadied. Realizing she was sleeping, he held her tightly against his body. Putting off the inevitable, he wanted to remember this moment. He couldn't bear the words he had to say to her soon.

After hours of restless sleep, the light of dawn whispered through the shadows outside the window. The time was near that she would leave. He had to tell her the truth.

"Leah, wake up." Joseph leaned down kissing her ear. His eyes hurt at the weight of no sleep. His mind raced to think of the words he would say to tell her of his deception.

Leah yawned twisting in his arms. "I forgot where I was. Is it morning already?"

Joseph's voice cracked. "Leah, I need to talk to you. There is something I must tell you." Leah tilted her head near his face. He rubbed her arms, afraid to let go. "There has been some news and I am feeling troubled." He struggled with his words.

Leah sat up breaking away from his arms and stared into his face. "What troubles you?"

Joseph swallowed hard. "My father... he troubles me. When I was younger, my education was about my obligations to be a duke. People respected my father because of his title, yet he was not the best of men. I wanted him to love me and tried to be the best son I could be, excelling in all my endeavors." Joseph paused to run his fingers through his hair, looking down at the bed. "His expectations of me were about duty and family."

Leah reached for him, stroking his face. He touched her hand, holding it in his.

He took a deep breath. "A little over a year ago, he became ill. Just like your father. He put a lot of pressure on me to fulfill my obligations to the family. He contacted the Earl of Rosenberg, his friend from Oxford. The earl did not visit London much, spending most of his time abroad when he was not in Kent. They arranged for his daughter to visit with her parents."

Leah's eyes narrowed as her body stiffened. Her breathing became labored. Joseph rubbed his lips together trying to finish.

"We spent a few days together at the request of our families. After a fortnight, my father asked me to do my duty. At that time, I did not know you. Never had I experienced love. Marriage to me was about obligation, not love. I agreed to the arranged marriage and proposed to Roslyn. She accepted and departed the next day. They were to visit her grandparents in Italy and travel for a year until the announcement of our engagement was made to the public. I received notice that she will be here on Saturday."

Leah's eyes widened. She scooted away from him on the bed, trying to find the floor. He bent over, reaching for her arm. "Leah, stop." She tried to jerk her arm away, but he held it tighter. He moved to the floor, bending on his knees in front of her, and placed his head in her lap as she sat on the edge of the bed.

"Tell me what to do, Leah. I barely know her, and I love you."

Leah's eyes were filled with tears dripping from her eyes. She looked torn between wanting to comfort him and wanting to resist him. Finally making a decision, she twisted her body away from him. He sat on the floor looking up at her as she stood.

"You knew! This whole time you made me believe..." She choked, wiping her tears. "Joseph, I must get Travis. My father needs me."

He stood up. "Leah, please let me explain."

She shook her head. "No! They warned me. Everyone warned me to stay away from you—that your intentions were not honorable. You made me fall in love with you just to throw me away. How cruel could you be?!"

Joseph's chest tightened, her words stabbing him like a knife. He reached for her, and she slapped his hand away. A knock on the door interrupted them. Leah went to the door to crack it open. It was Travis.

"Leah, I just checked the road and it's clear. Get dressed, we must go at once."

Leah nodded her head. "Of course, give me a few minutes and I will meet you downstairs." She turned around to see Joseph standing by the wardrobe. She picked up her dress. "Please leave me alone so I can dress."

His eyes were red as he stammered out his words. "I don't want you to leave. Not like this."

Leah closed her eyes. "You don't always get what you want. My father is dying, Joseph. Please show some respect and leave me alone."

Joseph pressed his mouth closed, staring at her. He finally stepped near the joining door and left the room. Leah took a rag, wiping her puffy face. She twisted her hair into a braid pinning it up, then put on her dress. She folded up the nightdress, leaving it on the bed.

Travis met her in the foyer. Joseph, Caroline, and John were waiting as well. Leah kept her head down, putting on her bonnet while she quickly curtsied to the three trying not to show her face. "Thank you for dinner, but we must be on our way." She pulled Travis's arm, walking out the door.

Caroline took a step outside. "Leah, are you ill? You don't look well."

Leah looked at her. "Just worried about my father."

Caroline nodded with concern. "Of course, please keep us informed. God be with your family."

Leah walked away and was assisted by Travis into the gig. Travis studied her face, but chose not to say anything as they rode away.

Caroline shut the door and looked back at Joseph. She walked near him touching his arm. "Does she know?"

Joseph stared at the carriage through the window, ignoring Caroline. John's usual banter halted as he went to pour a drink for his friend.

Caroline looked at John. "You're giving him brandy? It's seven in the morning. We should all go back to bed. Why are you up?"

John raised a brow. "I heard a vase break in Joseph's room which could have woken the dead. I decided to be of assistance." John looked at the drink and set it down beside Joseph. "My work here is done, and I will go back upstairs."

Caroline watched Joseph shoot a glare at John. He said no words, turning on his heel and headed to his study. Caroline followed him. "Joseph, talk to me."

He kicked the chair sitting by his desk. "I did my duty. I told her. Now leave!"

Caroline jumped back startled and left the room.

CHAPTER 17

THE RIDE HOME WAS LONG, and the gig faltered a few times but made it back to Leah's cottage. The two siblings rushed in to see their father. Leah's mother was sitting on the bed holding his hand. His eyes were closed, his breathing raspy.

Leah knelt beside her mother. Mrs. Johnson looked up. "Leah, are you well? Travis?"

Travis was in the doorway choking back his emotions. "I am well, Mother. The storm delayed us, but we are here now. I am sorry that we were not here sooner."

Travis walked in the room and put his hand on his mother's shoulder. "Take a rest, Mother. We will stay with him." Mrs. Johnson let out a breath. "I will only be a few minutes. He hasn't woken up since you left yesterday, Travis. The doctor was here last night, but said it's only a matter of a few days."

Tears streamed down Leah's face. Travis offered her the chair, dragging the other chair from across the room to sit beside her. No one spoke. Leah rubbed her father's hand not wanting to let go. Thoughts of her childhood entered her mind. The times he carried her on his back and helped her pick wild flowers for her mother. He was so generous that at times he would sneak coins to her to buy sweets or ribbons. One of her favorite memories was sitting with him at church as he helped her read bible verses. Her heart broke at the memories.

Leah's mother came back to the room an hour later. "Leah, you need to freshen up. You look exhausted after your trip home. I sent a message to my sister and they should be here within a few days. There is nothing more we can do for your father now but keep him comfortable. I suggest we take turns because we need to make sure we are also taking care of ourselves."

Leah nodded, walking out of the room. She washed up in the basin to freshen herself. Mrs. Freemont knocked on her door to tell her that Mr. Wilcox was waiting for her in the drawing room. She finished dressing to see him.

Mr. Wilcox sat on the settee, rising when she entered the room. He took off his hat. "Leah, I heard the news. How are you?"

Leah sat on the chair facing the settee. "We are preparing ourselves. The doctor says it might only be a few days more."

Mr. Wilcox cleared his throat. "I brought Jasper home. He is changing in his room. He will stay here with the family."

Leah looked down at her lap. "That is very kind of you, Mr. Wilcox. If you will excuse me, I need to get back to my father." Leah stood to leave the room, but Mr. Wilcox stood quickly and reached for her hand. He pulled it up to his mouth, kissing her knuckles.

"Leah, please understand that I am here to help you. I thought it was better not to mention our pending engagement during this time, but I think we must. The sooner we announce our intentions, the sooner you can be under my protection. Knowing you are under my protection, the debt collectors and others will think twice before bothering your family."

Leah's stomach dropped. This day had been the worst in her young life. Her heart was breaking by the only man she may ever love. Her father was on his deathbed, and she was being forced into a marriage of convenience. He was right though—his protection would help her family. She took a deep breath. "Soon, Mr. Wilcox, very soon." She turned and left the room.

Leah's father passed away a couple days later. The family prepared themselves with mourning dress for the day of the funeral. Their funds were limited for mourning wardrobe, opting instead for a black band on the arm after the first day. The funeral was a few days afterward, not large, only a few close friends and family. Leah's sister Betty made it in time for the memorial service. All four siblings gathered to say goodbye. Her mother's depression was a constant worry for Leah. Mrs. Johnson was unable to work at the bookstore, so they closed it for a few days. Mr. Wilcox tried many times to see Leah after her father's death. She avoided him at the funeral, feigning sickness afterward and closing herself up in her room and accepting no visitors.

CHAPTER 18

JOSEPH WAS IN HIS STUDY when his mother entered. "Joseph, it's too dark in this room. Come and give me a kiss."

Joseph rose and took a few steps before bending down to kiss his mother on the cheek. He sighed. "Welcome home, Mother."

She looked around the study. "Where is Caroline?"

A voice answered in the doorway. "I am here, Mother." Caroline strolled in and kissed her mother.

The duchess smiled, looking at Joseph. "I received the news that your betrothed will be here tomorrow. We will be very busy planning the engagement party and wedding." She took a seat wiping her gloves on her dress.

Joseph said nothing. He walked back to his desk to go through some paperwork. "Perhaps we should speak of the engagement at another time?"

The duchess huffed. "Why? It's a lot of work planning all of the events. It's been at least a year and we should be prepared."

Joseph grunted. "Plan whatever you choose. I don't care. The wedding is not important to me." He left the study.

***

The duchess raised her brow at Caroline. Caroline took a seat beside her. "Mother, there has been some news."

The duchess took a sip of tea and looked at her daughter. "What news? I received a letter directly from the Countess of Rosenberg. All the plans are set, and they will be here tomorrow."

Caroline rested her hands on her lap. "Mother, Joseph may need some encouragement. He has suffered recently and has questioned his attachment to his betrothed. I do believe he will do his duty but is not happy about it. Please be gentle with him."

The duchess squinted her eyes. "Suffered? What are you speaking about?"

Caroline took in a breath, whispering, "He met a new friend—a woman. Well, she's really a girl, beautiful but not from the *ton*. He has questioned his future."

The duchess tightened her lips shaking her head. "It's not uncommon, you know. Many nobles get caught up with common women, yet it doesn't stop them from marrying. He will do his duty, I am sure of it."

Joseph poked his head in the study. "Mother, I will be dining at the club tonight. The staff has prepared some of your favorites. I am sure Caroline will join you."

She rolled her eyes. "Very well, Joseph. I won't force you to dine with your mother who you have not seen in months."

The butler interrupted them. "Your Grace, the Earl of Rosenberg is here."

Joseph stepped into the doorway, turning to his mother. "Why would he be here?"

The duchess shrugged her shoulders. "I have no idea—the letter I received said tomorrow."

Joseph sighed. "I don't wish to see him."

Caroline told the butler they would be there momentarily. She touched Joseph's arm. "Today or tomorrow will not make any difference at this point." Joseph's face showed his anger, but he said no words. He followed his sister and mother to the drawing room.

The earl stood with his family. "Your Grace, we arrived today earlier than expected. We learned that our message did not make it to you—I hope you don't mind our intrusion."

Joseph's manners forced him to oblige. "Nonsense, you are welcome. We can ask the staff to prepare extra dinner at once. My mother and Caroline were going to dine alone, and I am sure they would enjoy the extra company. Unfortunately, I have a previous engagement."

Caroline and the duchess shot Joseph a disappointed look. Lady Roslyn blushed when she saw Joseph, who in turn briefly nodded when she curtsied. Her curly brown hair was pinned up, causing stray curls to fall along her face. Her dress displayed the height of fashion in London. Some may call her passably pretty by *ton* standards. But what interested most men was her bloodlines and flawless manners. She presented herself with the utmost aristocratic breeding—a perfect duchess.

The earl looked down. "Of course, Your Grace."

The duchess interrupted. "Please, won't all of you sit and have a drink? Joseph, would you like to take a seat by Lady Roslyn."

Joseph bowed. "Forgive me, but I must go. I am already late. I wish you a good day."

The duchess laughed nervously and spoke to the family, trying to make amends for Joseph's behavior. Caroline shot a look of sympathy for Lady Roslyn who was looking down at her lap through most of the conversation.

The duchess realized at that moment how hard it may be for her son to stop thinking about this other woman, but she would do what was in her power to make sure that he did his duty.

The next couple of days flew by for Joseph. He wasn't sure how he was going to go through with it. It's not just the wedding, but spending the rest of his life with a woman he barely knew. A woman he was not attracted to. He thought with time, she would be tolerable, but he knew his feelings would never change. Now that he knew what love could feel like—anything else was not acceptable.

Avoiding his family and wedding planning was the top of his priorities. With the family occupied, he took off to John's house. He had too much family companionship at his own house and craved John's bachelor lodgings—at least for a few hours.

Joseph arrived at the earl's house as he was leaving. "Joseph, I was just going to your house."

He let out a breath in frustration. "I came to borrow your home for the afternoon. I needed a break and thought we could have dinner at the club."

John winked. "I can't tonight. I am going to the theatre with Lady Casey."

Joseph snorted at his friend's whimsical reply. She had a reputation that proceeded itself. "Theatre?"

John smirked. "Yes, she is making me take her out if I want to continue to see her. Anyway, I was going to stop by to see you quickly because I ran into Preston. I am not sure how he found out, but Leah's father died. His funeral was yesterday morning."

Joseph closed his eyes. "I asked an associate to find out who his doctor was, and I was trying to get some news. That's horrible. I bet she is crushed."

John pulled on his reins. "I thought you should know, but I must take my leave because I am late."

Joseph turned from John's house and headed to Leah's to offer his condolences.

There was a knock on Leah's bedroom door. Mrs. Freemont poked her head in the doorway. "Leah, you have a visitor—it's a man. He left no name, just insisted upon talking to you."

She was mending some hose and held up her hand to the door. "I don't wish to see anyone. Please tell them I am not well."

Mrs. Freemont nodded her head. "He is very handsome and just said he is a friend of yours."

Leah perked up hoping it was Captain Jackson. No other males would visit her. She jumped out of bed. "Oh, tell him I will be down in a minute. I only wish to freshen up."

She practically ran down the stairs. Turning toward the drawing room, she gasped. There in her home stood the Duke of Wollaston. She looked at her mother and sister sitting on the settee. Jasper was sitting at the table drawing.

Leah composed herself. "Your Grace?"

Joseph cleared his throat and handed her some flowers. "I wanted to give you my condolences."

Leah slowly took the flowers, bewildered by his behavior. She straightened her shoulders lifting her chin. "Thank you. It was not necessary for you to come by."

He shifted his feet uncomfortably and ran his hand along the edge of his jacket. "If there is anything I may assist with, I would–"

Leah interrupted him. "We're fine, but thank you." She handed the flowers to Mrs. Freemont who put them in a vase.

Puzzled, Leah's family stared at the exchange. Remembering her manners, she looked back at them and said, "Mother, this is the Duke of Wollaston—Lady Caroline's brother."

Mrs. Johnson stood to curtsey. "It's a pleasure, Your Grace. Can I make you some tea?"

He smiled briefly before looking back at Leah. "No, thank you. I can only stay a few minutes."

Leah turned to her siblings. "This is Betty, my younger sister"—she pointed to the table— "and my brother Jasper."

Leah took a deep breath trying to fill the awkward silence in the room. "May I walk you out?" He nodded saying goodbye to her family.

They walked in silence to his horse when she finally turned to look at him. "Thank you again for the flowers. I am sorry you had to come to this part of town. It's a bit unsavory for someone of your status." She curtsied and turned around to walk away.

Joseph rolled his eyes blocking her path. "That was a bit uncalled for. I have never treated you differently because of your station."

Leah cracked a smile at the irony of his statement. "I beg to differ."

He hesitated, seemingly needing her to listen. "I need you to know that I never meant to be cruel to you. My intentions were not to hurt you. If I could change my circumstances then I would."

Leah snapped her eyes up at him snarling at the ridiculous defense of his actions. Sarcastically, she stepped away from him crossing her arms. "Poor Joseph and his circumstances."

Raising her brow in a feigned attempt of concern, she continued, "How is your fiancée?" Watching his expression closely, she attempted to get a reaction. "I read your announcement in this morning's paper. They are calling it the *match* of the season, perhaps even the wedding of the year. Congratulations. I hope you will be very happy together."

Joseph's face turned red, and he loosened his cravat. Trying to compose himself, he took a few deep breaths and reached for her as she winced and pulled away. "I didn't know about the paper. Honestly, Leah. You must believe me. She means nothing to me. I only love you."

Her tears escaped as she tried to wipe them away. He took her hands, tightly pulling her into his embrace. She tried to break away again, unable to resist his grip as he held her tightly against his chest. She couldn't catch her breath, relenting to let him hold her.

He closed his eyes as she trembled in his arms. She was sobbing loudly as he stroked her hair. After a few minutes, he released her and cupped her face. She looked up at him with tear-soaked eyes, searching for words. Finally, she lifted herself on her tiptoes and planted a kiss on his lips. She pulled back swiftly, taking a few steps away, out of his reach. "Goodbye, Joseph. You will always hold a piece of my heart."

Joseph stepped toward to her, but she kept her hand up. "Please just go and leave me alone."

He caught his breath. "Don't push me away. I love you."

She stared at him for a few seconds without responding. Gathering her thoughts, she whispered, "You don't love me enough." She turned away from him and ran to the house.

Joseph felt his chest tighten and his legs began to buckle. He took a few steps toward his horse and grabbed ahold of his saddle, trying not to show his emotions. He took a few deep breaths as he got ready to mount. He heard a horse behind him and he turned to see Travis coming to the stable.

Travis tipped his hat. "Hello, Your Grace." He gave him a stoic look as he stepped off his horse and led it to the stable.

Joseph nodded. "Hello, Mr. Johnson. I came to offer my condolences."

Travis nodded as he fixed the saddle on his horse. He turned to Joseph. "I appreciate your condolences." He looked away, searching for anyone around so he could speak privately. Seeing no one, he faced Joseph. "Your Grace, with all due respect, I must ask you to keep your distance from my sister. Leah is young and very innocent. She doesn't know her own beauty and is quite trusting of people. I read about your engagement in the papers. I don't wish Leah to get hurt."

Joseph tilted his head. "I don't have ill intentions, but I can respect your request. I do worry about her welfare, and it was that concern that prompted my visit today. I will do as you wish."

Travis looked down. "Thank you, Your Grace."

Joseph nodded appreciating the young man's nerve in asking a duke to stay away from his sister.

Joseph looked back. "Mr. Johnson, how is your family?"

Travis looked down masking his emotions. "We will take care of ourselves."

Joseph admired him for taking on the burden of being the man of the family. He was even younger than Leah. He was barely one and eight. "Will you be attending the University?"

Travis looked away sniffing his nose. "Not this year, perhaps someday. I must take care of my family first. My father had many debts."

Joseph's rubbed his lips. "Your brother Jasper, will he go into the military as Leah said he dreamed?"

Travis rubbed the horse not making eye contact with him. "No, he will work in the stables on Mr. Wilcox's property. Our welfare is not your concern, Your Grace. We will be fine."

Joseph respected his words and mounted his horse. He looked back to him. "Good luck to you."

CHAPTER 19

JOSEPH VISITED HIS SOLICITOR THE following morning regarding his newest cause. Afterward, he stopped by John's house hoping to avoid his mother. Her main residence was at the dowager house in the country, so she insisted on staying with Joseph when she was in town.

After a few hours with John, he faced the inevitable and rode home. When he arrived, he quietly snuck in the side entrance and asked his butler to send a tray to his room, yet his mother caught him in the hallway.

"Joseph, I have been looking for you. The earl has invited us to dine with them this evening. I told Lady Roslyn that you would take her on a ride today in the park."

Joseph huffed at his mother's imprudent gesture. "Then *you* can tell her that I won't be coming. I am otherwise engaged. Speaking of Lady Roslyn, did you tell the papers of our upcoming engagement?"

The duchess crossed her arms. "What does it matter? I may have told a few acquaintances. The engagement ball is next Saturday, what did you expect? That we could keep it a secret forever?"

Joseph's face turned red. "I expect you to stay out of my business. The gossip papers have us practically married."

The duchess's shoulders sagged while she studied her son. After a few moments, she tried to use her motherly tone on him, "Joseph, I heard about that girl, Miss Johnson—the one you have been dallying with. Really Joseph, don't you know that servants talk? Many great men have had liaisons with such women before. They are fun for a few months but hardly worth giving up a debutante. Lady Roslyn will make a great duchess. She is poised in a way that most women are not. Your fortunes and titles will make a powerful match, securing the legacy of our family. You made a promise to your father, and gave her family your word."

Joseph looked away from his mother trying to maintain his temper. "That *girl* is not your concern. Please don't speak of her again. I know my obligations."

His mother shook her head. "Very well, let's not quarrel. You can pick up Lady Roslyn at five for the ride. She will be expecting you, and that should fulfill your obligations for one day. I will make excuses for your absence at dinner if you insist on not attending."

Joseph turned on his heel and walked away from his mother. He went to his study to work the rest of the afternoon until he left to pick up Roslyn. His compromise with his mother was more than he should have agreed to. He had no desire to see the chit. Although a part of him felt sorry for her—it was not her fault he didn't want to marry her. His forced engagement was part of being a duke.

Roslyn dressed in a pale pink frock surrounded by lace. Her curly hair was pinned on the sides and fell on her shoulders. She smelled of lemons and brought a parasol to block the sun. Joseph chose the open carriage and assisted her into the passenger side.

The ride was short and bumpy. They struggled to make polite conversation as Joseph's thoughts were elsewhere. Lady Roslyn was poised with perfectly straightened shoulders as she ignored the bumpy roads and remained the picture of decorum.

She rubbed her lips. "Your Grace, what a beautiful day."

Joseph grunted adding no conversation to her comment.

Straightening her gloves, she tried again at conversation. "Your Grace, are you cross with me?"

Joseph did sneak a look at her then. He shook his head. "No, why would I be cross?"

She shrugged. "You have barely said two words to me the last few days. Do you wish not to marry me?" Her bright eyes searched his face with apprehension. He could see her bracing herself for his answer as she held on tightly to her reticule.

Joseph's breath caught in his chest. He did not know how to answer her question. He looked down for a minute. "I um... I made a commitment last year to uphold our families' wishes. That has not changed."

She looked down accepting his answer. It was not love or even friendship, but satisfied her concerned look. She smiled as people passed by offering their greetings.

They spent little time at the park, quickly departing back to her townhouse. She rubbed her hands on her lap smoothing her skirt. "Your Grace, some of my school friends are in London. They asked that we join them on Friday for dinner. Would you be able to escort me?"

Joseph shook his head. "Forgive me, I have another obligation that night."

She nodded her head remaining quiet the rest of the trip home.

Leah spent the day in her room, going over her last encounter with Joseph in her head. She couldn't bear to see him again knowing that he was with another. Her tears dried up after a night of sobbing. She knew she had to make some choices and they would have to be soon. Mr. Wilcox was growing impatient—she couldn't put him off forever.

A knock on the door disturbed her thoughts. Travis poked his head in the door. "Leah, there is a Captain Jackson here to see you."

Leah's breath caught in her throat. Relieved, she sat up quickly. "Show him to the drawing room. I will be there in a moment."

Leah practically ran down the stairs headed to the drawing room. When she entered, Captain Jackson was talking to her brother Jasper who looked so excited to speak to him about the military. The captain stood when he saw her. "Miss Johnson, you're lovely as always."

Leah smiled as he took her hand, kissing her knuckles. She beamed at him. "Would you care for some tea?"

He shook his head. "I would like to know if you could take a ride?"

She glanced at Travis standing behind them and he nodded. She donned her gloves and bonnet, following him out the door to his carriage. He assisted her up and they rode to the country.

He patted her arm. "I am so happy to see you again. You were in my constant thoughts."

She blushed. "My condolences on your grandmother. How is your family?"

He shook his head. "They are doing better. My parents left for America a few days ago, and my sister and I will join them soon. My uncle's shipping business is doing well, and he has invited my whole family to come to America. Melissa told me about your father. I offer you my condolences as well."

Leah's heart went into her throat. "Thank you, Captain." She tried to keep her breathing smooth. "America sounds like a fun adventure."

He smiled. "I am glad you feel that way. Please call me Clyde." He pulled the carriage over near to an open field with many trees and turned to face her.

She smiled. "As you wish."

He took her hand. "Leah, I don't have much time. I would love to court you properly as you deserve to be, but I leave in a fortnight. I want you to come with me to America."

Leah's sucked in her breath. "Are you asking me to be your wife?"

He smiled placing his finger across her lips. "Don't answer now. I need to speak to your brother. I also want you to think about leaving your family for America and spending the rest of your life with me. I have thought about nothing else. It's what I wish, and I hope you do too."

Leah nodded as he removed his finger before placing his lips upon hers for a chaste kiss. He touched her face. "I have a cousin who is a vicar. He lives near the port and can marry us before we depart—that way we can share my cabin. My sister has her own cabin. I know this is sudden, but we haven't much time before I must depart. We will have the rest of our lives to get to know each other. What difference would it make if we married next year or now?"

Leah stared at him as her eyes searched his face. This was sudden—but an answer to prayers.

He smiled shyly. "I already bought your passage in the hope you would join me. We will need to apply for a marriage license and that could take some time. I have a close friend who is a viscount, and he may be able to help us get a special license."

Leah's heart beat faster, unsure how to feel. "You've made me very happy. I will give you my answer tomorrow."

He took her hand and kissed her palm. "I thought about you every day since I left the house party. It may seem we are rushing things, but it is my wish to be with you."

Leah smiled. "I will speak to my family tonight."

After they arrived home, he kissed her hand goodbye, and asked Travis for a private audience. Travis agreed as they entered the drawing room alone. Leah smiled to herself taking the stairs up to her room to wait for Travis. A half hour later Travis knocked, entering upon her reply. He sat in the chair beside her bed. "How do you feel about him?"

Leah took a pillow, holding it in her lap. "I think I like him."

Travis cracked a smile at the corner of his mouth. "He seems nice, and I think he could provide for you."

Leah nodded. "He wants me to go to America. His uncle has offered him a job running his own ship, so his Navy training will pay off."

Travis sighed loudly. "Leah, it's up to you if you want to marry him. I would miss you terribly. However, there are other circumstances that you must consider."

She lifted her eyes blankly toward her brother. "What circumstances?"

Travis stood and walked to her dresser, sagging his shoulders with defeat. "I didn't want to worry you, but I have no choice." He turned to her taking in a deep breath. "Father's debts are substantial—more than we thought. The bookstore will not reopen as it doesn't make a profit. Mr. Wilcox purchased more of our debts, including our home. If you don't marry him, Jasper will be out on the street along with our mother. Miss Freemont will have no job, and our home will be sold. Aunt Margaret can take in Betty, but not all of us. Mr. Keels said I could rent a room over the shop. There is hardly enough room for just me, let alone a family."

Leah's chest felt like it was caving in. She'd allowed herself to be happy— to have hope after her conversation with Captain Jackson. But now, it was all crashing down on her. How could she marry Captain Jackson and leave her family destitute? Mr. Wilcox would not be kind to her family if she refused him.

Leah's pale face fell into the pillow. Travis came across the room and sat beside her on the bed. He tried to rub her back in comfort, but she pulled away and turned from him. "Please Travis, leave me alone."

Travis hesitated before turning to leave feeling as helpless as she was feeling.

CHAPTER 20

L EAH DRESSED EARLY IN THE morning after crying all night. She snuck out the back door to go walking through the woods. She needed to be alone, not wanting to see the anxious stares of her family awaiting her decision about Mr. Wilcox. He sent flowers the day before requesting her attendance at dinner tonight. She knew her time was up.

The cool breeze did not affect her as she was lost in thought, twisting through pathways, taking breaks to sit on the ground and praying for a miracle. She lost track of time, not knowing how long her walk had been when she finally headed back home.

When she reached the front of the cottage, she saw an unmarked carriage. She walked past it looking through the window before letting her presence be known. She noticed a sharp dressed man speaking to her brother inside by the front door. Curiosity overtook her, and she turned the doorknob to enter.

Travis's face lit up when he saw her. "There you are. We have looked everywhere for you."

Leah looked around the entryway at her family as the stranger nodded. Travis took her hand. "Leah, this is Mr. Dickerson—a solicitor. He knew Papa and came to tell us there was an investment that Papa made that has paid off handsomely."

He took both of her hands unable to hold in his excitement. "Leah, it was enough to pay off all the debts. Can you believe it? We are saved! Mama can stay at our home with Betty. There was even a letter Papa left to the solicitor in case it ever paid off. It said he wished to use part of the money for my University training, and another amount to buy a commission for Jasper. There was a small fortune in the account."

Leah was dazed, watching her family celebrate. Her insides twisted as she recognized Mr. Dickerson and knew where the money came from. There was no secret investment—she would be indebted to Joseph.

Her brother hugged her, taking the thoughts from her head as she embraced her family. Mr. Dickerson gathered his papers and walked to the door as Leah asked him for a private word outside. In her family's jubilance, they paid little attention that she left to walk him to his carriage. She took a few steps away from the house and turned to him. "I know who you are."

He tilted his head. "Pardon? I don't believe we are acquainted."

Leah crossed her arms. "You came to his house to drop off some papers. I remember passing you when I came for tea. You are *his* personal solicitor."

The solicitor stood with a blank face. After a few moments, he removed his spectacles and cleaned them as she waited for a reply. After replacing them on his face, he acknowledged her. "Let it be, Miss Johnson."

She breathed deeply holding her head high. There was her dignity to think about and she did not wish for his help. He had humiliated her, and she could not be bought. "I don't want his money."

He shrugged his shoulders. "He has plenty—a very rich man indeed. You can't give it back. It's done. He wants to remain anonymous. Will you oblige?"

Leah's mind wavered as she heard piano music from her home. She was trapped by her poverty, and her choices were taken away. She looked down, resigned to her fate. "I can hardly take it away from my family. Did you see their faces? He knew this, didn't he? That's why he had you talk to Travis instead of me."

He looked away not saying anything and cleared his throat. "Miss Johnson, in my line of work I meet many nobles. Most would not have cared. If you will excuse me."

Leah took a step out of his way, watching him board his carriage. Feeling guilty, she closed her eyes. "Mr. Dickerson?"

He looked over at her.

"Tell him, thank you."

Mr. Dickerson smiled and tipped his hat before riding away.

Leah entered the cottage to laughter. It was a sound she thought she would never hear again. She hugged her mother whose face showed peace and solitude. Joseph had given her family hope through his generous offering.

Her payment was a shattered heart.

Travis smiled, swinging his sister around, dancing with her. They were dancing to Jasper's singing and Betty's piano playing.

Their celebration ended abruptly as an angry Mr. Wilcox stood in the doorway. Miss Freemont had led him into the drawing room. Betsy stopped playing the piano as they all stared at him. He took off his hat. "Pardon my interruption, Johnson family. I have heard the news of your newfound fortune. I must extend congratulations and request a private audience with Miss Johnson." The family looked at each other as Travis led them out of the room. Leah stood by the piano.

Mr. Wilcox took a step forward, lifting his chin with determination in his demeanor. "Miss Johnson, I have come for your answer. I realize your father's debts were paid and Jasper is no longer in need of my services. But my offer still stands for your hand. I will provide you with a good life, and I will be a fair husband."

She felt exhausted at his persistence and her avoidance of his pursuits. She looked at his face for the first time as a woman not needing his protection. "What about love, Mr. Wilcox? Do you love me?"

Mr. Wilcox swallowed hard as he took his handkerchief to wipe his brow. "I am not sure I know what you mean. I would take care of you."

Leah suppressed a smile as she walked over and kissed him on the cheek. She touched his arm. "Your fondness is flattering, and your generosity helped my family in their hardest hour. I will always be grateful to you for that. I think there is a better match for you out in the world and I must decline your offer. I hope you can forgive me."

Mr. Wilcox stared at the ground. "I was afraid of that."

Leah walked to the door, straightening her shoulders. "If you will excuse me Mr. Wilcox, I must attend to my family."

Mr. Wilcox shoved the chair knocking it over. "Just like that? You dismiss me?"

Leah jumped back, a bit shocked by his outburst. "Sir, this is inappropriate. The debts have been paid. I wish you a good day."

Mr. Wilcox glared at her. "You led me to believe there would be a match. For weeks you made me chase you. You father gave his permission. I will not be trifled with, Miss Johnson."

Leah opened the door. "Sir, I am asking you politely to leave."

Mr. Wilcox narrowed his eyes and stomped off through the drawing room to the front door of the home, slamming it shut as he left.

Travis ran into the room. "What was that?"

Leah put up her hand. "Just Mr. Wilcox. He was a bit upset."

Travis nodded. "You can't blame him." He walked over and sat on the settee patting the seat beside him. Leah sat down beside him. "Are you going to accept Captain Jackson's proposal?"

Leah sighed. "He should be here later for my answer. After much thinking, I have decided to accept his proposal."

Travis stared at his sister trying to determine her thoughts. "You don't have to now. You can wait if you wish."

Leah wrung her hands, hoping her brother could understand her need to leave England. "I know, but I want to. My heart can't stay here. Travis, you guessed at my attachment that day with the duke, and I won't pretend with you. I can't see him with his new duchess—it would destroy me. I can't risk seeing him again, ever. Going to America is my chance for a new life."

Travis watched his sister struggle with her feelings. "Very well. I am happy for you, Sister."

Captain Jackson was announced a few moments later, and the siblings went to meet him. He arrived carrying a dozen roses. Leah was giddy with anticipation as she walked him into the drawing room for a private word. After closing the door, he bent on his knee holding a ring box. "Leah, please say you will marry me. Your brother has left the decision to you."

Leah's eyes filled with tears. "Yes, Clyde. I will marry you."

He stood up pulling her into his arms. He cupped her face, brushing a kiss against her lips. He whispered, "You have made me a very happy man."

Clyde slid the ring onto her finger as she smiled. They went to share their news with her family who were elated at their announcement. Hugs went all around the room. Clyde told Leah he would apply for a license the following day and their ship would leave in a week. He had to attend to some business before leaving but would be back the day before the ship left. His cousin would marry them in a small ceremony which was for the best because of their mourning period for her father. The family did not want to have a big event.

CHAPTER 21

JOSEPH AVOIDED HIS FIANCÉE AS much as he could by spending most of his time with John. His home was no longer a sanctuary, but full of women planning his wedding. The engagement ball was a bore, and he only danced once with his fiancée. She was biddable, never complained, and always had a smile on her face. She presented herself well, dressed in the height of fashion with impeccable manners.

Joseph couldn't stand her.

She was everything a duchess should be—picked out by his parents to be the perfect wife.

Caroline complained of his lack of commitment to his future wife. She spent countless hours with her future sister-in-law reassuring her about her nuptials. Her brother barely spoke to the poor girl, putting a strain on both families. The wedding was within a fortnight, and invitations were sent. The Earl of Rosenberg did not waste time—he booked the church over six months ago.

Joseph came home early and surprised his mother. She stared at him, bewildered by his presence. "Joseph? What a pleasure that you're home. Will you be dining with us?"

Joseph's clothes were disheveled, and he showed no emotion. His voice cracked and was filled with such pain and turmoil. "Mother, I must speak to you and Caroline in my study right away."

His mother found Caroline in the drawing room and asked her to accompany her to the study. Joseph had some news to share with them. Caroline followed her mother with lines of worry across her face. They entered the study to find Joseph at his desk with a glass and a bottle of brandy beside it.

Caroline took a seat trying to understand her brother's intentions. "Joseph, you look awful. Have you washed today?"

Joseph was annoyed by Caroline's voice. He snapped back at her. "I didn't come home last night. I was at the club and spent most of the night riding through town, ending up at John's."

The duchess wrinkled her nose in disgust. "Are you foxed?"

Joseph shook his head in irritation at their questions. "Not anymore, I slept it off. I have made a decision about my life that I wanted to share with you."

Caroline tilted her head in question. "What kind of decision?"

Joseph raked his fingers through his hair looking down at his desk. "I have thought about my life all night. Asking myself if I would always be this miserable? A duke has privileges, prestige, fortune, but without happiness it means nothing."

His mother interrupted him. "Joseph? Please. I—"

Joseph lifted his hand. "Stop! Please let me finish for once." He poured some brandy, took a drink, and wiped his mouth with his sleeve. "What kind of life am I living? I don't care about being a duke."

Caroline's eyes filled with tears watching her brother's painful speech.

Joseph threw the glass and it shattered against the wall. The duchess jumped. "Joseph!"

He stood up looking at both his sister and mother. "I will *not* marry her!"

Caroline's eyes widened as his mother shook her head. Joseph walked to the door as his mother yelled after him. "You can't do this. You made a promise and signed a contract that you would marry her. Everyone has been invited, and if you do not go through with the wedding, you will disgrace our family."

Joseph stopped in the doorway. "I choose to be happy. I want to marry Leah. I don't care about propriety or the dukedom. *She* is all that matters to me."

The duchess shifted in her seat, grabbing her chest. Caroline ran to her brother's side trying to beg him to reconsider. "Joseph, think about what you're saying. I liked Leah—she was a precious girl—but she is not duchess material. Many people depend on our generosity and employment. What about them? Even Leah understood the duty that you have. You don't have to love your wife, but you need a partner by your side that understands the responsibilities of nobility. Think about that! Roslyn can help you provide a living to our entire village."

Joseph stared at his sister holding back his anger. "It's my life. I will do what I please for once."

His mother sobbed loudly. "He will ruin us." Caroline's tears ran down her face as she comforted her mother and Joseph left the room.

Joseph mounted his horse, feeling free for the first time in weeks. His mind was made up—he would find Leah and tell her that he loved her and would marry her immediately. They could go to Gretna Green in the morning to elope, maybe even tonight. He kicked his horse into a canter to get to her house quickly. His body felt more at ease as he thought about her smile, the way she smelled, not to mention how her kisses tasted.

He stopped by his solicitor's office close in town to get some money and to straighten his clothes to be more presentable. The solicitor would help him get out of the marriage contract with Roslyn.

Leaving the solicitor's office, he noticed that the jewelry store was still open. He purchased a ring and bought some flowers from a lady on the sidewalk. He felt ready to see his true love.

The ride to Leah's took longer than he thought as he repeated the words in his head again. She would be his wife very soon. He knocked on the cottage door hoping she was home. After a few minutes, her sister answered. He smiled at her. "Hello, Is Miss Leah Johnson at home?"

She smiled as Travis walked up behind her moving his sister to the side. He nodded. "Your Grace. How can we assist you?"

Joseph sighed, noticing Travis's protective stance. "Forgive me. I do respect your wishes to stay away from your sister, but I have some urgent news that concerns her and is very important. I must ask your permission to speak to her at once. I promise I won't take long."

Travis looked to his little sister before answering. "Unfortunately, Leah has gone away."

Joseph flexed his jaw confused by his answer. "Away? Where?"

"Forgive me, I do not wish to upset you as I understand you have an attachment to my sister. But there is no easy way to say this–Leah went to America with her husband."

The color drained from Joseph's face as his heart pounding blared in his ears. He tried to catch his sudden loss of breath. "She is married? To who?"

Travis put his hand on Betty's shoulder as he answered Joseph. "To Captain Jackson. I believe she spent some time with him at a house party.

He returned to London a few weeks ago and asked her to marry him. He took a job in America and took her with him. That was about a week ago, and she has no plans to return to England. She said there were only bad memories here."

Joseph closed his eyes as he stood still on the porch. He struggled with his emotions and tried to compose himself. "If you will excuse me." He moved his feet one in front of the other in a daze until he reached his horse. Riding away, he didn't realize the conversation happening at that moment between the siblings.

Betty looked up to Travis. "Why did you tell him she married? They were not able to get a license and would not marry until they reached America."

Travis shrugged his shoulders. "What difference does it make. They would have been married if the license came through. They will marry within a few weeks when they reach America."

Travis pulled his sister inside to close the door thus closing the door on an alternate future for his sister Leah—the one she truly wanted.

Joseph rode his horse not remembering the journey home. He was at his front door not knowing how he got there. He opened the door stumbling into his foyer, untying his cravat. The butler rushed to assist him, but he waved him off. "I am fine."

Joseph found his study and grabbed the bottle of brandy, not bothering with a glass. While he was drinking his sorrows, the butler notified Lady Caroline of His Grace's arrival and she rushed to meet him. She was afraid to say anything, noticing the distant look in his eyes. He took the bottle and drank as much as he could. "Where's my pistol? It's not in the drawer." He opened all the drawers in his desk, throwing paperwork onto the floor in his search.

Caroline went to close the study door and whispered to the butler to send a footman to retrieve the Earl of Shepley, as John was the only one who could calm Joseph. She turned back around and began picking up the papers before she looked up at her brother. "I don't know where your pistol is and I am sure that you don't need it."

Joseph fell back into his chair. "Don't tell me what I need, Caroline!"

Caroline took a seat on the settee. "What happened?"

Joseph took a drink from the bottle. "I didn't love her enough. That is what she said." He took another drink, slurring his words he whispered, "I would die for her, but I was too late."

Caroline shook her head. "Too late?"

Joseph snorted. "She's married. Leah left for America with her new husband a week ago. She told her family that England held too many bad memories." He took a drink before swiping at his mouth. "Bad memories of me." He kicked his desk. "I have lost her!"

Caroline jumped and yelled at him, "Stop it! You have everything you need. You told me when my husband died that my heart would heal. I would never forget him, but my family would help me. You helped me out of that darkness, and I will help you. You will miss her, but your heart will heal. Most people in our station never know love, and you have. That's a gift, Joseph. I know it hurts, but it will get better. I promise."

Joseph stayed quiet, staring into the fire. His breathing quieted, his shoulders sagged as his eyelids felt heavy. His sister sat near him offering her quiet comfort. He knew she loved him, yet they never spoke of such feelings. He loved her too. When her husband died, he made sure she was not alone. He made excuses to invite her many places with him, hoping to keep her mind on other distractions. He knew she was going to help him get through this pain too.

Caroline answered the knock on the door and whispered to John for a few minutes before she left them alone to talk.

John let out a deep breath. "You look awful. Let's get you cleaned up and go get some dinner."

Joseph scowled at his friend. "I don't want dinner. Just leave me alone!"

John shook his head. "Tsk, tsk. You're stuck with me tonight. So, we can both sit here and look at each other for hours, or we can go get some dinner and entertainment."

He placed his hands on his head covering his eyes. "She's married. I can't think about anything else at the moment."

John took a seat facing his best friend. "I heard. It's not what you wanted, I understand. Destroying yourself will not make her unmarried. You have to let it go, my friend."

Joseph crossed his arms. "I was so close to happiness. It's not just her beauty. She was like a breath of fresh air, unspoiled innocence that I have never seen on another female. It rips me apart that another man is touching her."

John creased his brow trying to console him. "I do understand that you loved her. She will always be a part of your past—that kind of love does not ever go away. However, you will move on day by day, and the pain will subside."

Joseph cracked a smile. "John, I didn't know you were so philosophical."

John laughed. "I do have my moments, Your Grace. Now let's call your valet and get you cleaned up. I have a feeling it's going to be a late night."

CHAPTER 22

THE NEXT MORNING JOSEPH SLEPT through breaking his fast, meeting his family for lunch. Caroline seemed surprised to see him at all. He was dressed and enjoying some coffee.

The duchess sipped her tea, taking a bite of a crumpet. Caroline nibbled on an apple, waiting for someone to speak. Finally, she broke the silence. "What are your plans for today."

Joseph looked up from his coffee. "I plan to visit a few friends."

Caroline held in a breath. "I think you should speak to Lady Roslyn about your change of plans. The wedding is less than a week away, and we must notify guests."

Joseph wiped his mouth with his napkin, placing it slowly on the table. He looked at his mother. "As you know, Miss Johnson has married." Joseph paused looking down at his plate. "My plans to marry her are no longer an option." Joseph stood up shrugging his shoulders in defeat. "The marriage to Roslyn may move forward. I will honor the contract, but I make no promises or illusions that I will have feelings of love for my future wife and will not be pressured into it."

His mother nodded. "I understand. Your father would be proud that you are keeping your word."

Joseph glared at his mother's comment. He walked away from the table and left the room.

The next few days flew by as Joseph attended the mandatory wedding events but still managed to keep his distance from his fiancée. The wedding day finally came without too much commotion. Joseph hoped that it was all a dream, but waking up with his valet standing over him with his wedding suit in hand reminded Joseph that it was real. He dressed reluctantly, meeting John in the drawing room. The staff was running around preparing for the new duchess. The wedding breakfast would be at the earl's residence. They would come back to his townhouse afterward. He made no plans for a wedding trip. She could visit the country estates at her leisure. He would remain in town near his friends.

John stood next to Joseph as his best man. Half the *ton* was in attendance for the wedding of the year. Roslyn was dressed in head-to-toe lace, and it was a known fact in the top society of London that her dress came from the most prestigious dress shop. Her father walked her down the aisle, passing many well-wishers.

The vows were simple and standard. Joseph calmed his breath as his mind raced ahead thinking of his life without Leah. He stood beside a stranger, who he was promising he would vow to protect. She would have his children, carry his name, and be his duchess. Joseph was still woolgathering when the vicar pronounced them man and wife. He snapped back into reality facing his new bride and forced himself to bend down for a quick kiss on her lips—their first kiss witnessed in front of hundreds of guests.

Lady Roslyn, now Her Grace, smiled at her new husband in the receiving line. Joseph made no comments to her, only thanking each guest as they offered their felicitations. Dread came over Joseph as he snuck a peek at his bride, his heart tugged at what should have been Leah beside him. He had to clear his mind. Roslyn was a nice person, and it was not her fault that his heart was given to another. Friendship is what he would work toward. Hopefully he could do his duty and they would have an heir soon, so they could have less pressure with their union. He would be fair to her and generous with pin money as she liked to shop. Perhaps an occasional night out on the town would not be impossible. His heart was hardened, but he would try to provide a good life—even if it was without love.

CHAPTER 23

LEAH'S SEASICKNESS WAS FINALLY BECOMING tolerable. The last several days she had spent most of her time in the cabin that she shared with Lydia, Clyde's sister. The marriage license was unable to be secured, so Clyde reluctantly slept alone. They had plans to marry within a week of arriving in America—sooner if Clyde could arrange it. Leah felt horrible she could not spend more time with her fiancé. But the motion of the boat made her vomit if she stood up for very long.

After several days her body adjusted to the movement of the ocean, and she looked forward to leaving the compactness of her room. Her first outing was to meet Clyde and Lydia to break her fast. Dry toast is all she would eat, trying not to upset her stomach. Clyde's smile was contagious as he welcomed his fiancée to the table. "Your paleness has subsided. I am hoping to spend some time with you this afternoon. I promised the captain a conference this morning, but will look for you at the luncheon." He leaned over and kissed her on the cheek.

Lydia spoke up. "I will keep her busy." She was a young girl of eight and one and welcomed her new roommate, chatting unceasingly about the other passengers. Seeming excited to have a new sister-in-law, she held onto Leah and was anxious to introduce her to some new friends that she had met playing cards. Clyde excused himself and Lydia dragged Leah to a different table.

Her new friends were Susan and Rose, and they taught at an all-girls school in New York. They were traveling home to America from England. Leah enjoyed her visit with them and spent the next few days enjoying their company. Clyde spent most of his time with the captain of the ship, as he knew him from his days in the Royal Navy.

Leah met him for dinner most nights as they fell into a routine. After dinner, he would sneak her off for walks around the ship. He pointed out various areas, trying to impress her with his shipboard knowledge. His favorite part of his tours was finding a secluded area to steal kisses and other liberties. Leah liked Clyde—he made her feel special—but she did not feel the passion between them when she compared his kisses to Joseph's. She hoped she would with time as she could feel his tension mounting with her indifference.

One afternoon, the captain announced they should reach America within a week with favorable winds. Clyde invited Leah to dine with the captain, leaving his sister to eat with their friends. Leah dressed up in her lavender gown, donning her pearls. She smoothed the pearls thinking of Joseph.

The dinner was delicious, and she enjoyed hearing the war stories from the men. The captain smiled at the couple as he took bites of his meal. After the last course, he called for everyone's attention as he raised his glass of champagne toward her and Clyde. "Captain Jackson and Miss Johnson, may I congratulate you on your engagement. I never thought this old dog would leg shackle himself. You must be quite the lady."

One of the sailors snickered. "I will drink to that. He is a lucky man. Miss Johnson would make many men come up to scratch."

Leah blushed as a few of the guests chuckled at the comments.

Captain Jackson scooted his chair a little closer to hers. "Miss Johnson has made me very happy. We thank you, Captain, for allowing us to dine with you on this special evening and for the congratulations."

Leah and Clyde enjoyed the dessert then excused themselves for their customary after-dinner walk.

Clyde took her arm and put it in the crook of his elbow, he escorted her down a corridor, stopping in front of his cabin. He smiled. "Leah, I have something for you inside. Can you step in for a minute?"

She hesitated, looking around for other passengers. "What if someone sees?"

Clyde touched her face. "Leah, everyone knows we are engaged. We should have been married by now. Trust me, no one will say anything. Besides, we are alone."

Leah looked down as he pulled her inside and closed the door. She looked around the small room noticing the bed was too close for comfort. He asked her to sit down in the chair and removed his coat as he took a seat on the bed. He pulled a paper out of a drawer. "Here, this is what I wanted to show you."

Leah accepted the paper displaying a dozen roses drawn on top of it.

He studied her face, proud of his gesture. "There is nowhere to buy you flowers on the ship, so I made them for you."

Leah smiled. "You are so sweet, thank you."

He grinned with satisfaction. "Do you really want to thank me?" A gaze came over his eyes as they fell upon her breasts.

Her heart pounded in her chest because she knew exactly what he meant but chose to ignore the desire in his eyes. Pretending not to understand, she innocently looked at him. "Of course, I want to thank you." She stood up from the chair and leaned down to kiss him on the cheek. "Thank you."

She turned to walk away back to the chair, but he grabbed her waist pulling her on top of his lap. She tried to resist but gave into his kisses as he moved his mouth across her jaw to her neck. He rubbed her arms then moved his hands to the back of her dress and started loosening the laces.

He broke away trying to catch his breath. "Leah, I want you to stay with me tonight."

Surprised by his suggestion and reluctant to oblige, she shook her head. "I can't. We're not married yet. I want to wait."

He let out a breath of frustration. "What difference does it make? We are practically married already. I don't want to use you—I want to make love to you."

Leah's heart twisted. At that moment, she saw Joseph's face and she closed her eyes trying to erase the image in her mind. She opened them and stared at Clyde trying to think of an excuse. "We will have plenty of time to make love after we are married. It will be more special once our union is blessed by God."

He let out a sigh and squeezed her tight giving into her resistance. "You will be the death of me, my dear. Let's get you back to your cabin."

Leah agreed, and they snuck out unobserved. Her mind was racing at the predicament that she found herself in again: being courted by a man that she didn't want to marry. First it was Mr. Wilcox and now it's Clyde. This time she had agreed to the engagement. She twisted the ring on her finger unable to concentrate. Could she one day feel love for Clyde? Was it fair to him if she didn't love him?

Lydia had just returned to the room and asked if Leah wanted to play cards with their new friends. Since she didn't feel like resting, she agreed and accompanied her to their cabin—it was close quarters, but they had fun playing card games. Lydia only played one game, leaving the girls for a sailor she had promised a walk with. Leah wondered what her brother would say, but agreed to keep her secret.

Susan and Rose were quickly becoming great friends. Leah told them about her working in the bookstore for years and hoped that she could be more than a housewife when she reached America. They encouraged her to speak to Clyde. Leah shook her head. "I don't know if he would agree. He is anxious for me to start having babies."

Susan touched her arm sympathetically. "What's amiss? You seem sad about having a family."

Leah hesitated but needed to talk to someone. "I know I should not say anything, but please keep this in confidence."

Both women nodded.

"I don't know if I can marry Clyde."

Leah tried to avoid Clyde the next few days. She had a secret and was waiting for the right moment to share it with him. Her new friends convinced her to be their new library assistant at the school where they taught in New York. They were impressed with her knowledge of books and working in the bookstore would be a great background to work in the library. Their former library assistant was married last year and no longer worked at the school. Susan's cousin ran the girls school and was positive she could provide a job for Leah. It would not pay much, but room and board were included. That was all Leah needed to survive. She could sell the diamond necklace that Joseph gave her and live off the extra income for years if she was frugal. The pearls she would keep, but the diamonds could be her livelihood.

The captain announced they would be entering America the next day. Leah's heart knew she had to tell Clyde the truth. Marriage was no longer an option. She did not love him—she saw him as only a good friend.

That night she asked him to join her on the deck for a walk. He seemed surprised at her request as she had avoided their after-dinner walks since the night in his cabin. He smiled as he took her arm. They walked in silence for several minutes before finding a private alcove. He pulled Leah into his arms, pressing a kiss on her lips.

Leah stiffened, pulling away. "Wait, I think we need to talk."

Clyde slanted his head, "What's amiss?" He rubbed his finger over her lips. "I know you have been avoiding me. I thought you might be a little cross with me for wanting to consummate our relationship before the wedding."

Leah shook her head. "No, it's not that."

He tilted his head. "What is it? Are you a bit melancholy with the close quarters? We should be on dry land by tomorrow afternoon. All will be well." He tried again to brush his lips against hers.

Leah put her hands on his chest, pushing him slightly away. She stared into his eyes with guilt burning in her chest as she took a minute to compose herself. "Clyde, we have spent the last few weeks getting to know each other. In that time, I have grown fond of you and appreciate you taking me to America."

He smiled as he took her hands in his.

Leah pulled them away from his grip and looked up at him. She took a step back so she could concentrate. "I thought I could marry you and make you happy. You have become such a close friend—almost like a brother to me."

His eyes widened in realization at her comment.

She looked up at him watching his muddled expression. It was tearing her heart out to hurt him. Taking in a deep breath, she touched his arm. "It's hard for me to tell you that I don't... um... feel for you like a wife should feel about her husband."

He narrowed his eyes. "I don't understand?"

Leah wrung her hands. "I don't think it's fair for me to marry you when there may be someone else out there in America that could love you like a wife should love her husband." Leah looked down at her hand and removed the ring from her finger and placed it in his hands.

Clyde's eyebrows furrowed as his face grew red with anger. "Are you crying off? You are going back to England?"

Leah struggled with her words. "No, I won't go back to England. This was a very hard decision for me to make. But I am going to work at the all-girls school with Susan. She said I could live there at the school with her and Rose." Leah's voice cracked as she finally made eye contact with him, watching the hurt go across his face.

She reached for his hand. "Clyde, I want us to be friends. Please understand that I am not ready for marriage. I thought I was, but I would not be a good wife to you."

Clyde's breathing deepened as he stared at her. He shoved her hand away and shook his head. "I can't believe you. I was falling in love with you. Does that mean nothing?"

The lines in Leah's face narrowed with concern. "I don't think you could love me, Clyde. Not truly." She stepped near him, but he stepped away from her.

He walked past her a few steps. "Don't tell me how I feel." Clyde stomped off leaving her alone in the alcove. She waited a few minutes and returned to her cabin unescorted. Lydia was not in the room and did not return that night.

The next morning Lydia showed up early to attend to her bags. She made no conversation, only nodding if Leah asked her a question. Leah knew she must have spoken to her brother, so she left the cabin, allowing her to finish, and joined Susan for their departure. A sailor came to help Leah with her bags. She saw Clyde on the deck and approached him with Susan in tow. Lydia was next to him and refused to look at her. She whispered, "Captain Jackson, may I have a private word?"

He scowled at her but nodded. They walked a few steps away from the group. Leah bit her bottom lip as she looked up into his face. "I want to tell you that I am so thankful for the time we spent together. You are a wonderful person, and any girl would be lucky to call you her husband. I hope in time you can forgive me, and we can be friends."

He tightened his face looking away from her. "I hope you find what you're looking for, Miss Johnson. I can't be your friend, but wish you happiness." He made eye contact briefly and shockingly bent over and kissed her on the cheek. "Goodbye, Leah." He walked away taking Lydia by the arm and didn't look back.

Leah stood there as a tear dropped on her cheek. Susan patted her on the shoulder. "Are you, all right?"

Leah nodded. "I think I will be. I hope I made the right decision."

CHAPTER 24

5 years later – New York

"LEAH!" SUSAN SCREAMED WAKING ANYONE who was still asleep. She reached Leah's room with a teasing tone. "You have a visitor in the parlor."

She yawned stretching across her bed. "Visitor? Why so early?"

Susan shrugged innocently with a smirk. "*He* says he has a surprise for you."

Leah threw off the covers and got dressed quickly. "Tell *him* I will be down in a few minutes."

She dressed in a hurry and ran to the parlor to meet Bernard. He was tall with brown hair and matching brown eyes. Always dressed in New York's best fashion, he held a dozen red roses for her when she entered the room. He loved to spoil her and never showed up empty-handed. Their courtship was fast, making her head spin with all his attention and flattery. It had been years since she accepted the attention of a male suitor, often hiding away in the library not wanting to socialize. Five years was a long time to be away from home. Letters from England were infrequent after years of being away. Her new life in America consisted mostly of her students and a few friends. But now it was consumed with Bernard. She smiled, accepting the roses and putting them in a vase.

"Thank you, but you don't have to buy me flowers every time you visit me. Just you are enough."

He smiled, stepping closer to her. "I would buy you anything you wanted, love." He winked as he kissed her on the cheek. "I thought about you all morning and wanted to take you for a day of fun."

Leah cherished his fun days. "What kind of fun?" She waited impatiently for his answer.

He laughed at her impatience. "I will surprise you."

Leah took her cloak as he escorted her out the door into a waiting carriage. His new carriage was covered in deep rose cushions and matching curtains. Bernard sat beside her, taking her hand and kissing it. "Let us eat some food in the park and then go to the museum."

She would go anywhere just to be with him. "Yes, I would like that."

He smiled as they arrived at the park and went to feed the ducks. He bought them some food from a vendor, and they made a picnic on the bench.

She looked over at him remembering the day she first met him. It was an assembly dance a few months ago. Susan had made her go that night despite Leah's protest. She had lost a game of chess, and the wager was her attendance at the assembly.

Bernard insisted that she dance with him after she declined him several times. After his persistence won her over, he continued with his affections, showering her with gifts. Their friends were surprised at their quick courtship. At four and twenty, she was practically on the shelf, but always claimed she was not ready for marriage. When she met Bernard, her life changed. He was so full of life and very outgoing. Leah was shy and kept to herself. He tried for weeks to get her to go out with him until she finally relented and went to the theatre. His laughter was contagious, and she fell for him after a few weeks of courting.

He was new money, as they said in America. His family came originally from France, but he was born in America. His father made a fortune in the shipyards, leaving a sizable inheritance for Bernard. He dabbled in many business ventures adding to his fortune. He was always looking for the next amusement.

Bernard stopped Leah's woolgathering. "Are you set to go the museum, love?" She nodded, and he took her hand escorting her on their walk. They spent the afternoon laughing with each other and reading history. He loved history, especially talking to everyone about it. He became the designated tour guide as other patrons listened to his animated voice at each display. Leah felt lucky to be with him as people were drawn to his personality, often commenting on what a nice young man he was.

He took her to his home to dress for dinner and provided one of his maids to assist her. Leah felt pampered by his attention to her comfort. He planned a nice dinner party at his home that evening. Leah's wardrobe grew at Bernard's generosity. He sent a dressmaker to her home last week to dress her with ten new gowns. He wanted her to accompany him on many of his outings with business associates and friends.

The following weekend Bernard decided to take Leah for a weekend trip to the coast. She was hesitant, but some of his friends joined them, and Bernard rented a house on the beach. Leah's excitement grew as she loved the salt air and looked forward to spending time with him.

He picked her up early and they followed his friends' carriages on the trip that took several hours. Bernard was entertaining in the carriage. They stopped once to eat at an inn but arrived at night at the beach. Leah could smell the ocean and was excited to spend time watching the waves come in. Bernard offered to take her for a walk before retiring for the night.

Leah walked with him along the shore. "Oh Bernard, I love it here."

He smiled at her enthusiasm. "We must come more often, love. Perhaps I will buy a home here."

Leah took a deep breath looking over the water. "How lucky you would be to live next to the ocean."

Bernard rubbed her arm. "I would live in a shack as long as I was with you." He leaned down and kissed her. "We better get to bed, we have a long day tomorrow."

The next day they rested in the sand. Leah longed to swim in the ocean. She wished she could swim anywhere, as it was a desire she had since she was a child. They built sand castles and had a picnic watching the waves come ashore. Bernard took her on many walks that day holding her hand and making her laugh. They joined a local assembly later that night, dancing until dawn. Leah had never had such a momentous time.

Some local friends of Bernard's invited them for a dining party the following evening. He was acting very secretive, whispering to his friends and watching them smile at her. After a scrumptious, eight-course meal was served, Bernard asked for everyone's attention.

"Friends, may I thank you all for attending this evening." The group became quiet and looked up to Bernard.

Bernard turned to Leah and took her hand. "Leah, my love. These past few weeks have been the best in my life. I want to share so much more with you. I feel we can conquer the world together. Please say you will be my wife."

Leah's eyes widened with shock. He didn't say he loved her, but conquering the world and being his wife was enough for now. She knew she was falling in love with him, but they never spoke of love. Looking around the room, she noticed several pairs of eyes anticipating her answer and she felt the weight of the world on her shoulders. She had to say something. "Yes, Bernard. Yes!"

He smiled, hugging her in front of the table. He pulled back slipping a ring out of his pocket onto her finger. Leah's eyes widened at the size of the large diamond. Bernard bent down and kissed her on the cheek. The group clapped, congratulating them.

They played the piano and danced in the foyer of Bernard's friend's home. Leah laughed and enjoyed her time with everyone. She was sad they had to leave the next day. The ride home was long, and she slept most of the way leaning against Bernard as he held her. He woke her up when they arrived near the school.

Bernard whispered, "Sweetness, wake up. You are home—for now. Soon we will share a home together."

She smiled as she opened her eyes. "I can't wait."

He laughed as he walked her to the door. They stood outside, and as he bent to kiss her, the door opened.

Susan's jaw dropped. "Forgive me. I didn't know it was you. I was going out to check the gate before bed."

Leah smiled. "We were just saying good night."

Susan nodded. "Carry on. Don't mind me." As she started to walk away, she put her hands in her pocket. "Oh! I almost forgot! This letter came for you a few hours ago."

Leah accepted it, frowning as she read the return address.

Bernard raised his brows questioningly at her expression. "What's amiss?"

Leah felt uneasy. "It's from my brother. It's been a few years since I heard from him."

Bernard touched her arm. "Well what are you waiting for? Open it."

Leah nodded and walked inside to light a candle. Leah sat by the candle as Bernard stood beside her. After reading it, she gasped aloud covering her mouth with her hand. "It's my mother. She is very ill and is requesting to see me. They want me to come home at once."

Bernard sat beside her as she read the letter again. He rubbed her arm. "Leah, how long has it been since you have seen your family?"

Leah rubbed her lips together. "It's been a long time. A little over five years. I do miss them."

Bernard took in a deep breath. "Then it's settled. I will escort you to England. I will make arrangements and we will leave as soon as possible."

Leah looked at him bewildered. "I can't go unchaperoned."

Bernard shrugged. "We will bring a maid, and I will pay for them to travel with us. Don't worry, my love. I will take care of everything."

Bernard secured tickets to leave a few days later. Susan agreed to accompany the couple. She had family in England and wanted to visit them. Leah did some shopping and a lot of packing, hoping to get to England to see her mother, praying nothing would happen to her. England felt like another life and darkness clouded her memories. Her father was gone and soon her mother could be too. Travis's letter said her condition was grave. Going back to England weighed on her mind as she had held on to so many resentments and bad memories for years. So much had changed since she left all those years ago. Her letters home were less and less. The family had moved on without her. Travis was married and had graduated college. Jasper was doing well in the military and Betty was all grown up.

She shivered thinking about her closest friend Melissa. Mel had written her a scornful letter shortly after arriving in America. She heard about her breaking the engagement to Captain Jackson on their way to America and was furious at her lack of decency. She told Leah that she felt responsible for encouraging their relationship and hurting Clyde. Leah wrote her back and tried to explain to her about her reasons for not loving Clyde, but never heard back again. Her mother wrote her a few years later that Captain Jackson had returned to England and married Melissa's cousin. They were happy, and Leah was happy for them.

CHAPTER 25

BERNARD KEPT HER BUSY ON the ship on the way to England. His larger than life persona attracted many new friends. Their days were filled with sleeping late while evenings consisted of games, cards, and dancing. The time flew by until they reached England, getting there a few days earlier than expected. Leah's heartstrings pulled at the anticipation of seeing her family. There had been so many changes since she left. She was excited to meet Travis's wife. Her brother Jasper was promoted in the military, and she hoped he could come home for a visit. Her sister Betty was now a grown woman. Leah would stay at the cottage with her family, and Bernard rented a room at a hotel in London.

Their rented carriage took Leah the familiar way home. She sent a letter confirming her trip, hoping that it had been received before their arrival.

Leah's knock at the front door was received by a woman that she had to look at twice to recognize.

"Leah? Leah! Welcome home!" Betty squealed with excitement, tackling Leah with a hug as Bernard stood behind her smiling. He looked at Leah. "I think she recognizes you."

Leah giggled. "Let me look at you, Sister. You have grown into a beautiful woman." Betty blushed with tears in her eyes.

A man stood beside Betty. "You must be the famous sister that lives in America. I am so happy to meet you, Miss Johnson."

Leah smiled at the man looking back at Betty for an introduction.

She smiled. "Leah, please meet Mr. Soothers, my fiancé. Tom, please meet my sister."

Leah grinned. "So nice to meet you, Mr. Soothers. Please meet my fiancé, Mr. Williams."

Betty's eyes expanded. "We are both engaged at the same time!" The foursome laughed as Mr. Soothers offered to help Leah with her bags. Bernard walked with him to the carriage leaving the sisters alone.

Leah's smile faded. "How is Mother?"

Betty shook her head. "Not good, Leah. She doesn't leave the bed anymore. They say it's her heart."

Leah placed her arm around her sister. "I will see her now."

Betty escorted Leah to the room and stood outside so Leah could have some privacy with their mother.

Leah cracked the door and eyed the frail woman asleep on the bed. The last years had aged her mother to the point that Leah found her almost unrecognizable. Tears welled up in Leah's eyes as she took steps closer to the bed. Her mother's hair was gray, and her skin was the color of ash. Leah sat on a chair beside the bed watching her mother sleep. Her mother shifted slowly, lifting her eyes. The corner of her mouth moved up into a smile. "Leah?"

Leah smiled trying to put on a brave face. "Yes, Mama. It's me." She moved to sit on the bed beside her mother and took her hand. "It's been too long. I missed you terribly."

Tears ran down from her mother's eyes. "Oh, Leah. Thank God, you're here. God has answered my prayers."

Leah rubbed her mother's hand. "I am here Mama, and I brought a surprise."

Leah's mom started coughing. She held her mother up while rubbing her back. Memories of her father filled her mind. The room was dark and stuffy. Needing air, she walked to the window and lifted it a little for some fresh air. She took a pitcher of water and poured her mother a fresh drink. She helped her drink it before placing the glass on the table beside the bed.

She reached for her mother's hand again. "I am engaged, Mama. Can you believe it? My fiancé is downstairs. He came with me, and I can't wait for you to meet him."

Leah's mother smiled. "My baby girl. I am so happy for you. I was worried about you when I received the letter that you canceled your engagement with Captain Jackson."

Leah shook her head. "It was for the best, Mama. I didn't love him. I do love Bernard, although I haven't told him yet. He is a good man and provider."

Mrs. Johnson nodded her head. "If he makes you happy, then I will love him too." Leah took a brush from the nightstand and brushed her mother's hair. She told her about her job in New York and all about the friends she had made. Leah left her mother to rest, promising her she would introduce her to her fiancé later.

Leah returned downstairs to find Mr. Soothers and Bernard talking about local business ventures. Bernard rose upon seeing Leah and kissed her on the cheek. "How is your mother?"

Leah shook her head. "Not good. I will take you up later to meet her. She is resting now."

Bernard nodded, not sure what to say. "Of course. I will travel to the inn. Mr. Soothers has offered to accompany me, and I will be back a little later to take all of you out to dinner."

Betty smiled at his generous gesture. "That sounds like fun. We will be ready."

Leah and Betty dressed together. She let her little sister borrow one of her gowns. Betty was in awe of Leah's wardrobe. She explained to Betty that they were gifts from Bernard—that she only recently could wear such luxury.

Bernard escorted them into London. The four had a big dinner at a famous London hotel. Mr. Soothers suggested that they continue their night out and they ended at a local dance assembly. The four danced most of the night as Bernard made some new friends. Leah was in awe of his ability to attract people everywhere they went. She was shy and did not converse easily with complete strangers. Perhaps that is why they were attracted to each other.

Over the next few days, Leah chose not to go out but spent time with her mother. Travis and Jasper were due home by the end of the week, and Leah could hardly wait to see her brothers. Bernard stopped by each day for a few hours but left before night. His meeting with Leah's mother was brief. He was charming, but not too engaging. Leah had hoped that he might stay home one night with her, but his new friends, including Mr. Soothers, kept him busy. Bernard was always attentive toward her—claiming his devotion, smothering her in kisses. To Leah's disappointment, he never uttered the word love but was openly affectionate with her. His hands were always full of presents when he arrived for his brief visits. She missed him, but to her resolve, she was invited to go with them but did not want to leave her mother.

Travis and Jasper finally arrived on Saturday. Leah could not hold in her excitement to see her brothers and practically tackled Travis in the doorway. He grabbed her hand, holding it up to turn her around in a circle. "Sister, let me look at you."

Leah stepped back keeping a hold of his hand. "I missed you so much, Travis."

He laughed. "Me too. I'm so glad you are home."

Travis brought his wife, Julia, a lovely young woman with red hair and green eyes. She smiled. "I am so happy to meet you, Miss Johnson."

Leah waved her hand. "Oh, please call me Leah. We are sisters now after all."

The young woman smiled as she embraced Leah.

Behind the couple, Leah saw a large man walking up the pathway. She gasped, barely recognizing her little brother. Jasper's stature had practically grown twice the size from how she remembered him to be. She took a few steps near him as he picked her up in a big hug.

He squeezed her tightly. "My big sister is finally home."

Leah laughed. "You're huge! I would hate to come across you in a dark corner. How is the military?"

Jasper rubbed his stomach. "Treating me well, but I miss your cooking."

Leah laughed. "You shall have it, my brother."

Leah was disappointed that Bernard was not there to greet them. Betty was with Mr. Soothers at the park when they arrived, but came home shortly afterward. A few hours went by, and Leah spoke to Mrs. Freemont about supper plans when Bernard finally arrived with a big smile on his face. He introduced himself to Leah's brothers, offering to take the whole family to a nice dinner in London. Leah was upset at him but chose to ignore the nagging feeling in her gut. She put on her rose gown with a scoop neckline. Bernard's eyes widened when he saw her. "You look beautiful."

Leah shrugged. "I am surprised you even noticed." Lifting her chin nonchalantly, she feigned indifference.

Bernard's brows creased as he held out his arm to escort her outside.

They boarded into different carriages, leaving Leah and Bernard in their own. Bernard sat beside her trying to snuggle close to her, but she leaned away from him. "Bernard, I am cross with you."

Bernard made an exaggerated sad face. "Why are you cross?"

Leah squinted her eyes in annoyance. "You have not spent any time with me. You go out every day with your new friends, leaving me alone. You were not even here today to meet my brothers when they arrived."

Bernard cracked a smile. "Leah, I was only trying to give you some time alone with your family. Forgive me, my love. I want to spend all my time with you. Now please give me a kiss."

Leah smirked, pulling away from him. Bernard reached over tickling her until she was wrapped up in his arms. "Kiss me!" he said with a laugh.

She leaned over and kissed him on the cheek. He pulled her face closer to his lips and kissed her on the mouth. He deepened his kiss as he opened his mouth to taste her. She closed her eyes, enjoying his closeness and she looked forward to when they were finally married. He let go, taking a deep breath. "Now, enough of that. I am looking forward to a nice dinner with your family." Leah nodded as the carriage pulled up to the restaurant. The family enjoyed the dinner and their time together, thanking Bernard for his generosity.

CHAPTER 26

His Grace, the 10ᵗʰ Duke of Wollaston, finally arrived at his townhouse in London. His two-week reprieve at one of his country estates was not enough time away from all the business of London. He looked forward to some alone time in his study. Correspondence was piled high on his desk and demanded his attention. He pushed aside tons of invitations. He needed to send a missive to his solicitor letting him know he came back early and was ready to start on some business deals.

A few hours later, a knock on the door interrupted his thoughts. "Good, you're here. I ran into Caroline and she said you might have arrived early." The Earl of Shepley's normally jovial demeanor was stoic.

His Grace creased his brow. "Why such a serious face?"

John reached for a glass and the bottle of brandy. "Do you remember that dandy we met at the club before you left? A Mr. Soothers? The one that practically begged for an introduction to you. He seemed to want some advice about some business deal with that chap from India."

Joseph accepted a glass from his friend taking a sip. "Barely."

John took a drink while looking at Joseph. He smacked his lips. "Well, I ran into him last night again. He was at the club speaking about his fiancée with Preston. I also saw him this morning."

Joseph shrugged uninterested in the conversation. "Is there a point to this story? I don't know the guy and have no interest in giving him an introduction to Baker. He's my contact for India."

John smirked at Joseph's annoyance. "It's not him, but his fiancée you may have interest in hearing about."

Joseph took another drink, raising his brow at the mention of a female.

"Not likely. I keep my women private, and I would not dally with another man's fiancée."

John watched for his friend's reaction as he divulged a little more of his story. "Her name is Betty Johnson."

Joseph shrugged, downing the rest of his brandy. He stood up to end this charade and attempted to move on to more interesting subjects. "I wish him congratulations. Now, I need about an hour to wash up and then we can go to lunch."

John looked at his friend with his final blow. "Her sister's name is Leah."

Joseph slowly looked at his friend. His breath caught in his throat. He sat back down and stared at John in disbelief.

John nodded. "He told me that Leah is back in town."

Joseph reached for his glass trying to take a drink before realizing it was empty. He looked up at John. "All these years. Why is she back now? Is her husband with her?"

John sat down looking at his friend. "Apparently, she never married."

Joseph shook his head. "That's impossible. Her family told me she was married and went to America."

John nodded pouring more brandy in Joseph's glass. "She went to America, but per Soothers, she cried off. The wedding never went through while she was in London because they were unable to get a license. They were to marry when they reached America, but she met some new friends and called it off. She works at an all-girls school in New York. Her mother is very ill and is not expected to make it, so Leah came back to pay her respects."

The duke's forehead creased. Overwhelmed by the news, he shifted in his chair digesting the information. He whispered. "Poor Leah—to lose both of her parents when she is so young."

John wiped his mouth after another drink. "There is more."

Joseph looked up at him. "Don't keep me waiting. What is it?"

John paused. "She didn't come alone."

"I don't understand?"

"She is engaged to some rich American. Rumor has it that he is making several business inquiries here in London—trying to meet with a lot of important people in society. If Leah doesn't share with him about her past with you, he will probably call upon you very soon. They say he is very rich and likes to have a good time—often showing his money boastfully wherever he goes."

Joseph crinkled his nose. "Hardly her type."

John lifted the corner of his mouth. "I happen to have on good authority that Leah will be at Hyde Park at two o'clock today with her sister. Soothers is escorting them while her fiancé meets with a supplier."

Joseph rubbed his lips together looking into his glass. "I may take a stroll later. I will see you tonight at the club."

John laughed at his friend's apparent change of heart.

Leah felt the breeze blow across her face. Her visit to Hyde Park brought back memories of her walks when she was younger. Betty and Mr. Soothers accompanied her, persuading Leah to get out of the house. She wanted to stay to read to her mother, but they insisted she go. Bernard was meeting with some new business associates and was trying to get some contracts for a shipping company. He had scheduled a meeting with a supplier, and couldn't go with her to the park.

Betty was escorted by Mr. Soothers on one side, holding Leah's arm on the other side. "Leah, tell Tom about the time you helped me get out of that tree I was stuck in. You ripped your dress and Papa was so mad, but then he ripped his pants climbing it after me to help me get down."

Leah giggled at the memory of her papa's trousers ripped down the seam. He had just finished scolding Leah about her dress when he ripped his pants as well. Even Papa laughed at that scene.

Leah started to tell Mr. Soothers when she caught a familiar face out of the corner of her eye. She looked closer and the blood drained from her face. Her heart beat faster as he approached their group.

"Your Grace!" Mr. Soothers approached the duke excitedly. "A pleasure to see you this afternoon."

Leah tried to stabilize her breathing, trying to remain calm. He looked so handsome—his shoulders had filled out even more than she remembered. The same warm smile lit up his whole face.

He stopped to join the group and nodded at Mr. Soothers. "Thank you."

Betty smiled as Mr. Soothers presented her to the duke. She curtsied, and he bowed at her.

He then turned to Leah. "This is my fiancée's sister, Miss Johnson."

Joseph cracked a smile. "I am well acquainted with Miss Johnson, we are old friends."

Mr. Soothers' forehead creased in confusion. "Forgive me, I was not aware you were acquainted."

Joseph turned to him. "If you would allow me a private word with Miss Johnson. I won't be too long."

Mr. Soothers nodded. "Of course, we will walk near the fountain and meet you there."

Joseph turned to Leah as the couple walked away. "Your sister has grown up."

Leah smiled. "Yes, I can't believe it. She is getting married and has turned into a beautiful young woman."

Joseph winked at her. "Like her sister."

Leah blushed and looked away.

He took a few steps toward her as they walked to the bridge that looked over the water—it offered a little more privacy than the main path. He looked over at her with admiration.

"How are you, Leah?" She looked away at the water.

Finding her voice, she answered, "I am well, but my mother is not. That is why I am here—her illness has taken a turn for the worse, and I came home to see her. It's a bittersweet visit."

Joseph frowned. "That's terrible. If there is anything I can do, just say the word."

Leah shook her head. "We just want to make sure she has no pain and spends a lot of time with her children."

"How are your brothers?"

"They are great. Travis graduated college last year, and Jasper received a commission in the military. Travis married a nice girl a few months ago. It seems a wealthy gentleman provided for them before I left for America, so they were able to do what they had always dreamed of doing. But if I am being honest, I must thank you for your generosity."

Joseph looked at her questioningly. "I don't know what you mean?"

She shook her head. "I know it was you, Your Grace. I recognized your solicitor when he visited my family that day. He practically confirmed it. It's okay. I will keep your secret. I just wanted to say thank you for everything you have done for my family. I am not sure why you would do it?"

He looked down. "My reasons are my own, but I would think it was quite obvious."

Leah ignored the comment and decided to change the subject. "How is your family? Caroline?"

Joseph took a deep breath and kept his eyes focused on hers as if he was afraid she would disappear. "She remarried a few years ago and had a son. It was good for her to join society again."

Leah smiled. "That's wonderful. What about you? How is your wife? Do you have any children?"

Pausing before he answered, he turned away from her to look at the pond. "Roslyn died a few years ago, giving birth to our daughter."

"Forgive me. I did not know. I am sorry for your loss."

"She was a good person and deserved better than me—she deserved someone who could love her."

Leah looked at him trying to absorb what he was telling her.

He hesitated before asking, "Why didn't you tell me that you were leaving England?"

Leah closed her eyes not wanting to have this conversation. "It made no difference. You were to marry, and I needed to leave." She looked away for a second, wanting to tell him more. "The truth is that my heart couldn't take staying in London and taking a chance of seeing you with her. Every paper spoke of your relationship. It was too much."

She wrung her hands as she looked down at the ground. "When Captain Jackson asked me to go with him, I thought it was my opportunity to leave everything behind. But we were unable to secure a license to marry in England, so planned to marry when we arrived in America. On our journey, I realized I did not love him. I stayed with some new friends in America and never looked back."

Joseph reached down to touch her face, but she pulled away. "Leah, I came back for you. I told my family I would not marry Roslyn. Despite their protest, I came for you. I wanted to marry you and take you to Gretna Green."

Leah's mouth dropped open in astonishment. "I didn't know."

"You're the only girl I ever loved. My heart shattered that day when your brother told me that you married another. How could you not tell me? I wanted to marry you. How could you do that to me?"

Leah lifted her chin up trembling. "Do that to *you?* You never mentioned marriage to me. Never! How dare you!"

She took a deep breath, trembling, thinking about the secrets she kept that he never knew. The humiliation of her circumstances kept her silent for so long.

It was time.

Straightening her shoulders, she answered him. "Did you know that my family was forcing me to marry a man twice my age because my father owed him money?"

Joseph's mouth opened, he shook his head, shocked at her admission.

She nodded. "Yes! His name was Mr. Wilcox—a farmer who inherited a small living. He was my only prospect to save my family. The sacrifice was tearing me apart. He was courting me when I was secretly seeing you. I was humiliated and never told you."

Leah started shaking as tears welled up in her eyes. "I secretly wished that you would save me and want me as your wife." She let out a breath, putting up her hand to silence him as he made a move to say something. "Any dream I had was taken away that day at your house. What choice did I have? When Captain Jackson came to me with honorable intentions, it was better than Mr. Wilcox. You made your intentions clear—you were to marry your perfect duchess—so I left you alone."

Joseph's voice pleaded with her. "I would have helped you. I have never stopped thinking about you. I love you still."

Leah's heart broke. "Stop it! You can't still love me. It took me years to get over you. But I did. In fact, I've met someone else who makes me very happy. I was finally able to let you go. I am now engaged to be married."

Joseph was breathing heavily. "I only want your happiness. But I still believe that there is another reason you came to London. It could be our second chance. Look at my scarf, Leah. Do you remember when you made this for me? I have always cherished it."

Leah glanced at the scarf before looking away. It meant nothing. She crossed her arms. "Joseph, I don't wish to hurt your feelings. I know most people don't say *no* to you. But trust me when I tell you that you're too late. I don't love you anymore. I am engaged to a wonderful man that's not ashamed of his feelings for me."

Joseph looked as if he was holding back his anger. "Very well, I just ask one favor." His chest rose and fell as he looked like he was trying to compose himself. "If you claim you don't love me, then spend one day with me to prove it."

Leah's eyes widened in disbelief. "I hardly think that would prove anything."

He touched her arm. "Just one more day. After a full day together, if you still feel that you don't love me, then I will pay for your wedding to your fiancé."

Leah snorted. "That's ridiculous. I do not need to prove I don't love you. It's been *five* years, Joseph. People change. Besides, he doesn't need your money—he has plenty for our wedding."

Joseph smiled. "What are you afraid of? You told me on our last night together that I would always have a piece of your heart. Did you mean it?"

Leah shook her head. "I was young and naïve. I am not that same little girl that you fell in love with years ago."

Joseph lifted the side of his mouth. "Just one more day. It will be like a previous time, when all we knew was each other."

Leah tilted her head. "I can't, Joseph. It's inappropriate. My fiancé is here in London with me. I will not dishonor him by spending a day with you. I won't live in a previous time, I have changed."

Joseph reached for her hand bringing it to his mouth. "Leah, don't be afraid. I only need one day to prove to you that our love did not end."

Leah pulled her hand away. "No, Your Grace. I must go." She turned, and walked swiftly to her sister, not looking back.

When Leah approached her sister and Mr. Soothers, he asked, "I didn't know that you were friends with His Grace."

Leah shrugged, trying to calm herself after the encounter.

Mr. Soothers turned around to look for the duke. "Do you think you can arrange a meeting with him? He is next to impossible to talk too. Many of my friends try to do business with him but are unable to get an appointment. The ION club is very exclusive, and you must have his permission to join. He has made a fortune, and his influence could really help me get my foot in the door. I could learn a lot from him."

Leah rolled her eyes. "We were old friends, but not anymore. I doubt I should see him again."

Betty turned to Leah. "I remember him. He came looking for you when you left for America. Travis told him you were married. The poor man looked positively shocked."

Leah turned her head to her sister. "Are you sure it was him?"

Betty nodded. "Oh yes. Hard to forget. He said it was of the utmost importance that he spoke to you."

Leah looked back, but Joseph had disappeared. She shivered, pulling her shawl closer to her as the breeze was cold that day.

CHAPTER 27

BERNARD WAS WAITING FOR LEAH when she arrived home. He gave her some flowers and kissed her on the cheek. He was entertaining Travis and his wife with stories of New York. Leah put the flowers in a vase and took off her cloak and bonnet. She took a seat next to Bernard on the settee.

"How was the park, love?" Bernard popped some tarts into his mouth. Leah's heart beat faster as she didn't want to tell him about Joseph. She shrugged. "Refreshing."

He nodded then turned back to Travis to finish their conversation. Leah sat beside him shifting in her seat, trying to keep Joseph out of her head.

After a few minutes, Bernard rose to bid the family goodbye. He turned to Leah. "I retained a solicitor here in London. I think it is better to have a man of business that understands the law of the country. I want to make some investments. He said he would secure some invitations for me to meet some other prominent businessmen here in London."

Leah straightened her mouth. "I thought you were here to support me. I didn't realize it was a business trip for you."

Bernard looked uncomfortable at her comment. "Can we go somewhere and speak privately?"

Leah nodded, escorting him to the back door. They went out on the side of the house to finish their conversation.

Bernard reached for her hands when they were outside. "Leah, I don't understand why you are cross with me? Doing business in London could give us more opportunity to travel abroad to see your family. I thought this would please you."

Leah looked down, feeling foolish. His pleas made sense and she would like opportunities to see her brothers and sisters more. She smiled. "Forgive me, I just miss you."

He bent down and brushed his lips against hers. "Forgive me, but I must take my leave. I will take you to dinner tonight. Just the two of us so we can spend time alone."

She smiled. "I would like that. I will be ready by eight."

Bernard grinned and mounted his horse to leave.

Leah went back inside to spend some time with her mother. She was having a better day, not refusing to eat and enjoyed the chicken soup that Mrs. Freemont was feeding her. Leah offered to help and took over the care of her mother to give Mrs. Freemont a rest. Leah's mother smiled as she entered the room. "My dear, you look lovely this day."

Pouring her mother some water, she smiled. "Thank you, Mama. I took a walk in the park with Betty and Mr. Soothers."

Leah's mother swallowed as she looked at her daughter. "How was the park?"

She shrugged. "Fine. It looks the same to me."

"Did you run into any old friends? I hear Melissa had a child a couple of years ago. I was hoping you could mend your friendship."

Leah's eyes enlarged thinking of Melissa pregnant. "Yes, I remember your letter about that. Betty told me she is away in Italy with her husband right now. I wouldn't know what to say to her anymore. She blamed me for crying off with Captain Jackson. It was for the best. I heard his wife is lovely."

Mrs. Johnson nodded her head. "She is a nice girl. You would have liked her."

Leah sat back. "It matters not." She thought about the events she had missed over the years. Her friend Mel was the closest ally she had growing up. She thought about her mother's discerning comment regarding old friends. She took some sewing out of the basket as she spoke to her mother. "I did run in to the Duke of Wollaston. Do you remember his sister Caroline who I spent some time with before going to America?"

Leah's mother rubbed her lips. "Of course, he came by to give us his condolences after your father passed."

Leah looked down at her sewing not making eye contact with her mother. She was afraid her expression would give away her folly. She took a few minutes then looked up from her sewing. "He is well. His wife passed away a few years ago."

Leah's mother creased her forehead. "I heard about it in the papers. They did not speak kindly of their relationship. He was never around her much leaving her to go to many social events alone, and there was speculation throughout the town that it was not a love match. Their only daughter is left for him to raise, poor dear. The papers have him linked to many different women, trying to see who he will pick to have his heir. His fortune is renown throughout London. I would not envy him with every mother in the town pursuing his every move."

Her throat burned a little with the hurt she was feeling. She tried to push the feeling away—they were dormant the last few years—but with seeing him today, some feelings were starting to come back. She masked her thoughts and cracked a smile. "Mother? Are you reading the scandal sheets?"

Leah's mother smiled. "I try not to, but Ellen tells me about them." Leah laughed with her mother enjoying their afternoon together.

Leah dressed for dinner with care. She wore her apricot gown and the gold necklace Bernard had gifted her with a few days ago. She took care with her hair, braiding it in a bun on top of her head with tendrils falling along her neck. Bernard complimented her when he picked her up in a new carriage he had purchased earlier that day. He claimed it was better to have their own transportation while in London instead of renting all the time.

He picked a new restaurant that he found on one of his outings. Leah enjoyed his full attention. They laughed and indulged in delicious food. Toward the end of the meal, a man came over to the table. He addressed Bernard. "Mr. Williams, I believe we met yesterday at Mr. George's office?"

Bernard nodded. "Yes, Lord Riverton. Good to see you. May I introduce my fiancée?"

Lord Riverton looked over to Leah. "We are acquainted."

Leah blushed. "How are you, Lord Riverton? It's been a long time."

He smiled. "Indeed. You are still as beautiful as ever."

Bernard cracked a smiled. "I am a lucky man."

Lord Riverton looked back at him, "That you are. Here is my card. Come by and see me this week. We share the same solicitor, and he said we have similar business interests. Perhaps I could introduce you to some of my acquaintances as well."

Bernard smiled. "Indeed, I look forward to it."

Riverton nodded and then turned to Leah. "It was a pleasure, Miss Johnson."

Leah smiled while watching him walk away. She knew he was good friends with Joseph. She hoped that everyone would keep propriety and past mistakes would be forgotten.

Bernard stared at the card and then tucked it into his pocket. He rose to pay the bill and to escort Leah outside. He smiled. "I thought you said you were not acquainted with the London society?"

Leah shrugged. "I am not acquainted with them. I met Lord Riverton once, but we were not in the same station. I worked at a bookstore, which is looked down on by the aristocrats. My father was a solicitor, so on occasion, we would see them at functions. I met Lord Riverton at a house party of a friend's family. We were surprised he attended as most of his station would not be at that event. I believe they were buying some horses from the host and stayed over a few days."

Bernard let out a breath. "I may not be noble, but I am rich. They will not shun us from attending their social outings. Trust me."

Leah looked out the window. "Indeed."

He grunted with a mocking voice. "You must have made an impression that he remembered you after all this time."

"He was only being polite."

Bernard laughed, shaking his head. "You have no idea the effect you have on men. I must keep you close by my side."

Leah flirted back. "How close?"

He embraced her, kissing her in the carriage.

CHAPTER 28

JOSEPH WAS IN HIS STUDY when Lord Riverton was announced. John was spread out on the settee going through some paperwork conversing with Joseph. There were some mining opportunities they were investing in throughout Europe.

"Good day, gentlemen." Lord Riverton took a seat in the wingback chair.

Joseph smiled. "Riverton, what brings you here? Can I offer you anything to drink?"

Riverton shook his head. "No, I can only stay a few minutes. I wanted to speak to you about a new fellow from America looking to invest a pile of money. I spoke to him at my solicitor's office, then again at dinner last night. He introduced me to his fiancée—you may remember her from that house party years ago—a Miss Johnson."

Joseph smirked to hide his discomfort. "Miss Johnson, you say? I am not sure."

Riverton cracked a smiled. "Oh, come on Joseph. Everyone at the house party knew you were smitten with her. She is a beautiful woman, hardly a girl anymore. The whole restaurant noticed her."

Joseph steadied his breathing. "You had dinner with him?"

Riverton shook his head. "No, I saw him at a restaurant. He is interested in doing some business, and I thought we could speak to him."

John looked at Joseph raising his brows in question while Joseph took a drink of his coffee. "Interesting. Why don't you invite him to dinner tomorrow night? I will host a small dinner party. Tell him to bring his fiancée and everyone can bring a partner. We can get to know him socially to see if he is someone to do business with."

Riverton nodded and rose to leave. "Very well, I will send him a message and see you tomorrow."

Joseph smiled at John once they were once again alone. "I won't let her go again."

"Joseph, she is engaged. She may not be the same girl you fell in love with."

Joseph ignored his warning. "Do you know any decent women that I can escort to my dinner party? No one looking for a love interest as I don't need any complications—only one dinner. I can't show up alone as I would look desperate. If I ask Caroline for help, she will go overboard trying to marry me off."

John busted out in a laugh. "You are asking me to find a woman for you? You are the most sought-after bachelor in London, and you need my help?"

Joseph gritted his mouth. "I don't *need* your help with getting a woman. I need your help finding one that won't expect anything from me. Preferably someone easy to look at as well."

"I know someone, but you will owe me. My fiancée has a married cousin that is visiting from Scotland. She is passably pretty and waiting for her husband to come back from the military. She came to have some fun but is low on funds. I am sure she could be persuaded to be your partner for a price."

Joseph shook his head. "This is ridiculous. How much?"

John smirked. "Probably a new gown would be acceptable."

Joseph crossed his arms. "Done. Just make sure she is here on time tomorrow night."

John laughed as he gathered the papers. "This is going to be fun. See you tomorrow."

Leah woke up early the next day. She brought her mother breakfast reading to her from a new novel she brought from America. Betty interrupted them when Bernard arrived and was waiting in the parlor for her. Leah excused herself to meet with him.

Bernard was dressed in a new navy coat and black trousers. His hair was slicked back showing off the dimples on his face. "Leah, excuse my early arrival. I know we have plans for luncheon this afternoon, but we need to reconsider. I have the best news."

Leah smiled at his excitement. "What news?"

Bernard motioned for her to take a seat on the settee. "I have received our first invitation to a dining party with prominent members of society. This could be the ticket we need to invest in some of the lucrative business deals my solicitor told me about."

"What kind of dining party?"

Bernard shrugged. "I am not sure to be honest. He said to bring my fiancée. They wanted it to be a social dinner with business associates."

Leah clarified, "Who said?"

Bernard paused. "Forgive me, I was so anxious I forgot to tell you. It was Lord Riverton, the man we saw at dinner. He came to my hotel last night and invited me. My solicitor told him where to find me. It's at some duke's house and if we can establish some kind of friendship, this could open doors for me. Apparently, he has a lot of influence and you practically need his approval to do business in this town. He could ruin you if he chose to."

Leah felt her heart pound in her ears. She closed her eyes trying to compose herself. "Did he say which duke?" There was a small possibility it could be someone else. Leah tried to calm herself.

Bernard rubbed his lips together. "Walton or Wilkinson—something like that."

Leah could not believe this was happening. Her voice cracked, "Wollaston?"

Bernard snapped his finger. "That's it. The Duke of Wollaston."

Leah's head was spinning. There was not a chance she would attend the dinner. Excuses would be made, and he would have to understand. She looked at Bernard. "I can't come tonight. I have other plans..."

Bernard looked frantic. "Please Leah, it's a social event. He specifically mentioned you. They want it to be a friendly get-together and he knows you. Can you not change your plans? This could be my one chance."

Bernard's pleas tugged at her heart. She relented. "Fine. I will go. But I must warn you that I briefly met the Duke of Wollaston and his family. They were customers at the bookstore I used to work at. They may seem familiar with me, but trust me when I tell you that we are very different people. I don't wish to stay long."

Bernard kissed her hands. "As you wish, love." He stood up. "I will pick you up later tonight. I must see my solicitor and let him know. He will be most pleased with my invitation."

Leah watched him leave the parlor before leaning back on the settee and closing her eyes. In all her dreams, she never thought she would be escorted to Joseph's house on the arm of her new fiancé for dinner. She didn't know what game Joseph was playing. Did he know Lord Riverton invited them? She felt nauseous.

A few hours later, Leah stared at her wardrobe hoping the perfect gown would magically appear. Careful not to ask her too many questions, Betty offered to help her dress. Leah was firm when she told Betty and Travis she did not want them to mention the duke around Bernard. In fact, she preferred they not mention him at all. Although, her future brother-in-law would be salivating to know about the invitation. He made his desires known on developing an acquaintance with His Grace. Leah would not help anyone social climb with Joseph. She did not want to be associated with him. It hurt too much.

Leah turned her thoughts to Bernard—feeling content as she thought about marrying him. He may not proclaim his love, but his devotion was evident. Leah never told him she loved him either, but she would soon. Her love for Bernard was not a schoolgirl infatuation like she had with Joseph. She thought back to her first encounter with the Duke of Wollaston—how smitten she was to catch the attention of a powerful duke, not knowing he was deceiving her the whole time. She shivered thinking of the day he told her he was to marry another. The devastation that tore her heart apart and left her unfit to love in the same way again. What she had with Bernard was real. It was not an infatuation. They would marry soon, and they would live a happy life in America. Perhaps Betty and Mr. Soothers could come visit them. She smiled at the thought as Betty braided her hair on top, allowing the back of her hair to cascade down her shoulders.

Leah squinted creasing her forehead. "You're not going to pin it all up?"

Betty scrunched her nose. "Nah, you're not a young miss. This hairstyle suits you. You have beautiful dark golden hair and should show it off. We will pin up the sides. Take a chance tonight."

Leah felt unsure but left the style alone. Her light green dress showed off her eyes and the sapphire necklace that Bernard gave her in America.

CHAPTER 29

JOSEPH PACED HIS STUDY ANXIOUSLY waiting for John. He was late as usual. The staff worked all day diligently on the preparations for the impromptu dining party. He kept the small party a secret from Caroline. He didn't need any advice or judgment from his devoted sister. She was on a quest to see him married again so he could have an heir. Joseph had no desire to leg-shackle himself unless it was with Leah. He didn't care about her station—the *ton* could hang.

John knocked on the door then peeked inside. "You alone?"

Joseph stepped near the door pulling it open. "Come in. Is Miss Woods's cousin here yet?"

John stepped inside closing the door behind him. "Not exactly. She had a prior engagement. I even offered a new dress and money, and she wouldn't budge. I brought another girl who is in the drawing room as we speak."

Joseph groaned at the prospect of John's other girl. Hopefully it wasn't someone's mistress. "Who?"

John patted him on the shoulder as if trying to soften his response. "Miss Jacobs."

"Is this a jest?"

"It was either her or a trollop. Who else could I get to come here on a few hours' notice? She is my fiancée's friend."

Joseph ran his fingers through his hair. "I avoid her and her mother at every social event. She is very pleasing on the eye, but not for me."

John took in a breath. "That's not all."

Joseph raised his hands in defeat. "What now?"

"Lord Riverton brought his cousin Miss Rogers as well. She practically invited herself. In order to even out the men and women, he extended another invitation to Mark's son. He asked me if I thought it would be okay, and I said yes."

Joseph let out a breath perturbed with all the people getting in his way of spending time with Leah. He grunted. "Why not invite all of London? Come, let's go get a drink."

Leah's anticipation mounted as she turned into the familiar drive of the duke's townhouse. Sweat moistened her palms as she flexed her gloved hands. Bernard shifted in his seat excited for his meeting with the businessmen of the town. Leah spoke little on the ride over, choosing to listen to Bernard's big plans to make a splash in London's society. The mention of the ION club was always on his lips. Leah's mind wandered—suspicious at his motives of coming to England. She snuck looks at him through her eyelashes, relishing in the memories of their time in America. He obviously cared about her— but she wanted love.

Her woolgathering was interrupted by the footman opening the carriage door. Bernard stepped down offering his hand to help her out. Leah's nerves jumped in her skin as they entered the front door. A butler smiled at Leah as he welcomed Bernard and escorted them to the parlor. It was full of laughter as they entered. Feeling faint, Leah braced herself as Lord Preston approached them.

He smiled politely at the couple. "Miss Johnson! Welcome back to England. I am glad you could make it. You always did light up a room."

Leah was unsure how to take the compliment, but remembered her manners. "You're too kind, Lord Preston."

He turned to his side, looking at a pretty woman with dark curly hair. "May I introduce you to my friend, Miss Carlton?" She nodded smiling at Leah and Bernard.

Leah grinned. "Nice to make your acquaintance."

A blonde woman walked up behind them on the arm of John. Leah recognized him immediately and shifted in her shoes uncomfortably. John smiled at her before turning to Bernard for an introduction.

Lord Preston introduced Bernard to John and he smiled at Leah. "Miss Johnson, it's been too long. I had heard you were back from America. What a pleasure to see you tonight. May I introduce my fiancée, Miss Woods?"

Miss Wood smiled. "It's a pleasure to meet you Miss Johnson, and I do remember you from trips to the bookstore. You read to the children."

Leah blushed at the familiarity. She looked very young for John but happy. She must have been no more than one and nine. Leah cracked a smile. "I do miss the children."

Miss Woods turned to a lady beside her with red hair dressed in a very fashionable blue dress with a low neckline. She nudged Miss Woods who looked back tightening her lips. "Miss Johnson, may I introduce you to Miss Rogers."

Miss Rogers lifted her chin barely nodding an acknowledgment. With obvious flirtation, she turned to Bernard offering her hand for him to kiss. Leah wanted to strangle her for her wanton behavior. Unable to stomach her display, Leah took Bernard's arm and led him away.

A few other couples lingered near the fireplace, not making introductions. Leah eyed a blonde woman conversing with a few other women who kept staring at her without attempting to approach her for an introduction. She looked like a polished porcelain doll. Her stares made Leah uncomfortable, and she chose not to look at her.

Bernard excused himself and engaged in some conversation with other men. Leah tried not to let her eyes wander at where the duke may be. She overheard John telling another gentleman that he was saying goodnight to his daughter. Leah's heart tugged at the devotion. Most men in his station would not be involved in the nighttime ritual.

Miss Woods approached her without John. Leah liked her demeanor and felt comfortable. They spoke of the children and books until they heard the room quiet as the duke entered. Leah's heart skipped a beat trying to act casual. She couldn't help but notice that his perfectly tied cravat highlighted his flawless looks.

John introduced the duke to Bernard, and she watched Bernard's whole face light up as they spoke about business. Leah turned her head noticing a woman by the fireplace walking to Joseph then taking his arm. Leah looked away as Miss Woods studied her face.

She whispered, "That's Miss Jacobs, who seems to be marking her territory with His Grace. Although, I don't think he will marry her. Please don't think I am awful for saying it."

Leah shrugged trying not to stare. "I don't really follow London society."

Miss Woods lifted the corner of her mouth. "I understand. *Trust* me. John is like His Grace's brother, so I did hear about your prior acquaintance."

Leah raised a brow. Miss Woods covered her mouth with her hand. "Forgive me and my mouth. I should not have said that."

Leah shook her head, not sure how to take Miss Woods. "It's quite all right. My acquaintance with His Grace is in the past."

Miss Woods bit her lip. "I know you don't know me, but I wanted you to know that he speaks highly of you."

Leah was taken back by her comment. Trying to reassure her stance, she answered, "I was only friendly with his sister many years ago. We have both changed a lot since then."

Miss Woods met her eyes, challenging her honesty. "Perhaps you have changed." She gave Leah a genuine smile. "You're nice, Miss Johnson. That's rare with the women in this group. John was right about you."

Leah smiled as Bernard approached them with Joseph in tow. Joseph's eyes held amusement as he smiled at her. "Miss Johnson, you are lovely as ever. What a great coincidence that you're Mr. William's fiancée. I could hardly believe it when Lord Preston told me of the news. I wish Caroline were here to see you as well."

Leah curtsied. "Your Grace. Thank you for having us."

Joseph smiled then looked to the woman on his right. "May I introduce Miss Jacobs?" Miss Jacobs nodded her head, and Leah smiled. "A pleasure."

Joseph peeled his eyes away from Leah when the butler entered the room. "Dinner is served, Your Grace."

He smiled. "Very well. Let's enter the dining room. Miss Johnson, will you do me the honor?"

Leah saw his outstretched elbow and raised her eyes to Bernard in question. Bernard smiled nodding as Miss Rogers took his arm. Leah was fuming inside but held her composure accepting Joseph's escort. The dining table was arranged with assigned seats and Leah was set next to Joseph on one side and Bernard on the other. Miss Jacobs sat beside Joseph with John and Miss Woods across from them.

Leah tried hard not to look at Joseph. She knew what he was about. At least he didn't put Bernard at the other end of the table. Leaning over, she turned her body to her left to be closer to Bernard. He was oblivious to her closeness and was engrossed in a conversation with Mr. Myers.

Glancing over, she noticed Miss Jacobs shooting daggers at her across the table while John and Joseph held a conversation with each other. Leah was relieved when the footman entered with the first course. She was famished, and the potato soup would soothe her nerves.

Joseph's conversation quieted as he ate his soup, and he turned to Leah. "Miss Johnson, how is your mother?"

Leah swallowed, lifting her eyes to Joseph. She hoped Bernard did not hear his question and ask how the duke knew about her mother's illness. Clearing her throat, she answered, "She has good days and bad days, Your Grace." She glanced over to Bernard who was laughing with his new friend.

"Please let me know if I can provide any assistance. I could send my personal doctor."

Leah shook her head not wanting to ever be indebted to him again. "You're very kind to offer, Your Grace. But Bernard has provided a new doctor that is trying some different treatments."

Joseph took another bite of soup as Miss Jacobs put her spoon down. She turned to Joseph trying to engage him in conversation. "Have you seen the new opera? I heard it was wonderful."

"I am afraid not."

She looked at Leah as the duke's attention seemed focused on her. "Do you enjoy the opera, Miss Johnson?"

Leah shrugged not wanting to engage in conversation. "I am not sure, Miss Jacobs. I have enjoyed a musical soiree but have never attended an opera."

Miss Jacobs brought her hand to her chest as if in shock. "Oh, dear. Are you not use to London society? Forgive me—I thought at your age—you would have attended many by now."

Leah laughed at her cutting remark. "Yes, my advanced age of four and twenty should have prepared me for more than an upcoming pension."

Joseph snorted at her banter. "Some women improve with age."

Miss Jacobs glared at Leah before turning to Joseph. "Oh, you must go. Perhaps we could go together. Papa will let us use his box."

Leah's eyes widened at the impulsiveness and impropriety of the young woman's invitation. Joseph raised his brows with surprise and Leah suppressed a laugh.

"Miss Jacobs, your invitation is tempting, but I have my own box and made plans with some acquaintances to attend. Perhaps another time?"

Miss Jacobs looked down. "Of course, your Grace." She took another bite of soup looking at Leah. "Miss Johnson, how are you and His Grace acquainted?"

Bernard's conversation ended as he looked at Leah for her answer. Leah looked at Bernard as John looked their way as well.

The group stared at her anticipating the answer. Leah's heart beat faster as thoughts raced through her head. She finally breathed in, thinking of an answer. "We actually met accidently when I was working at a bookstore. He became a customer and introduced me to his sister."

The group looked at her for further explanation. Leah took a drink of water. "His sister and I enjoyed the same books and liked to speak of our favorites. His Grace accompanied us a few times. That was a long time ago as I went to America several years past and lost touch." Leah took another drink hoping that was the end of the questioning.

Bernard smiled. "I am a lucky man that she went to America."

Joseph took a drink. "Indeed."

Leah muddled through the next few courses carefully not looking to Joseph. Bernard whispered a few endearments during the courses as he kept up a conversation with John and Joseph. Joseph announced the port as Miss Woods led the women into the drawing room. Leah took a seat on the settee as the women spoke of the Wilson's ball coming up in a few days.

"Miss Johnson, are you to attend the ball?" Miss Jacobs cracked a sly smile.

Leah shook her head making sure not to gaze too long at the young woman.

Miss Woods watched the exchange, indignant at her friend's behavior. "You're welcome to come as my guest, Miss Johnson. Katherine Wilson is a dear friend of mine. I will have her send you an invitation right away."

Leah smoothed her hands on her dress not wanting the conversation to be focused on her. "Thank you, but I am sure I have other plans."

Miss Woods frowned her displeasure. "Oh, you must come. His Grace will insist upon it." She whispered loudly, "It will help us to persuade *him* to attend."

Leah's eyes widened as everyone in the room was silently listening to their conversation. Leah blushed at the insinuation. "I am sure His Grace has no opinion on my attendance." She stood up to take a glass of wine from the footman who smiled at her. Recognizing him, she acknowledged him with a half-smile.

A deep voice rumbled behind him. "What about His Grace's opinion?" Leah sucked in a breath as she turned to look at Joseph. Bernard was laughing with Lord Preston by the doorway unaware of their conversation.

Miss Jacobs tightened her mouth. "Miss Woods has tried to convince Miss Johnson to accept an invitation to the Wilson's ball. She thought you would insist she accept the invitation if you were to be there. Miss Johnson disagrees."

Joseph glanced at Miss Jacobs then between Miss Woods and Leah. "She is correct. Miss Johnson and I are old friends, and I insist that she come if she wishes."

Leah held up her hand trying to stop the maddening conversation. "I have no wish to attend a London ball. You are very polite, Your Grace, to suggest such an invitation. But please accept my regrets."

Bernard walked up behind her. "Your regrets about what love?"

Leah could tell that Joseph did not like Bernard's term of endearment when he tightened his jaw, trying to mask his disgust. He grabbed for a glass of brandy and tightened his hand around the glass.

Leah looked up at Bernard. "It's nothing. A ball, not an event I wish to attend."

He smiled at Leah. "We should not turn down any invitations when we are so new to London society. If we receive one, we should go."

Leah grew annoyed at the conversation and let Bernard know it. "We will speak about this later."

Miss Jacobs walked over to the piano to play a few pieces as the group conversed. Bernard was soon led away by a few guests who had questions about American business. Leah excused herself to take care of some private needs not noticing that Joseph watched her as she left the room.

After a few minutes, Joseph told his group he needed to check on his daughter, leaving out a separate set of doors. He quickly found a back way to see if he could locate Leah. He saw her walking down the hallway. "Leah?"

She turned around. "Joseph?"

He smiled as he approached her. "May I have a private word?" He opened the door to an empty chamber, motioning her inside, then locking it behind him.

He faced her. "I just need a few minutes."

Leah looked down. "This is improper, Joseph. Please speak quickly because I don't want to be caught alone with you." She huddled by the door awaiting an escape.

He swallowed hard trying to find the words to convince her how he felt. Part of him wanted to embrace her but he held his hands to his side. He slowly let out a breath to calm his nerves. "Leah, please say you thought about my request. Can you honestly say you have no feelings left for me at all?" He rubbed his knuckles across her face.

Leah winced turning her cheek to the side. "I can't answer that. It's not proper, Your Grace." She pulled her head away from his touch, trying to deny the feelings it stirred within her.

Joseph took a step closer. "My name is Joseph. Did you forget? We are alone." He touched her chin, turning her face to him. "Leah, you're the only woman I have ever told that I loved." His gaze moved over her face searching for answers. "Please think about what I said in the park."

She looked away, eyeing the door. He moved his head trying to capture her eyes. "It's only one day of your life. I would never tell your fiancé about our past. That's ours to share—no one else's. My feelings have not changed for you."

Leah's hands shook nervously as she met his eyes trying to compose herself. "Please don't say such things to me. I can't live in the past—it took me years to get over you. I won't spend any time with you, and even if I did, it won't make any difference."

Joseph leaned down closer to her and she shuddered, not moving away. "Leah, I am not the same man. I learned a hard lesson when you left England. You said I didn't love you enough—but I came back for you. I still want you. But not like before. This time I want to do it right—I want to marry you. I want you to be the mother of my children."

Leah's heart sank in her stomach. Tears welled up in her eyes. She had wished for those words years ago hoping that he would rescue her from Mr.

Wilcox. Her heart could take no more—she could not chance it. She would marry Bernard.

Lifting her eyes up, she finally made eye contact. "I don't wish to hurt you. Please just leave me alone. Why can't you understand that I don't feel the same way about you." She lied as she trembled with his hand still on her face.

He bent down brushing his lips against hers. She pulled away pushing against his chest, "Please don't. I can't do this Joseph. I don't love you anymore." She choked out a cry as she turned her back to him reaching for the door handle.

Joseph stepped behind her, pulling her back against his chest. She felt him breathing on the back of her neck. He whispered in her ear, "I love you, Leah."

She closed her eyes, tears escaping. "I have to go. They could be looking for us."

Joseph closed his eyes and sighed. "Very well. You go first, and I will wait a few minutes and join the others from the side door. I went to check on my daughter."

Leah said nothing as she opened the door and fled.

⁓⁓⁓⁓⁓

She entered the drawing room unnoticed. Bernard was surrounded by a group of men as the women spoke by the piano. Leah took a glass of wine and sat quietly on the settee listening to the music. Bernard came over and sat beside her drinking a glass of brandy. He whispered, "This has been a most productive dinner party."

Leah took a drink of wine trying to calm her nerves. "I wish to go now if you are done doing business."

"Why do you want to leave so early? Let's stay and have fun. A quiet night at home alone does not appeal to me tonight."

"I don't wish to stay. Perhaps I can get a carriage to take me home. You can stay."

Bernard's frustration was evident. Joseph entered the room telling John that his daughter was sleeping soundly before his eyes met Leah's from across the room—his eyes showing his concern for her.

Joseph approached the couple. "What's amiss?"

Bernard shook his head. "My fiancée wishes to leave because she is not feeling well. She insists that I stay."

Joseph gazed at her. "You are welcome to rest in one of our chambers or I could have one of my footman escort you home in my carriage."

Bernard smiled. "That is most kind, Your Grace."

Leah looked at Bernard and shook her head. Standing up from the settee, she faced Joseph. "Thank you for your kind offer of an escort, Your Grace. I would be much obliged."

Bernard walked behind Leah as Joseph spoke to his footman. He walked the couple outside. "They are alerting the stable staff, and will have a carriage in a few moments."

He looked at Bernard. "We welcome your company, Mr. Williams, but understand if you wish to tend to Miss Johnson."

Bernard smoothed his coat. "With your permission, I would like to stay. Leah assures me that she prefers to return home to rest."

Joseph lifted a brow and turned to Leah as the carriage approached. He took her hand and brushed a kiss across her knuckles. "It's always a pleasure, Miss Johnson."

He nodded to Bernard. "Mr. Williams, we will see you inside shortly. Let's play some cards."

Bernard nodded. "Looking forward to it, Your Grace."

Bernard assisted her into the carriage. "Good night, love."

Leah snorted as she sat down refusing to say anything.

Bernard shook his head while closing the carriage door.

CHAPTER 30

L EAH WOKE UP EARLY THE next morning to make breakfast for her mother because Miss Freemont had to visit her sister for a few hours. Miss Freemont left the eggs for her and Leah scrambled them with some bread and tea. She delivered them to her mother who was awake reading a book.

Leah smiled at her mother. "You look better today, Mama. Perhaps we can get some food inside you and open the window for a while."

Mrs. Johnson yawned. "Oh child, I had a nice visit with Ellen yesterday. The doctor told me that my heart is doing better. Perhaps the new medicine is working."

Leah's heart filled with hope. "Let us pray, Mama. I will bring some hot water and give you a bath."

"How was the dining party last night? Did you see the Duke of Wollaston? The papers would love to know who he will marry."

Leah was amused by her mother's question. "Mother, you can't believe what you read in the papers. I did not see his sister last night but did see him. He was very polite and a perfect host. I left early and did not get a chance to ask him who he would marry." She laughed, and her mother giggled with her.

"I hear he is very handsome. I don't remember him much when he came to visit us as I was distraught over losing your father. Is he as handsome as they say?"

Leah rolled her eyes. "I will not answer that question. I am an engaged woman and don't notice other men." She busted out laughing as her mother smiled.

"I guess I have my answer." Leah blushed and shook her head avoiding her mother's gaze.

"I will fetch the water, and perhaps we can fix your hair as well."

As she walked down the stairs, Bernard had just arrived and was waiting for her. She was cross with him for not escorting her home but gave him a small smile.

He went and took her hand. "Leah, you look well rested."

She held in her contempt. "Are you hungry?"

He shook his head. "I ate at the inn. I came to let you know that I need to leave for a few days to go to Bath. One of my business associates from America is there and has some papers for me to sign. We are going to inquire about a factory close to that area."

"Indeed?"

Bernard leaned over and kissed her on the cheek. "I will miss you, love. I know you're cross with me, but I wanted you to take this money and buy a new gown for the ball. Miss Woods practically insisted that we attend, and we don't want to appear rude." Bernard took out some money and handed it to Leah.

Leah shook her head. "Bernard, London balls are not like the balls at home. Everyone is very pompous and judged by their station. I don't wish to attend."

"Leah, I want to go. It's important to me. You are my fiancée and it would not look right if you did not attend with me. Many of my new acquaintances will be there."

Leah closed her eyes feeling guilty. She realized how important this was to him and would not be able to get out of going. "Very well, I will see you in a few days."

"That's my girl." He kissed her and left.

Leah filled the basin with water to take to her mother. She wished Bernard would have stopped to visit her mother before he left on his trip. He had not seen her since their first day in London.

The next few days flew by. Leah's mother was getting anxious to be outside. Her legs were weak, but she stayed awake longer each day. Travis carried his mother to sit outside to enjoy the fresh air.

Leah had reluctantly gone shopping for a new gown. Betty helped her pick out new gloves and shoes as well. The night of the ball came quickly, and Betty was more excited than Leah. She made Leah wear the jewelry that Bernard had bought her and helped her with her hair. Leah was enjoying spending time with her younger sister as they were both young women now with more in common than when they were children. Betty showered her with many compliments before she came down the stairs to wait for Bernard. She had not heard from him since he left and hoped he was still coming to get her. She drank some water in the drawing room snacking on nuts and talking to Betty when Bernard entered the room dressed in a new coat. His brown hair was brushed back showing off his handsome features. Leah stood as he approached her watching as his eyes widened with delight. "You look beautiful."

Leah blushed. "Thank you. You clean up nice yourself."

He greeted her sister and escorted Leah to the waiting carriage. He assisted her inside taking the seat beside her. "I missed you, love."

Leah kissed him on the cheek. "I missed you too."

"I hope you have an enjoyable time tonight. I received a formal invitation when I was gone. I have it in my pocket. Lord Riverton asked me to play some cards later tonight with his group of friends. You don't mind, do you?"

Leah felted trapped. She didn't wish to attend the ball and now to find out that part of her evening would be fending for herself while Bernard played cards made her uneasy. She looked out the window ignoring the question hoping Bernard realized that her silence was answer enough to how she felt.

They arrived a while later to a huge house with wrought iron gates. The circular drive was full of carriages and ladies were assisted out with ball gowns far fancier than Leah's. Leah's stomach hurt thinking of the scrutiny of the town—especially the other women.

Bernard escorted her inside, and they were introduced to Lady Katheryn Wilson and her parents. She was charming and welcomed the couple. They were announced a few minutes later, and Leah was given a dance card. Bernard signed her card for the supper dance and soon met with some acquaintances. Leah felt left out scanning the ballroom for a friendly face. She didn't wait long before Miss Woods embraced her arm.

"Miss Johnson, what a lovely gown."

Leah smiled. "Thank you. Your gown is beautiful as well."

"I wish I could wear that gold color. My mother insists on me wearing pastels since I am unmarried. Yet, she knows I am engaged to John."

Leah giggled. "Enjoy your youth, Miss Woods. It's gone before you know it."

Miss Woods barked at the implication. "Please, Miss Johnson. You're hardly older than I am. Do you want to walk with me? I could use some lemonade."

Leah looked back at Bernard who was engrossed in a conversation with someone she was not acquainted with. She pulled his arm motioning that she would be going with Miss Woods, and he nodded his head. She turned to take her arm and they walked together to the refreshment table.

Miss Woods wiped her brow. "It's so hot in here. I wish we could have an outdoor ball."

Leah thought about the cool breeze outside. "Yes, under the stars would be fun, Miss Woods."

She smiled as they slowed their pace at the table. "Please call me Janet. I know we will be great friends."

Leah squeezed her arm. "Very will Janet, please call me Leah."

Janet whispered, "Don't look now, but Lord Crawford is coming up behind you."

Leah looked up to see a blond man approach. "Miss Woods, may I steal a dance with you?"

She handed him her dance card, and he signed it before asking for an introduction to Leah. Miss Woods introduced Leah and she gave him her dance card as well.

He smiled. "I don't recall seeing you at any balls as I would have remembered you."

Leah blushed at the way he stared at her. "I came from America a few weeks ago."

He raised his brows. "Indeed?"

Leah looked at Miss Woods. "I have been gone several years."

He stroked the beard on his face. "I look forward to hearing about America."

Miss Woods pulled Leah away from Lord Crawford and directed her toward the corner of the ballroom. "He is one of the most sought-after bachelors this year. He is an Earl and looking for a wife. It must be time for an heir. Be careful as he seems to be on the hunt."

Leah laughed. "I am engaged, Janet. I hardly think he would be interested in me."

She smirked. "Well, you're not married yet."

Leah followed her around the ballroom and Janet introduced her to several new people. Her dance card was quickly filling up with dances. John caught them before all their dances were gone and Joseph came up shortly afterward.

"My Miss Johnson, you are certainly the talk of the ball."

"Your Grace, you do flatter me."

"Do you have any dances left?"

Leah gave him her card, watching his mouth turn up into a smile. "There... I wrote my name for the next waltz."

Leah stared into his eyes as they looked at each other for a few minutes before speaking. He leaned down and whispered, "You look very beautiful tonight."

John stood beside Miss Woods and slipped her hand into the crook of his arm as they watched the exchange between Leah and Joseph.

Leah bit her lip. "I should go find Bernard."

John looked over the crowd. "I think he is in the cardroom getting an early start."

Leah curtsied. "Thank you. If you will excuse me, I will see to the ladies drawing room."

Joseph wanted to stop her, but manners dictated otherwise. "I will find you later for our dance." Leah nodded as she walked away from the group.

Joseph looked at John raising his eyebrows while Miss Wood laughed. "She is a treasure. She didn't even notice the attention she was receiving. Everyone has asked me who she is. Lord Crawford fell all over himself trying to get an introduction." She looked up at Joseph. "I can't believe you came as you swore off attending balls years ago. She must be special, although I think you make her nervous. I can see it when you are around her and how she fidgets."

John let out a breath. "Let us dance, dear." He pulled her arm leading to the dance floor.

Joseph stared after Leah while taking a drink of champagne.

Leah found herself dancing every dance. She was having a wonderful time but needed a break for her poor feet. Bernard had not surfaced from the cardroom, forcing her to spend her time with strangers. Miss Woods saw her a few times to wave, but Leah mostly danced.

The waltz was soon announced, and Leah's hands felt weak. Joseph was at her side quickly guiding her toward the dance floor. He pulled her waist into his arms closer than appropriate. He moved her around the dance floor to the music. She noticed people watching them. She hoped their prior relationship was not evident.

Joseph leaned down to whisper, "Miss Johnson, are you enjoying the ball?"

"It's better than I thought it would be. I must confess it's my first London ball. I have only attended parties and a few assembly dances. I did go to Baron Morgan's ball, but nothing like this. This is so extravagant that I feel out of place."

"You should never feel out of place. No one here can hold a candle to you."

"Indeed, Your Grace. You can be a flirt."

Joseph whispered, "Only with you."

Leah tried to keep a straight face while Joseph turned her around the dance floor a few more times. He watched her intensely. "How is your mother?"

Leah smiled that he remembered. "She is better. The new medicine seems to be making her feel better and lifting her spirits. Travis carried her outside for a few minutes yesterday and she enjoyed the fresh air. I have been reading to her and she loves that."

Joseph grinned. "Your romance novels?"

Leah ignored his jest. "No, she enjoys poetry and I am embarrassed to say… the scandal sheets."

Joseph laughed out loud. "You don't say?"

Leah looked into his eyes with amusement. "She has read about *you* in the papers. You really should be more discreet, Your Grace."

Joseph shook his head. "Tsk tsk, my dear. I don't even know what they say. I guess I should read one to make sure that I am living up to my reputation."

Leah laughed as the music ended. She curtsied, and he bowed. He was about to ask her to take a walk but was interrupted by Mr. Crawford who asked Leah for their dance.

His jaw tightened at the man's eagerness to take Leah's hand.

Leah thought Mr. Crawford was charming, though a little too forward with his compliments. He was handsome and asked to call on her, yet she denied him due to her engagement. Leah graciously left him to pursue some much-needed refreshment when a familiar voice came up behind her. "Miss Johnson, imagine seeing you here."

Leah sucked in a breath. "Mr. Wilcox?" His brow sweat was dripping near his spectacles. Leah forced a smile. "Good to see you. I didn't realize you were acquainted with these types of events."

He creased his brows seeming confused. "Why ever not? I served with Lord Wilson years ago in the military. I come to their ball every year."

Leah tried to recover from her comment. "Of course. Pardon me if I offended you."

Mr. Wilcox wiped his brow. "I see you have not changed. Unmarried is what I heard. Perhaps you have led others on as well?"

Leah opened her mouth in surprise. "How dare you. I didn't lead you on."

Seeming to change his mind, Mr. Wilcox asked, "Can we speak privately?"

"I don't think so, Mr. Wilcox."

"Forgive me if I offended you. I didn't get a chance to tell you how I felt before you left. I did a lot for your family, Miss Johnson. I think you owe me a few minutes of your time to say my peace."

Feeling guilty, Leah agreed and followed Mr. Wilcox out the terrace doors. There were a few other couples outside.

He looked around nervously. "Do you mind if we take a walk down the path. I don't wish for others to hear."

Leah complied, walking behind Mr. Wilcox down a path through the garden. He stopped abruptly pulling Leah near a bush. She jerked her arm away from him. "Unhand me, or I will leave."

Mr. Wilcox lowered his voice to a growl. "You thought you could just throw me away. Some benefactor paid the debt, but what about all those months that I supported your family? Your father gave me permission to marry you. I had his permission! You belonged to me." His voice was shaking, and she could smell the alcohol on his breath.

Leah tried to pull away. "Stop this at once. I am not a piece of property. I don't belong to anyone."

Mr. Wilcox squeezed her arm tighter. "You will honor me, Miss Johnson." He pulled Leah toward the bush, and she lost her balance falling to the ground, scraping her cheek. He grabbed for her ripping her dress as she tried to crawl away. She slapped him, screaming as he held her down by sitting on top of her while trying to press a kiss against her mouth. He was heavy, taking the breath from her.

She twisted in his arms as she heard a voice behind her. "Let her go now if you value your life." Mr. Wilcox let her go and faced Joseph.

Joseph looked at Leah with rage in his eyes. He took Mr. Wilcox by the collar smashing his fist into his face and kicking him as he went back down to the ground. Leah yelled for him to stop.

Mr. Wilcox held his stomach as he tried to get up to look for his spectacles. Blood dripped from his mouth. Joseph went after him again as Leah tried to hold him back. "I will ruin you if you come anywhere near her again. I am the Duke of Wollaston."

Mr. Wilcox's eyes widened as he stood up. "She is a nobody, Your Grace, and should not even be here. She is not a lady, but a whore."

Joseph's jaw flexed as he went to hit him again, but Leah jumped between them.

She yelled at Mr. Wilcox. "Get out of here, before he kills you."

Mr. Wilcox ran away toward the back of the house assumingly to leave the ball.

Leah fell to the ground unable to keep her balance anymore. Joseph leaned down to the ground beside her. "Are you hurt?"

She tried to catch her breath, gasping for air. He reached for her and held her against his chest. "We need to get you some help."

Leah grasped at him frantically. "No! Please don't tell anyone."

Joseph shook his head. "Leah, we need to make sure he doesn't hurt you again."

Leah cried, pleading with him. "Please, Joseph. Don't tell anyone especially Bernard. I am so ashamed. I just want to go home."

Joseph sighed with frustration. He wanted nothing more than to hold her all night. He helped her stand and bent down to meet her eyes. "I don't understand? He will pay for this as soon as I find out who he is."

Leah sobbed, trying to catch her breath. "I know him. He was the man who saved my family who I was to marry. He felt I owed him and tried to take what he thought was his."

Joseph clenched his fist. "I will kill him."

Leah grabbed his hand. "Please, I just want to forget. My dress is ripped, and I can't go back inside. Can I use your carriage to take me home?"

He rubbed her arm. "Leah, of course. You can have anything you need. May I escort you?"

Leah shook her head. "No, I need you to tell Bernard that I fell outside and went home. I don't want him to know about my past. Please, Joseph."

He took a deep breath. "I would do anything for you, but I don't think we should forget this. That man needs to pay for hurting you. Take my coat to hide the rip in your dress. Let's go to my carriage."

Leah accepted his coat, and he walked her to his carriage. He told his footman to return for him after seeing that Leah got home safely. Leah tried to give him back his coat. He shook his head. "Nonsense, you need it more than me right now. I will send for it later." He touched her face where a welt was rising from hitting the ground. He bent down and kissed her cheek. She flinched but did not pull away.

He smiled sadly. "I will go tell Mr. Williams of your departure."

"Thank you, Joseph. For everything. Promise me you won't do anything to Mr. Wilcox. I just want to forget about tonight."

Joseph nodded and kissed her hands. "Be safe, Leah." Joseph went back inside without his coat. He spoke to Lord Wilson who let him borrow one of his. He found Miss Woods with a group of women and asked her for a private word.

She excused herself, walking away with Joseph. "What's amiss, Your Grace? There has been talk that you have only danced once with a mysterious blonde woman who has since left the party. Do you have no plans to dance with anyone else? The tongues are wagging."

Joseph rolled his eyes. "I don't care about the gossip of the *ton*. You know my intentions. However, there is another matter we must discuss."

Miss Woods smirked. "Very well, Your Grace. What matter is that?"

Joseph sighed. "I need your help, with little to no questions."

Miss Woods raised her brows in question.

"Miss Johnson had an accident near the terrace and ripped her dress. She doesn't want anyone to know. I witnessed it and was sworn to secrecy. She needs Bernard to know, but I don't want him to know that I was with her. Are we clear?"

Miss Woods' smile grew across her face. "Very well, how did she leave?"

Joseph whispered, "I had her take my carriage with my coat. Please find Bernard and tell him. It sounds better coming from another female."

"Very well. Let's go find him."

They met John at the card table as they watched Mr. Williams in a high-stakes match. Joseph had to admit that the guy was good. How attentive he was to Leah's needs was another story.

After the round finished, John asked Bernard to speak to them privately. Bernard excused himself approaching their group. Miss Woods grabbed his arm to whisper near his ear. "Mr. Williams, your fiancée Miss Johnson had a small accident on the terrace and asked me to discreetly tell you that she had to leave."

"Leave?" he questioned. Miss Woods looked down. She hid her conversation with Mr. Williams with her fan. "Yes, unfortunately, her dress was ruined. The poor girl needed to change and asked that you be notified."

Bernard looked back at the table. "Did she say if she wanted me to leave?"

Miss Woods looked at Joseph then back to Bernard. "Actually, His Grace allowed her to use his carriage. I think you need not leave right away."

Bernard nodded. "Thank you, Miss Woods. I will return to my game now."

Joseph turned to John. "He has no idea the treasure he has waiting for him at home."

John patted his shoulder trying to stir Joseph away. "Let's go, Your Grace."

Leah arrived home and ran up the stairs avoiding any questions. Betty was not home yet making her happy not to have to share the bedroom at the moment. She cleaned herself up, changing her dress and got into bed. Betty came in a few hours later, but Leah feigned sleep to avoid speaking of the night.

CHAPTER 31

THE NEXT MORNING LEAH WORE her hair down trying to cover the mark on her cheek. She told her family that she fell accidentally. Bernard sent a message with Mr. Soothers that he would be by that night to take her to dinner. He had a business appointment during the day. Leah tried to catch up on some sewing, making that her afternoon plans.

Betty came home after a morning stroll with Mr. Soothers, then found the chessboard to play with her fiancé. Miss Freemont came into the room a few hours later to announce a visitor at the door for Leah. Leah followed Miss Freemont to the front door and lost her breath for a moment as she saw Joseph standing in the doorway with a bag in his hand.

"Your Grace, what a surprise. Please come in."

Joseph stepped through the doorway. "I hope you don't mind me stopping by."

Miss Freemont curtsied and left them alone to prepare the luncheon.

Joseph handed her the bag. "I brought a poetry book for your mother."

"Thank you. She will love it." She took the book out of the bag turning a few of the pages. "Your Grace, would you like to give the book to her yourself?"

"Of course."

Leah wondered how her mother would react to meeting the man she hears about in the papers. She led him up the stairs to her mother's room and peeked inside. "Are you well enough for a visitor?"

Her mother nodded. "Yes, who has come?"

Leah smiled as she showed Joseph into the room. She looked at her mother. "Mama, this is the Duke of Wollaston."

Her mother widened her eyes. "Oh Leah, I look a fright. Excuse my appearance, Your Grace."

Joseph smiled tenderly. "It's quite all right, Mrs. Johnson. I can clearly see where your daughter gets her beauty. I brought you a gift."

Leah's mother blushed trying to smooth her hair with her hand. Leah snickered at her mother's nervousness around the duke. He handed her the bag and she opened it. She covered her mouth with her hand in surprise. "I love poetry. How did you know?"

He smiled. "I must confess that Leah may have mentioned it."

Her mother nodded, and Leah noticed that she did not acknowledge that he called her by her Christian name.

"We will leave you to rest, Mama. I will send you some luncheon soon." Leah guided Joseph down the stairs.

Miss Freemont approached them. "Will His Grace stay for some luncheon? We are having sandwiches and pudding."

Leah looked at Joseph raising her brow.

"Yes, I believe I will. That sounds delicious." Joseph graciously accepted.

Leah was surprised he would accept an invitation to dine with her family. She set the table as he watched her in the kitchen. Mr. Soothers was very excited when he approached the table to find Joseph eating with them. Betty also had problems masking her surprise. Miss Freemont took Mrs. Johnson's food to her on a tray. Travis was working at the shop store, but his wife joined them. Jasper was out with friends.

Mr. Soothers tried to keep Joseph's attention, but the duke kept steering the conversation toward other topics besides business.

"This pudding is delicious. Do you cook Miss Johnson?"

Leah smiled. "Occasionally, I help Miss Freemont."

Betty snorted. "Don't let her fool you. She is a wonderful cook."

Joseph looked at her in amazement. "I would love to taste your cooking."

They ate the rest of their lunch while laughing with her siblings. Leah thought how it was such a contrast to the dinner she had at his house. His meals always seemed so formal, yet he did not act pretentious at all, he was very gracious and appreciative of the meal he was having with her family. After they ate, he asked her to take a walk with him. She agreed ignoring the curious glances from her family.

Leah asked him to wait a moment while she retrieved his coat from her room. She handed it to him, placing the coat across his arm. "Thank you for last night."

"Anytime. It was my honor to be able to help you."

She guided him to the stable. "I want to show you something."

He followed her into the stable and spotted a white horse.

"Do you remember her?"

He laughed, petting the horse. "Of course, I remember her."

"I was right you know. She proved to be the most loyal companion."

Joseph stared down at her, studying her face. She looked up at him, her eyes focused on his mouth. Her chest rose and fell as she watched him step away.

Leah walked him back outside. "I just want to thank you again for helping me last night and being discreet."

Joseph touched her face lightly, moving her hair out of the way. He clenched his jaw at the red mark across her cheek. "I wish I could take your pain away."

His voice was so gentle, and she had to tell herself to guard her heart. "I will heal. I must go and get ready for Bernard. Thank you for the poetry and visiting my mother."

"Leah?" He took a moment, seemingly changing his mind.

"Yes?"

He shook his head. "It's nothing. I hope to see you soon."

Joseph mounted his horse and left.

Leah prepared a bath and got ready for her dinner with Bernard. Most of her washings took place in a basin, but today she wanted to soak in a tub. It would be nice to have help again with chores such as hauling buckets of warm water up the stairs to fill up a tub. Bernard planned to hire many footmen after they were married.

The work was worth it as she enjoyed the steamy bath, relaxing all her sore muscles from last night's debacle. How could Mr. Wilcox treat her like that? She wanted to scrub her skin as she thought of him forcing himself on her. What if Joseph had not been there? She shuddered at the thought.

Leah finished her bath and quickly readied herself. She chose her lavender gown with silver earrings. She wore her hair in tendrils trying to mask the mark on her face. It was nearly impossible to hide the damage, yet Mr. Wilcox's face probably looked a lot worse.

Bernard showed up a little early and was playing chess with Mr. Soothers when Leah arrived in the drawing room. He stood and went to kiss her on the cheek. He stopped short when he saw the mark. "What happened to your face?"

Leah touched her face. "It was part of my fall last night on the terrace. It's only a scrape."

"Are you okay, love?"

Leah forced a smile. "Yes, just really hungry. Are you ready to go?"

He took her hand. "Of course, let's go."

They went into the carriage and Bernard grinned. He took her hands. "Leah, my love. I have some great news."

Leah smiled at his excitement. "What news?"

He leaned down brushing a kiss on her lips. "I made a decision. Living in an inn is becoming uncomfortable, so I met with my solicitor this morning and bought a townhouse in London. Can you believe it? You will love it. I think we should get married within the next few months here in England. I don't think we should wait any longer."

Leah felt her breath escape. "What about America?"

"I still have my homes there, but we will be able to visit both places. Your family is here and that should make you happy. My new business deals will make me happy. We should stay in England for a time."

Leah's mind raced between living in the same town as Joseph and her wedding plans. Looking at Bernard, she smiled taking in the news. "It looks like I have a lot of planning to do and we must get a license." Her memories shifted to Captain Jackson and the delay in the license. It's been a long time since that day and fate brought her all the way back to England. She will marry an American near her family home. A real wedding full of flowers and friends.

"That's my girl. I am glad you agree. We can see the townhouse tomorrow. You can have any type of wedding you want. Spare no expense." Bernard leaned over caressing her lips softly with his mouth, rubbing his tongue against hers. He pulled her closer, opening his mouth wider and letting out a moan. He broke away slowly, placing his forehead on top of hers. "Let's talk about what I am really looking forward to." He rubbed her arms with his hands giving her chills. "The wedding night."

Leah's eyes widened. "Bernard!"

He laughed, watching her blush. "I mean a wedding trip. I think we should visit the ocean. I know how much you enjoy that."

Leah's face was glowing with happiness. "If we are together, I will be happy."

He took her hand in his, rubbing a circle around the top. She placed her head on his shoulder, dreaming of their wedding.

"I would like to help you with the planning, but I need to go to York on some business for a fortnight. I leave the day after tomorrow."

Leah's shoulders sagged. She didn't know why he had to leave all the time. Would this be a sign of what was to come?

"Bernard, must you leave? Don't you want to stay with me?"

"Of course, my love. When I am not with you, I am always thinking about you."

She stuck out her lip. "Then stay here in London until after we are married."

He shifted in his seat adjusting his cravat. "You know I want to stay with you. I can't as I have other commitments."

Leah bent over and kissed him on the cheek. She whispered near his ear, "Please stay."

He rubbed her shoulders pushing her slightly away. He bent down to meet her eyes. "Leah, you know I would stay if I could. I have people counting on me. I must go."

Leah moved away from him and looked out the window.

Bernard took a deep breath in frustration. "Leah, stop this. You are acting like a child."

Leah snorted. "Just take me home. I lost my appetite."

Bernard's face turned red as he pounded his fist on the ceiling to alert the coachman. The carriage slowed as the footman answered the door. Bernard told him to take them back to Miss Johnson's home.

The rest of the ride was spent in silence. Bernard walked Leah to the front door turning to her as he reached for her hand. "Leah, please forgive me. I don't want us to be cross with each other."

She looked up at him. "Forgive me too. I am just very tired."

Bernard leaned down and kissed her on the cheek. "I will pick you up tomorrow morning to see the new townhouse. I must see my man of business to help secure a license—provided you still want to marry me."

Leah smiled. "Of course, we only had an argument. I will be ready for you."

He kissed her hand and walked back to the carriage.

CHAPTER 32

L EAH MET BERNARD THE FOLLOWING morning. He took her to visit the townhouse he had purchased. His excitement was contagious as he showed off each room hoping to impress his fiancée.

The townhouse was decorated in pale shades throughout all the rooms. Leah took note of changes that would have to be made with the decorations. Many of the fireplaces needed a deep cleaning and servants would have to be hired to ready the place before Leah could move in. New furniture and dishes would have to be purchased. Bernard said to spare no expense, so Leah had to go shopping as soon as possible.

After the tour, Bernard turned to her. "Did I do good, love? Can you believe you will be living here soon?"

"It's a beautiful home, Bernard. I just wish I would have helped you choose a home for us."

Bernard shrugged casually. "I buy the house—you decorate it. This will keep you busy for years." He stepped closer to her bending down to kiss her on the lips. "You must trust me that I know what is best for us."

Leah turned from him and walked around the room. Her memories of her family's cottage tugged at her heart—the laughing, dancing, and many meals together. She felt him approach behind her, placing his arms around her waist. He placed his chin on her shoulder as he warmed her back with his body heat. She leaned back onto his chest. "I do like it. It's just very big, but we can make it a home. I just want a place to spend time together and watch our children play. That's all I need."

He squeezed her tight. "I knew you would." He turned her around to face him. "Love, I have to leave in the morning for my trip. I will think about you every day until I return in a fortnight. Once I return, I promise I will stay in London until after we are married."

Leah leaned her body into him breathing him in with closed eyes. "Very well."

Bernard kissed the top of her head. He showed her the ballroom and swung her around laughing and speaking of all the entertaining they could do. Making the right alliances was very important to him. As the wife of a prominent businessman, she would be expected to host many social gatherings. Leah was uncomfortable with such responsibilities, but Bernard encouraged her to hire the help. His business plans seemed to grow daily and now included several trips abroad.

Leah enjoyed her evening with him. It was a rare occasion they spent time alone since arriving in London. A fortnight would go by quickly. They would be married shortly after that, but it was still hard to say goodbye.

The next day Leah went into town to shop. She wanted to find some material for drapes, and she also needed a wedding dress. Bernard had left a lot of pin money and told her to open accounts in his name. Betty accompanied her as they walked down Bond Street.

Betty giggled. "This is better than window shopping. I can't believe we can buy anything we need in any shop we desire."

Leah scolded her little sister. "Betty, we must not be frivolous."

Betty shrugged. "Do you always have to be so practical? Enjoy yourself, Leah."

Leah laughed. "Very well. Let's get some tarts at the bakery."

Betty smirked. "Let's get extra everything!"

Leah looped her arm around her sister's as they walked down the road.

Betty saw Jasper's friend Mr. Tollway coming out of the bakery. He was a big man with a slight Scottish accent. "Mr. Tollway, how nice to see you."

He tipped his hat. "Good day to you, lass. Your looking bonnier every time I see you. I just saw Jasper a few days ago and enjoyed his military stories."

Betty blushed. "We were so happy he could join us for a few weeks."

Mr. Tollway tucked his purchases under his arm. "Aye, we spoke of our time on Mr. Wilcox's farm. We had a great time working in the stables. Did you hear about Mr. Wilcox?"

Betty looked at Leah who was trying to hide her discomfort. "I don't believe we have seen him for a long time."

He took off his hat and wiped his brow. "I heard there might have been some trouble at his place the other night. Some folks said that he was escorted out of his home yesterday, and has apparently left for America all of a sudden. His farm is being sold."

Leah's face went pale. She coughed at her shock as she knew that it had to be Joseph. He warned he would ruin Mr. Wilcox. It was his way of protecting her. She held her composure, wishing Mr. Tollway a good day.

Around the corner, they heard a woman's voice. "Miss Johnson?" Leah turned around taking a moment to recognize the woman in front of her. "Lady Caroline? It's so nice to see you."

"Oh! Leah. You look so beautiful. America must have been a grand adventure. I heard you were in town. It's nice to have you back."

Leah chuckled. "That it was—definitely an adventure. Look at you! I heard you are married with a child."

"Yes, it's wonderful. I was told *you* were engaged."

Leah blushed showing her the ring. "Yes, in fact I am shopping now for my new home."

Caroline looked at her finger. "The ring is beautiful! Congratulations! I am so happy I saw you today. Perhaps we can have tea at my home soon?"

Leah agreed. "I would like that. Thank you."

Betty stayed quiet, watching the exchange. After Lady Caroline left, Betty asked, "How do you know her?"

"She is Lady Caroline, sister to the Duke of Wollaston. Forgive me for not introducing you." Leah moved to walk as Betty touched her arm.

Betty whispered, "Indeed. His name is always mentioned lately. There are rumors you know."

"Please don't tell me you are reading the scandal sheets. Who is he with this week?" Leah straightened her bags, pulling her sister forward.

Betty stared at her sister hesitantly before answering. "You."

Leah stopped abruptly. She turned to Betty feeling light-headed. "What did you say?"

"You are. But it's not being said in the scandal sheets. Someone mentioned something at a tea party at Lady Barker's home that I attended with some friends of mine. I denied it of course."

Leah shook her head in denial. "I don't understand. I was friendly with His Grace several years ago, but I hardly speak to him now. I am engaged to Bernard. Why would anyone speak about me? Especially in those circles?"

Betty tucked her arm around Leah's once more to finish their walk. "Leah, you're my sister and I love you. But your past with the duke is not such a secret. Tom told me that his friends say that he is still in love with you. The rumor is that he hasn't been to a ball in years, yet he attended one a few days ago. The only woman he danced with was *you*, and it was a waltz."

Leah huffed. "That's absurd. He is not in love with me."

"Is it possible that you deny his affections because you are trying to make yourself believe that you have no feelings for him? I am not a little girl anymore, yet I remember the day he came for you. He was a man in love."

Leah stayed silent. Her little sister was too observant for her own good. When did she grow up so fast? Leah cleared her throat. "I don't wish to speak of it."

Betty said no more, and they boarded the carriage for the cottage.

CHAPTER 33

MRS. FREEMONT HAD DINNER ALMOST ready when the girls arrived home. Leah put her purchases away looking forward to dinner with her family. The smells of roast beef filled the home. Her mouth watered at the thought of the meal. It was Jasper's last day in town before he had to join his command. They celebrated with his favorite dish.

Mrs. Johnson joined her family for dinner, and the family was amazed at her recovery. It was a slow healing process, but each day brought them more hope. Travis and his wife had an announcement they wanted to share during the family meal. Leah imagined it was probably baby news—a new life would bring such joy into their family! Mr. Smoothers entered just as Travis stood up to address his family.

"My family… it's been too long that we all sat around this table. Our lives have taken us in different directions, but we all made it back home to be together for our mother. Tonight, my wife and I have exciting news to share as we want to announce that we are having a baby."

Leah's heart filled with joy as everyone stood to hug and congratulate the happy couple. As everyone sat back in his or her seats, Jasper continued to stand, as he was next in line to speak.

"It's been a great joy to spend these past few weeks with all of you. My military commitments will keep me away from both of my sisters' upcoming nuptials, but my heart will be with you. Perhaps someday—not too far in the future—it will be my turn. I am so lucky to be here tonight. I will miss all of you."

Tears fell from Leah's eyes. The happiness and closeness of her family were the most important things to her. She wished Bernard could be there to share in her joy—although his family obligations were not the same as hers. He was not close to his family and enjoyed going out on the town more than spending time with his family. She felt concern for their future—she couldn't recall a time that Bernard stayed home. Would he settle down once they had children? Would her life be filled with one social event after the other? Did he enjoy country life, or would he rather spend all his time in London? Perhaps she needed to speak to him to clarify where he saw their future. They could surely work everything out before they got married.

"Leah?" Betty asked laughing, "did we catch you woolgathering?"

Leah's face blushed. "Pardon me. Is it my turn?" She stood up to face her family. "I could think of nothing more than leaving London a few years ago. My time back home has shown me that no matter how far you go, you can't replace that emptiness that can only be filled by family. I am so happy I am here with you tonight. I can think of no place that I would rather be."

Betty stood up to hug her. "My sister, my best friend, my family—I love all of you."

The family finished their meal. Jasper went to the piano and started playing as they danced around the house. Leah relished these times with her family. Betty helped Mrs. Freemont with the dishes while the rest of the family retired to the drawing room.

Mr. Soothers approached Leah and asked her for a private word. She invited him to stand next to her by the fireplace. He whispered, "Miss Johnson, as Betty and I grow closer to a wedding date, I want to give her a more appropriate diamond. The ring I gave her was just something to hold her over until I could secure some more funds."

"That is lovely, Mr. Soothers. I am sure she will love anything you give her."

He lowered his voice so no one else could hear. "I am in a bit of a quandary. You see there is a special jeweler who has a beauty of a piece available at a price that I can afford. I must pick it up on Saturday or risk the chance of him selling it to someone else. He lives a few hours from here, but I have a business meeting that I can't miss. Is it possible that you could go? I do trust you and would provide a carriage and footmen to accompany you."

Leah spurted out. "Me? Is there not a friend or family member that would be more appropriate to help you?"

He shook his head. "I don't trust just anyone to go in my place. I want it to remain a secret for Betty, and it would require them to carry a considerable sum of money for me. Please, Miss Johnson. Can you do it for Betty? I can't wait to see her face."

Leah took a deep breath. "Very well. I will do it."

A huge smile tugged at his face. "Thank you, Miss Johnson. I will not forget your kindness. Please remember to keep this our secret."

Leah whispered. "Of course."

CHAPTER 34

SATURDAY MORNING CAME QUICKLY FOR Leah. She made an excuse of wedding shopping while dressing to leave. Leah rode the gig to the new townhouse, then took Mr. Soothers' carriage. She did not want to raise suspicion with having his carriage pick her up at her family cottage.

The ride was bumpy as the roads became less traveled. Leah brought a novel with her to pass the time. Peeking out the window gave her picturesque scenes of the English countryside. She missed the country and her homeland.

She thought of the diamond for her sister. Although feeling reluctant at first, Leah was happy to oblige to help her sister's fiancé. The carriage slowed as Leah looked out the window spying a home in the background that looked somewhat familiar. She felt apprehensive as she thought the jeweler would have had a shop in the village. Twisting in her seat as the carriage approached, she finally remembered the home. Her mouth dropped open as fury came over her at the deception. She had been tricked! Her breathing became labored as she seethed with anger. The doors opened, and Joseph was standing outside with an innocent look on his face ready to help her out of the carriage.

"Leah, please let me explain." He held out his hand to help her out.

"How could you? Did you deceive Mr. Soothers as well or was he part of your ruse?" Leah refused his hand as she stepped out of the carriage. Joseph told the footmen to wait by the stable.

He turned back near her. "Forgive me for my deception. I was desperate to spend one more day with you. This lodge held so many memories. Do you remember our time here? Please, Leah. I wish you no harm."

"Joseph, this is inappropriate," she said, not realizing the causal use of his Christian name.

"I know it could look that way, but I have nothing inappropriate in mind. I know I don't deserve to spend the day with you and if you want to go home now, I will fetch the footmen to escort you. My only hope is that you will find it in your heart to spend the day with me."

Leah stared at him as her mind raced with all the reasons she should turn around and get back into the carriage. Looking at his desperate face, she conceded. She gave an exhausted sigh. "If I spend a few hours here with you today, will you promise to leave me alone?"

"Promise."

She looked around the house and grounds. "I remember this place well."

He whispered, "Let's take a walk." Leah took his arm as they walked along a path through the woods. After taking her through the path into the trees, he smiled fondly. "I walked through these woods for years after you left remembering our special time here." He slowed his pace, stopping in front of a tree and pointed at the carving. "Do you remember?"

Leah's heart beat faster looking at the tree. She took a step toward it while taking off her gloves to rub the carving. She whispered, "Joseph loves Leah."

"It is still true."

She turned around taking her hand off the tree. "We can't go back, Joseph. I am not the same person, and neither are you."

He stared at her for a second, looking away, he pointed toward the lake. "Come, let's go to the lake. I have a surprise for you." Leah took his hand as they walked through the woods and down the pathway toward the water. She remembered the dock and stepped on it, looking across the lake. There were two baskets next to it. He grabbed one that included two blankets. He spread them out on the dock and handed her the other basket.

She opened it finding a pink muslin gown. Looking up at him in confusion, he laughed. "It's a bathing gown from France. It's popular for sea bathing, but I thought it would be perfect for swimming today. You told me once that you dreamed about swimming. Today that dream comes true. I will teach you."

Leah's mouth dropped open in shock. "I don't know what to say. It's not decent."

Joseph shrugged. "Who will know? The woman I used to know was not afraid of getting wet. Need I remind you of the day in the mud? I can turn around while you change, or you can go behind that tree."

Leah hesitated biting her bottom lip. She had always wanted to swim, but it was most improper. After deliberating in her mind, she took the dress, resolved to have her day of fun. "Fine. I will go behind the tree, but I want you to turn around as well." Leah changed into the dress. taking off her chemise, petticoat and corset. not wanting to get them wet.

When she was done dressing, she approached Joseph who was sitting on the dock with his feet in the water waiting for her. He must have changed while she did as he only had his breeches on. "I am ready."

Joseph turned around and looked her up and down. She could feel his gaze from the tip of her head to the bottom of her toes. "Leah, do you trust me?"

Her heart was racing in her chest to see his bare, muscular chest. Sweat perspired in the palms of her hands at the sight of him. She tried to look away as her face burned with embarrassment. Her voice cracked. "Should I?"

He suppressed a smile, seeming to enjoy her discomfort at his state of dress. He turned away from her and suddenly jumped into the lake. A few seconds later, he surfaced from the water splashing near the dock. "The water is cold but refreshing. The best way to learn to swim is to just jump right in. I will catch you and promise I won't let you go."

A frightened look came across her face. "I can't jump in. What if I drown?"

Joseph laughed. "You won't, and I promise I will catch you. Don't let the fear stop you from learning to swim. It's what you have always wanted to do."

Leah looked at the water, hesitating for a moment. He was right, and she would not let fear stop her.

Closing her eyes, she jumped.

Joseph reached for her pulling her toward him as she came up out the water. She coughed and gasped for air swinging her arms until she felt his hands reach for her.

"I have you, sweetheart. I won't let you go under." He took her in his arms as she opened her eyes with a smile on her face.

"It feels so cold but good. I don't ever want to get out." Her lips shivered as a chill went through her.

He chuckled. "We will live in the water as you wish."

Leah did not let go of him as he swam with her in his arms near the edge where he could touch the bottom with his feet. The mud slipped through his toes as he held Leah firmly, turning her around and pulling her back against his chest.

"Every good swimmer learns by kicking first and trying to float on their back. I am going to hold you while you try to float."

Leah arched her back as Joseph kept his hands on her waist. She kicked her legs and giggled. He moved her through the water as she closed her eyes enjoying the sensation of swimming. He stared down at her lovingly. After several moments of floating he turned her around pulling her toward his chest. "Do you wish to go under again?"

She looked up at the proximity of his face near hers. He looked so handsome even when wet. His muscles shimmered in the sunlight. "I will try."

"Hold your breath when I count to three, and I will pull you under with me."

Leah nodded her head as he counted. When he got to three, she held her breath and he took her under with him. She came out of the water laughing.

Her infectious laugh made him off balance, and he grabbed her tighter bringing his face next to hers. Instinct made him brush his lips against hers. And for once, she didn't pull away.

His expression turned serious as he moved her wet hair away from her face, bending down to pull her against his chest for another kiss. The kiss deepened as he opened his mouth searching for her tongue.

Leah melted into him, wanting to get closer, ignoring the warnings in her head. His kisses went from her mouth to her neck as she trembled in his arms. Feeling limp in his embrace, her conscience finally took hold of her causing her body to tense. Realizing her folly, she pushed away from him breathing hard.

They stared at each other in silence. Not saying a word, he searched her face but did not speak. He twisted his arm around her waist and began swimming for the dock. She kept quiet as he moved them through the water. He lifted her onto the dock and then brought himself up. They sat there soaked, still not speaking.

Joseph finally broke the silence. "Do you want to jump again?" He turned to her.

Leah raised her brow. "Yes. I just wish women had something practical to wear during swimming. This gown grows heavy."

She watched his gaze as it went down her body, falling upon her perfectly round curves, barely concealed in her wet gown, he was unable to hide his desire. He sighed. "Perhaps once you're married, you can dispose of the gown when you swim."

Leah's face turned red as she turned away from him and stood to get away from his scrutiny.

He chuckled at her embarrassment. "Although not sure how much swimming would get done if you didn't wear a gown. You can try it here if you wish."

Leah smirked. "I am not as naïve as you think. It would serve your teasing if I discarded it. Wouldn't you be shocked?"

Joseph stood and took a step toward her whispering in her ear, "Shock is not the word for it."

Leah ignored his comment. "Are you ready to jump?"

He reached for her hand. "We can hold hands, or I can carry you."

She held up his hand. "Hands."

The couple ran off the dock holding hands. Once they entered the water, their hands broke away. A slight panic came over Leah, yet quickly went away at the feeling of Joseph's hands on her waist. She surfaced spitting water, yet laughing.

"Let's do it again."

Joseph pulled her close to him. "You will be the death of me. But there is nothing I would deny you. Let's do it again."

They ran, jumped, and swam for another hour until Leah was finally exhausted.

"Take this blanket, and we can change at the house."

Leah accepted the blanket holding it around her. She leaned up and kissed him on the cheek. "Thank you for today. That was more fun than I've ever had."

His mouth opened slightly at the shock of her affection. Taking her arm, he led her up the hill to the house.

Embarrassed by her kiss, she couldn't speak. It was instinct and felt natural. The feel of his arm was familiar and comfortable. Confused over the feelings she had for this man while engaged to another unsettled her. She felt young again as old feelings surfaced and she tried to push them away.

"I have a tub in the kitchen because I am without servants today. May I prepare you a bath?"

"Are you serious? Do you even know how to boil water?"

"Tsk tsk, Miss Johnson. I may be a duke, but I can do some domestic chores. At least for you, I can. The kitchen has a door, and you can take a bath while I start a fire. After you finish, then I will bathe." As if sensing her hesitation, he added, "I won't peek."

Leah smiled, "Very well. I would love a bath. Prepared by His Grace." She pulled the blanket around her as Joseph went into the kitchen to prepare her bath.

Leah relaxed in the steamy water watching vapors rise out of the tub. Closing her eyes, she listened to Joseph starting a fire. There may be no soap, but a good soak would make her feel clean. The burning smell soon filled her nostrils—the fire would be welcomed when she finished her bath. Thinking about the man in the next room gave her much to wonder about. Her mind struggled with many reasons she should end this charade and demand to return to London, but her heart would not listen. She wanted to stay.

Joseph knocked on the kitchen door. "Leah, do you need anything?"

She opened her eyes wiping the water away. "Some soap would be nice."

He chuckled. "Ah. Please accept my apologies, my lady. I have no soap. But can volunteer my services of filling up the bath with more hot water."

She snorted. "I am fine, Your Grace. I will get out shortly."

"No hurry."

She heard him moving some furniture around in the other room. The water was becoming chilled, so she finished up her bath and dressed quickly. After a few moments, she appeared.

"Come sit by the fire. I will go wash up and join you shortly." Joseph stood and helped her sit down on the blanket. He took his blanket and dry clothes to retire to the kitchen.

Leah felt so relaxed. She helped herself to some of the wine and cheese he had put out on the blanket while running her fingers through her hair trying to dry it by the fire. The wine warmed her as it moved down her throat. She reached for a piece of cheese and nibbled on it as she waited for Joseph. The time was going by quickly and the footmen would arrive soon to take her home. Guilty feelings tried to penetrate her content mood, but she quickly suppressed them. This day would not define her future— only give her the affirmation she needed to move on with her nuptials with Bernard.

Leah lay down on the blanket as her eyes became heavy. She propped her head on her arms, turning to the fire. Her thoughts took her back to the day she left London. It was the right decision. There were no promises made and no talk of marriage. Her childish fantasies of her knight rescuing her were for novels. Joseph told her he was to marry someone else—a noble woman—and it wasn't her. They were not meant to be.

Her voyage from London was full of reservation and excitement. Crying off from Captain Jackson was not part of her plans. She made a rash decision in desperation. Telling him it was over was as much for him as it was for her. They could pretend through life, but what if there was a chance at real love? She had to be truthful. Sadly, it had cost her friendship with Melissa. Her thoughts turned to Bernard. He was full of life, and he brought out the fun side of her. She loved being with him. But was it love? Or was he a replacement for someone she thought she could never have? No, she could not be wrong again. Marriage to Bernard is what she wanted. Listening to the fire crackling, Leah slowly drifted off to sleep.

Joseph entered the room to a find her sleeping on the blanket. An empty wine glass beside her had fallen over. He bent down to lay on the opposite side to watch her sleep. Her eyelashes rested on her cheeks as she breathed heavily. He scooted his body closer to hers, gently pulling her hair back to whisper in her ear. "Leah?" He watched her stir as he placed a kiss on her cheek. "My dear, are you hungry?"

Leah opened her eyes slowly at first then they snapped open as she realized where she was. She yawned. "Forgive me. I was just so relaxed, I must have fallen asleep."

Their faces were close together. He moved his hand to touch her cheek. "You needed rest. Swimming will make you tired."

She smiled. "Swimming was so much fun. I loved it."

Joseph leaned down, placing a quick kiss on her lips like it was the most natural thing in the world. He sat up reaching for the basket and pulled out the bread. He tore off a piece for her and then one for himself.

"More wine?" He pulled out another bottle offering her some.

She shook her head. "I shouldn't, but will have one more."

Leah accepted the glass and took a sip. "It is dry, but tastes good. I don't usually drink too much."

"I enjoy brandy more than wine. But today's adventure seemed to call for wine." Joseph leaned back on his elbow as he took a bite of his bread. He stared at her, studying her face.

"I wish I could stay here with you forever. I won't pretend this is not what I want."

Leah closed her eyes. "Please don't say such things. I am engaged to another man. I don't know what you want from me."

"I think you do. Follow your heart, Leah."

Joseph reached out pulling her into his arms. Tears welled up in her eyes as he cradled her. "Don't cry, Leah. Please stay with me tonight."

He brushed his lips against hers and pulled her tighter against his chest. She moaned, opening her mouth to accept him as their kiss deepened. She stirred in his arms as he loosened his hold to kiss her neck. It was not gentle kisses, but ones full of desire and need. She did not protest but responded to his touch. He took his hands and began exploring her body. Leah did not resist. Moving his finger down the neckline of her gown, he moved her dress further down and loosened the ties on the back to place kisses on her chest. She responded to his touch, caught up in the moment. As he was removing her gown, there was a knock on the door that split them apart. They both breathed deeply and stared at one another.

Leah's forehead etched in worry, she straightened her gown to cover herself. Joseph fixed his shirt and answered the door to a footman. "Your Grace, we have arrived for an escort back to London."

Frustrated, he took a deep breath. "Of course, please give me a few moments." Joseph closed the door turning to Leah. She was picking up her reticule, folding the blankets and replacing her gloves.

"This was a mistake. I must go at once." She tried to rush past him to the front door.

He blocked her way to the door. "Don't say that. Leah, please look at me." Touching her arm, he begged, "Leah, I don't have much time. I leave next Saturday to go to India for at least a year. I can't stay in London and watch you marry Mr. Williams. I lost you once—my heart can't lose you again. Don't you know that I would do anything for you? I love you and want you to be my wife. I would spend my life trying to make you happy. Marry me."

Leah's chest felt like it was going to cave in. "Joseph, I..."

Joseph put his finger across her lips. "Shh. I will wait for your answer. Come see me next Saturday before ten in the morning. If it's yes, we will go to Gretna Green that day."

Leah stared into his eyes. "I don't wish to hurt you." She reached her hand up and touched his face.

Taking her hand, he kissed the inside of her wrist. "Then don't. Follow your heart."

She opened her mouth but said nothing. The footman was waiting, and she had to go. Pulling her hand from his touch, she opened the door. Looking back, she said, "Goodbye, Joseph. Thank you for today. I shall always remember it."

He crossed his arms. "By next Saturday, I will have your answer."

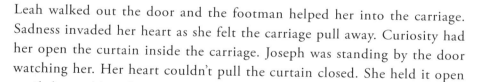

Leah walked out the door and the footman helped her into the carriage. Sadness invaded her heart as she felt the carriage pull away. Curiosity had her open the curtain inside the carriage. Joseph was standing by the door watching her. Her heart couldn't pull the curtain closed. She held it open until she could see him no more.

CHAPTER 35

SHE FELT LIKE SHE WAS in a daze on her ride back to London. The carriage took her to Bernard's townhouse where she'd left the gig that morning. She entered the townhouse and heard voices—deep voices and she stopped at once.

"There you are, love. I heard from Mr. Soothers that you did an errand for him." Bernard stepped near her and kissed her on the cheek.

Leah touched his face. "You're back early. I wasn't expecting you."

"Hopefully it's a good surprise. I thought about what you said, and I wanted to come back as soon as I could. I missed you, love." He leaned down and kissed her on the lips.

Mr. Soothers coughed gently to interrupt. The couple turned toward him. "The jewels were not for sale after all, Mr. Soothers. You are better off without them."

He stared at Leah apologetically. "I hope the trip was not a waste of your time and you would understand my intentions."

Leah removed her bonnet. "The jeweler showed me two different jewels—it would be hard for any girl to choose."

Bernard clapped his hands to get their attention. "Let's have a drink, shall we? The hotel is not far from here, and we can get some dinner."

"Thank you for the invitation, but I must go see to Betty. She is expecting me for dinner."

Leah turned to Bernard. "I am actually very tired from my journey. We should go to my house and get something to eat."

"Very well. I guess we will dine at home tonight." He held out his arm for Leah to escort her to his carriage with Mr. Soothers following in the gig close behind.

The next few days flew by for Leah. Bernard was attentive and spending a lot of time with her. The park was now a favorite past time of his since he discovered that afternoons in Hyde Park was a social event for the *ton*. Leah also enjoyed the trips to the park as they spoke to many acquaintances.

One day she saw a familiar face as they walked a well-traveled pathway near a fountain. Leah peeked at the woman, recognizing Melissa.

"Mel?" Leah's stomach fluttered at the chance of being rejected by her friend.

"Leah? Oh, it is you. I heard you were in town." She walked over and hugged her. "You look so beautiful."

"I was afraid you might not speak to me."

Melissa smiled. "Don't be a ninny. I am so happy that we can finally speak. I felt positively awful over our quarrel."

Leah looked up at Bernard. "This is my dearest friend Melissa and her husband Captain Shockley."

Bernard bowed. "Nice to make your acquaintance."

"This is Mr. Williams—my fiancé."

"You must come for dinner tonight. We are having a small dinner party. Please say you will come."

Leah looked at Bernard for his consent. He patted her hand in approval. "Of course, we will be there."

Bernard enjoyed social events, and they were starting to receive many invitations now that word was out that he had money to invest.

The ride to Melissa's kept Leah on edge. Her heart fluttered with nervousness. Melissa's beautiful home was a wedding gift from her father. The footmen greeted them as they entered the front doors. Melissa practically ran to her. "Leah, I am so happy you came. Please, have some champagne." Leah took the glass as Bernard handed her cloak to the footman. Melissa's family all welcomed her although she felt uneasy due to her calling off her wedding to their family friend. Unmoved by prior events, Captain Shockley kissed her hand to welcome her.

The couple then addressed Bernard. "Mr. Williams, we hope you are enjoying London?"

"Indeed. I have decided to make it my second home. With my travels, I will feel more at ease with Leah near her family when I am not here to accompany her."

Leah looked back at him smiling. Captain Shockley offered Bernard some brandy, and they conversed for a few moments. Melissa leaned into Leah's ear and whispered, "After dinner, let's take a walk outside. I feel we have much to say to each other."

"Are you sure it's okay? I thought you were the hostess."

"Bah. It's a small dinner party with close friends and family. I will not be missed."

Leah smiled, taking another drink of the sweet champagne that slid down her throat easily. The footman announced dinner a few moments later and the crowd went to the table. Most of the couples sat together instead of in assigned seats. The first course of soup was delicious, and the main course of roasted chicken was very tender. Baby potatoes and asparagus topped off the side dishes leading to the decadent desserts.

Bernard did not know a stranger and kept a jovial manner throughout the meal. Soon the ladies dismissed themselves to leave the men with their port. The women were led to the drawing room for after dinner conversation. Melissa made excuses and took a walk with Leah outside.

The air was brisk, pulling the girls closer together as they walked along the path near some bushes. "Leah, I wanted to apologize for my cross words with you regarding Captain Jackson. I regretted our quarrel for years and missed our friendship."

Leah shook her head in protest. "I am to blame. I should not have agreed to the marriage. I want you to know that I did not pretend affection for Captain Jackson. I thought I could love him one day. I realized after a few weeks on the ship it was not going to work, so I thought best to end it."

Melissa reached for her hand. "I understand. Perhaps it worked out for the best. My cousin is smitten and very happy. She settled in America quite nicely. I should have trusted you. Can you forgive me, my friend?"

Leah squeezed her hand. "There is nothing to forgive. You will always be my dearest friend."

"I hope you mean that because I have something else to say and it may not be my place."

"What's amiss?"

Melissa took a deep breath. "I may have been wrong about another matter as well." She looked at her friend with affection. "My life has changed these last few years. I started some work with charities and had served on some committees with Lady Caroline. I also have followed the papers and heard the talk of the *ton* regarding the Duke of Wollaston."

Leah looked down and bit her bottom lip. "I don't understand."

Melissa touched her arm. "I think you do. He does not have dishonorable intentions toward you. I was wrong. Lady Caroline has spoken to me about you. He loves you still. I guess he always has."

"I am engaged to Mr. Williams. I can't believe you out of everyone would do his bidding." Frustration grew within her causing her face to turn red. "Is that why you invited me here tonight?"

Melissa shook her head. "Please, Leah. I invited you because I want us to be friends again. I am not doing his bidding. Lady Caroline told me he was going to India, so he would not see you get married. I felt at fault for telling you to stay away from him. I just wanted to clear my conscience. If you love Bernard, then marry him. I will be your friend no matter what choice you make." She waited a moment looking at Leah and added, "Don't deny yourself love because you were hurt many years ago and don't marry Bernard because you like him. Marry for love, Leah."

Leah looked away from Melissa. "I wish to marry Bernard because he is honorable. He is a good man and will be a great provider."

"Those are admirable qualities. He seems to get along with everyone and from what I heard has good business sense. A great catch if you love him too."

"I would like to go back inside now."

Melissa nodded her head. "As you wish."

Leah walked ahead of her, opening the door to hurry inside. She found Bernard on the settee speaking to a few gentlemen.

"There you are, love. They told me you took a walk outside." Bernard stood and kissed her on the cheek.

"I am well. I thought to take in some air." Leah smiled at him, hiding any indication that she was uncomfortable.

Melissa patted her on the back. "It's good to be with my friend again. Let's play some music."

The couples listened to music for another hour before Leah announced they were leaving. She thanked her friends for the wonderful time.

CHAPTER 36

BERNARD WAS QUIET ON THE way home, pulling Leah next to him as they rode along the streets of London.

"Just a few more weeks, love, and I won't be taking you home anymore. You will be coming home with me." Leah put her head on his shoulder thinking about her conversation with Melissa.

"Bernard, why did you ask me to marry you?" Leah's heart flipped in her chest waiting for his response.

"Are you jesting?" Bernard looked confused shifting his body away from Leah.

Leah sat up and looked at his face. "No, I want to know."

Bernard shrugged. "I thought it was time. Our relationship was ready for the next step. I need a partner by my side for business, and I want children. I adore you and think you are a beautiful woman."

Leah stared at him with confusion as he never mentioned *love*. "I am just nervous that is all. A lot of planning is still to be done. Perhaps we should forget the wedding and run off to Scotland to get married."

Bernard crinkled his nose. "Where is the fun in that? I want a big party."

Leah smiled as the carriage slowed near her home. She kissed him on the cheek. She knew sleep would be hard to come by tonight as she had some decisions to make.

The Duke of Wollaston looked around his bedchamber one last time before departing. His trunks were already packed, and he was ready to go.

She didn't come.

He waited all morning, and it was already eleven—an hour later than he told her to come and now he had to leave for his trip to India.

Caroline and his mother waited for him with his daughter by the doorway. He kissed his daughter. Caroline would take care of her in his absence. The duchess kissed her son on the cheek.

He addressed them both. "I will be out of touch for a few months but will write as soon as I can."

Caroline nodded. "Be safe, Joseph."

Joseph bowed and took his leave, looking around one last time to see if Leah would come. There was no sign of her, and his heart broke as he waved goodbye to his family.

The shipyards reeked of trash. Joseph stayed at the inn waiting for the cargo to finish loading. They were running a few days behind on deliveries, postponing his trip. Playing cards with the crew became old. He was happy that it was the last day of his stay and they would depart soon. After luncheon, it was announced that they could board.

Joseph gathered his bag as his trunks were already on board. He walked across the docks hearing loud voices behind him. He turned around as the wind caught his hat, blowing it off his head. He bent down to see a woman running toward him on the pier. He looked closer as his heart stopped.

It couldn't be?

She came closer, holding onto her bonnet trying to reach him.

It was Leah.

His knees felt weak as he moved toward her. She jumped on him hugging him tightly, and he spun her around.

Unable to control his surprise, he put her down. "What are you doing here?"

Leah cupped his face. "You didn't leave? They told me you were gone."

Joseph held her waist. "Who told you?"

Leah looked back pointing at John and Caroline. "We had a broken carriage wheel and couldn't get to your house that day. My sister and Mr. Soothers took me the next day, but we were too late. They all wanted to come to help me—to help us."

He shook his head not understanding. "Help us?"

She smiled touching his face. "You told me to follow my heart, and it led me here. I chose love. I choose you."

Joseph closed his eyes holding her tightly. "I am never letting you go again."

She brought her head back and kissed him on the pier in front of their family. The crowd came over to congratulate the couple. He kept a hold of her hand.

She looked up at him. "Scotland?"

He smiled. "On the hope, you would say yes and show up to my house that morning, I secured a special license. I say we go back home and get married with just our family in attendance. What do you say?"

Leah hugged him. "I can't wait."

A few days later, Leah walked down the stairs of the duke's home to a crowd of family and friends escorted by Travis. She eyed her mother sitting in a chair near the front. Happiness surrounded her as she saw her groom smiling at her as she walked toward him. Melissa was seated near the front, and Caroline was holding her niece's hand as Leah bent down to give her new stepdaughter a bouquet of flowers.

Joseph took her hands and made a vow to love her for the rest of his life. The ceremony was beautiful, and she had no regrets.

She thought back to her conversation with Bernard. He was surprised by her decision but accepted it gracefully with the assurance that the duke would still support his business ventures. He was a good man, but not the love of her life.

During the receiving line, Joseph made several excuses to touch his new wife. After the crowds had passed, he leaned down. "Your Grace?" he whispered.

Leah smiled, not used to her new title yet. "Yes, my love."

He kissed her on the cheek. "Thank you for today."

Leah kissed him back. "You can have all my days."

EPILOGUE

"**Y**OU CAN'T WEAR YOUR NIGHT clothes to the ceremony." Leah stared down at her two sons not wanting to dress appropriately for their Uncle Jasper's wedding. "Please put on the new clothes I gave you yesterday."

"I don't want to dress in those clothes. They make me itch." Joseph Junior crossed his arms, challenging his mother. "Besides, Uncle Jasper may want to go fishing. I can't fish in these clothes, Mama."

Leah placed her hands on her hips trying to suppress a smile. Junior was a spitting image of his father. "Young man, you will get dressed right now and help your brother. Or I will send Mr. Morris to deal with you two. Your father's valet will make sure you are buttoned up tightly. Uncle Jasper will be getting married today. I doubt fishing will be on his mind."

Leah narrowed her eyes at her youngest child. "Garrett, go with your brother at once."

With an exhausted breath the boys took their clothes to the wash room and closed the door.

"Mama?" Leah turned around to see Margaret at the door. She looked beautiful in her new green gown. Her blond curls reflected the same color as Leah's, as she could easily pass for her natural daughter. Leah treated her as her own.

"Oh! Margie, you look like a princess." Leah walked over hugging the young ten-year-old.

She blushed. "Papa asked me to check on the boys. He is in his study with Uncle Travis."

Leah shook her head, "Hmm. Wonder what the two of them are up too?" She bent down and kissed her on the nose and headed towards the study.

Leah knocked and opened the door. Travis scowled, "Why knock if you are just going to enter?"

Leah walked over and playfully punched her brother. "Why are you here so early?"

Joseph stood and kissed Leah on the cheek. "We are putting together a gift for Jasper. Since his military obligations are over, I have purchased Old Mr. Wilcox's farm and am giving it to him for a wedding present. Travis purchased a few horses and is having them delivered before the wedding."

Leah's mouth slightly opened. "That is a wonderful idea! He will be thrilled. He loves horses and will be a great neighbor to my mother."

Travis put on his hat and kissed Leah's cheek. "I will see you two at the chapel." Leah walked him to the door and wished him a good day.

Turning around she gazed at her husband. Her stomach still flipped when she looked at him. "You are so generous with my family."

He walked over to her and kissed her. "They are my family too. Besides, they gave me the greatest gift." He pulled her closer to him.

"Papa!" Garrett ran into the study being chased by Junior. Sliding between Leah and Joseph, he stuck out his tongue to his older brother. Junior lunged at his little brother holding a single shoe, only to be swept away by his father who held him tightly.

Joseph tightened his face trying to discipline his boys. "Stop this quarrelling at once!"

Leah took the shoe out of Junior's hand. "Enough! You will both be sent to your rooms after your uncle's wedding for the rest of the day if you don't start acting like you have manners."

Joseph carried Garrett and held Juniors hand taking them out of the study and up the stairs and handed them off to his valet. "Please make sure the boys are dressed and ready to go within the hour."

Turning around he climbed back down the stairs to speak to Leah. She was laughing uncontrollably. Her sound was infections and Joseph started laughing too. "I am so glad you took them away. Did you see Garrett sticking out his tongue?"

Joseph's grin turned into a smile that took up his face. "It's so hard to be cross with them when they remind me of myself at their age."

Leah tried to compose herself. "Your mother would be mortified by their behavior."

Joseph shook his head. "Perhaps we should send them to stay at the dowager's house for a few days."

Leah covered her mouth. "She would never forgive you."

Joseph dragged his hand over his face. "It's tempting."

Leah reached out and hugged him, placing her hands around his neck. "Not a day goes by that I am not thankful for our life together. I wouldn't change a thing."

Joseph placed his head against her forehead. "You still take my breath away. And I thank God for one more day."

THE END

ABOUT THE AUTHOR

GG Shalton has been writing short stories most of her life. Often entertaining friends and family. At their encouragement she wrote her first novel in 2016 for publication. Although, she received her Bachelor's degree in Business Management, her real passion is history. Her fascination with different time periods is the inspiration for most her stories. GG is an avid reader and can often be found in various hiding places around her home enjoying a good book. She loves happy endings and most of her free time is spent developing story lines and writing. She is married to a wonderful husband who inspires her to pursue her passion. They met while both of them served in the US Navy. Her heart belongs to her two sons who both promise that one day they may read one of her books. She thanks Jesus for her multiple blessings each day, especially the gift of storytelling.

Authorggshalton@gmail.com.
https://www.facebook.com/gigi.shalton.7